A Matter
of Time

∫

SCEPTRE

Also by Catherine Feeny

The Dancing Stones
Musical Chairs

A Matter
of Time

CATHERINE FEENY

SCEPTRE

Copyright © 1997 Catherine Feeny

First published in 1997 by Hodder and Stoughton
A division of Hodder Headline PLC
A Sceptre Book

The right of Catherine Feeny to be identified as the Author of
the Work has been asserted by her in accordance with the
Copyright, Designs and Patents Act 1988.

10 9 8 7 6 5 4 3 2 1

A CIP catalogue record for this book is
available from the British Library.

ISBN 0 340 68256 6

Typeset by Palimpsest Book Production Limited,
Polmont, Stirlingshire
Printed and bound in Great Britain by
Mackays of Chatham PLC, Chatham, Kent

Hodder and Stoughton
A division of Hodder Headline PLC
338 Euston Road
London NW1 3BH

This novel is lovingly dedicated
to my father, Patrick Feeny.

Acknowledgements

Thanks as ever to my agent Sara Menguc for her unerring guidance and her ability to perceive what it is I actually want to say, especially amidst the initial fog of ideas. To my editor, Carolyn Mays, for the work she puts into my writing and for her constant faith and encouragement. My partner Ray Ffoulkes for his practical help with the text and his supportive presence. Special thanks to my sister, Sarah Feeny Welch who, as a Renaissance scholar, provided a wealth of information about the literature and drama of that time and the situation of women during the period. This she invariably found herself having to do without prior warning and whilst surrounded by toddlers. Her uncanny ability to switch attention from cereal to sonnets at the drop of a hat is testament to her fine and generous intellect.

Lastly I would like to thank my wonderful friend, Amanda Shepherd who, in addition to gins, pickles and Lady-Nights has given me every kind of support possible.

Poor naked wretches, wheresoe'er you are,
That bide the pelting of this pitiless storm,
How shall your houseless heads and unfed sides,
Your loop'd and window'd raggedness, defend you
From seasons such as these? O! I have ta'en
Too little care of this. Take physic, pomp;
Expose thyself to feel what wretches feel,
That thou mayst shake the superflux to them,
And show the heavens more just.

William Shakespeare, *King Lear*

Let us possesse our world, each hath one, and is one.

John Donne, *The Good-Morrow*

A Backpack of Despair

If he hadn't spent much of his adult life in Pitsbury, David Marsh would have considered attempting to conceal himself behind a bit of Roman ruin or the trunk of an oak. That way, if Clementine did come out of the cathedral, he would have time to decide whether or not to reveal his presence.

Unfortunately, however, David had lived in Pitsbury long enough to be familiar with the stories about the strange effect its cathedral sometimes had on people. For those already near the edge, apparently, the sight of a vast religious edifice could prove to be the last straw. Perhaps, David reflected, his eyes automatically scanning the great building for weather damage, because it suddenly hit them that some poor bastard was responsible for the maintenance of all those acres of cathedral roof.

Whatever the cause, though, a consequence of the spasmodic descents into madness of Pitsbury's more impressionable visitors was that anyone spotting David Marsh engaged in furtive behaviour in the precinct would be likely to assume they were witnessing his final crack-up. Which would confirm the undoubtedly myriad rumours about the direness of his situation. Which might be bearable if Clementine had come to Pitsbury, but could only serve to make a bad situation worse if she hadn't.

Concealment therefore not being an option, David had had

to choose what to wear, taking into account the impression it would make on Clementine – always supposing she was there to see it.

On good days, David could fancy himself, at forty, a Bogart type with the added bonus of plenty of light brown hair. A rugged, intelligent, slightly sardonic face. A broad body, rather muscular for his line of work. Today, however, when he'd viewed himself in his wife's mirror, in jeans and that heavy sweater she'd given him last Christmas – knitted by Icelanders out of hand-spun, greased goat's wool the label said – it had seemed to David that he was more likely to be taken for an unsuccessful Arctic fisherman whose youth had been worn away by cruel weather. Though even the manly potential of this had had to be negated by a sheepskin jacket, it proving so bitterly cold when he finally stepped outside.

Typical of Pitsbury, thought David, to time its Arts Festival – of which today's event in the cathedral was the supposed zenith – in order to milk the last possible dregs out of the tourist season. The oak he would have hidden behind was virtually leafless. A biting little wind whipping round the precinct made his eyes water. Every last thing was grey and moribund.

But suddenly, in buggersome contradiction, the sun came out. Light glittered on the saints and gargoyles of the cathedral's north tower and bounced off the razorsharp edges of the flints embedded in the Roman ruins. The medieval cloisters cast aqueducts of shadow onto the precinct's lawns and across the walls of the adjoining Queen's School – Pitsbury's apology for Eton; the educational establishment favoured for their offspring by its bank managers, solicitors and more successful shopkeepers.

David Marsh wasn't prone to looking on the bright side. He couldn't quite call himself an atheist because of a belief in a God of vengeance, wrath and utter bloodymindedness. When his thoughts turned to Pitsbury's architecture it was usually, as just now, to contemplate the sanity-threatening effect that the upkeep of an old building could have on a person or to deplore the soul-numbing hideousness of the modern constructions the city was pocked with. Since Clementine, however, there were occasionally these moments when he was forced to concede

Pitsbury's incipient beauty, to acknowledge that not all of it had been constructed by the dictates of backhanders according to the aesthetics of a multistorey car-park.

Involuntarily, David smiled. He experienced a vague surge of optimism. Saw in his mind's eye the city in spring. Its chilly clumps of daffodils and pale blue evening skies. The swollen Ebb plunging down the weir by the Cock and Hen.

Swollen.

David's smile fixed, then faded. The brisk, reedy river gave way to an image of the bulging ceiling that had served as inspiration for this morning's hideous realisation. Merely, of course, the most recent among many but the only possible explanation for this and the other hitherto inexplicable household horrors; the mould, the drips, the leaks, the mysterious pools of water: David's roof tiles were porous.

In spite of the cold, he started sweating.

Why oh why, at the end of the twentieth century, did human beings persist in hooking tablets of pottery onto rows of sticks and hoping they would cope with being frozen, rained upon, frizzled in sunshine, snowed all over, and still provide impermeable shelter? Why oh why did Pitsbury Council insist that these tablets be not new ones, which might have stood some hope of fulfilling this function, but old, clapped-out ones, in keeping with all the other old, clapped-out ones that offered virtually no protection atop Pitsbury's listed buildings?

In keeping with the poor, broken, clapped-out people that lived in them.

David would have implored the Heavens to rain curses upon him, had he been able to cope with the idea of any more water, and had they not been so much more than obliging in that respect already. He should have known. He should have known better than to allow himself a vision even of the vaguely endurable, let alone the pleasant, given his awareness that the tiniest image of past pleasures only accentuated his present overloaded backpack of despair. He shouldn't have relaxed his guard even for a minute. He couldn't afford to. Optimism was the enemy. Without it, and with an unwavering but generalised focus on existence's awfulness, you could shuffle along fairly tolerably. Especially if armed with sarcasm, cynicism and irony

– all the things that Clementine had come along and made a temporary mess of.

Though she had appreciated his wit – something to which everyone else seemed oblivious.

Were there other things about him that she might have appreciated? David wondered. Had she admired his loyalty? Probably not. Unless it was to themselves, loyalty wasn't a virtue women had much time for. She must have liked his books, though; or at least the thought of the fingers that might have touched them.

The fingers that might have touched.

The cathedral doors opened.

The cathedral bells started to clang savagely.

The presence of Clementine. The absence of Clementine. The impossible mayhem of the one. The inconceivability of the other. The soft, irresistible little tap of hope upon the psyche. To combat which David forced himself to think of everything that he loathed about Pitsbury. To focus, not on the sturdy grace of the city's churches or the fry-ups they used to do at the bus station café; the merry peasants in the cathedral's stained-glass windows or the cobbled back-alleys. Instead, he contemplated the High Street's burger outlets with their strip lights and plastic menus. The one-cup teapots and textureless scones of the ersatz tea rooms at the bottom of it. The undeveloped stretch of wasteland at the end of Weaver Street. The postcards of the Archbishop in the cathedral gift shop. The Mayor. The Conservation Officer. The Pitsbury Arts Festival.

The Pitsbury Arts Festival, which the crowd now emerging from the cathedral had theoretically been in there to celebrate – though Pitsbury's apparent love of the arts didn't manifest itself in a desire to purchase any substantial number of volumes from David Marsh Antiquarian Books. David's eyes moved feverishly from group to group, person to person, sifting through nondescript men and women in beige and navy, the Archbishop, lay clerks, a gloved batch of Worthy Ladies, the Mayor of Pitsbury, the Lady Mayoress.

The bells stopped, but in David's head the clanging continued. Barely breathing, he waited.

Out into the sunlight came Harriet, Duchess of Pitsbury, deep in conversation with Tony Gilbert, who taught Media Studies at the University. They stood in the cathedral's great doorway, a terrible, earnest expression on Gilbert's face, his long, obscenely healthy body blocking David's vision of who was behind him.

Gilbert and the Duchess took a few paces forward. David glimpsed a cluster of dazed-looking, suntanned people in light fawn mackintoshes: the contingent from Pitsbury College, Canada, surely. The people that Clementine would have come with, if she had come.

At that moment a vicious gust of wind threw grit into David's eyes. The crowd, the cathedral, the ruins turned into a blurred fog of shapes and colours. David had the absurd feeling that in this visionless moment he could choose whichever reality he wanted to be the case when his sight came back to him; then the awful realisation that he did not know what that would be.

By the time David could see again, the Canadians were standing in the sun examining their cameras. The Duchess had moved on from Tony Gilbert and was accepting flowers from a group of primary school children and a scattering of Brownies. She shook hands with a fat black person, someone in a wheelchair and various curtsying ladies in hats. People waved little flags. The entourage disappeared around the side of the cathedral to watch a dance extract from the Queen's School's Francis Partington Day production of *Loving Wisely Well* by Hermia Mowbray. The play had been performed in April. David had gone to it.

His heartbeat slowed. The number of people coming out of the cathedral had thinned to the pious and one or two cathedral groupies; they liked to help gather up hymn-books. The wooden NO ENTRY sign was removed and a queue of tourists began to shuffle in. A verger appeared from the cathedral, with the air of someone about to shake a duster. Business as usual. The wind carried small bursts of something Tudor, played on a recorder. The ever-present criss-cross of scaffolding which lined the north tower vibrated. At its feet lumps of masonry awaited cleaning or sticking up among the angels.

David abandoned his last hope – that Clementine had let her

colleagues proceed without her, preferring to wander alone around the cathedral. She had not come.

He felt hollow and exhausted. The Icelandic sweater was itchy. Clementine had not come and this pointless search for her would probably have rekindled Fay's suspicions. Those suspicions that he had for so long grimly, bitterly and – yes – credit where credit was due, what little could be taken – affectionately endeavoured to quieten.

Credit.

Clementine being here would, at the very least, have shaken everything up. Changed the priorities. As it was, all remained exactly as before, demanding ever more insistently that David deal with it.

He had better go home. There was nothing to stay for. Everything would continue unaltered. In his pocket was a letter from the bank, his name and address firmly centred in the see-through box. Some time today it must be looked at.

As he set off back to Weaver Street, David was not heartened to remember that, at eight o'clock, he was due to attend Henry Pearl's Mongolian Evening.

2

Mongolian Evening

The visit of the Duchess of Pitsbury to Pitsbury Cathedral had been in order to unveil a plaque in memory of Renaissance playwright, Hermia Mowbray, who, tradition had it, was born in Pitsbury and, rather more certainly, died there, in a house which was pulled down by Pitsbury Council in 1986. The site of the demolished building was now occupied by a closed Estate Agent's.

This Renaissance connection was, presumably, the explanation for the display in the window of Domicile Department Store, one of the Pitsbury Festival's principal sponsors according to the local paper. Behind the glass, on an enormous rose-printed sofa, a Tudor sort of hat and a wooden musical instrument shaped a bit like half an onion lay side by side. A hand-written card on an adjacent occasional table read 'Pitsbury Arts Festival Window Display Competition – First Prize'.

As he paused to look at this, David's nose was assailed by the aroma emanating from another of the Festival's backers, Bigga-Burgers; a subtle mix of burning fat and onions, with an aftertaste of slightly off meat. Bigga-Burgers had sent down Bozo, the official Bigga-Burgers' clown who appeared in its television advertisements, for the opening Saturday of the Festival. An attempt, David supposed, to upstage the contribution of another of the Festival's sponsors, Burger-Fish ('A New, Lighter Eating Concept', shamelessly cashing in on the food scares). Burger-Fish, according to the paper, had provided a complimentary banana milkshake to each member of a barbershop quartet from Hastings, bussed in for the occasion courtesy of Can-Do Computers. In the window of Can-Do Computers, David noted a Pitsbury Arts Festival 'Honorable Mention' certificate, proudly placed on a hard-disc-drive.

The performers provided by the Quik-Potato Literary Fringe had been of a similar calibre. Comedian Reggie Bell and model Kandy Lam had read from their new novels. A photograph in the window of Fay Marsh's ex-employer, Langley The Chemist – an area which in the past had been occupied by displays of trusses and corn plasters, but which nowadays was filled with pictures of bark-pounding natives and reflexology diagrams – showed Reggie Bell crowning the new Miss Pitsbury, who had apparently won 'A Langley's Makeover'. As David walked disconsolately past Quik-Potato, with its list of forty toppings, including the 'new tomato curry flavour', he saw that its formica tables were occupied by dozens of emaciated teenage females, all toying with their 'lo-cal cottage-cheese and apricot' toppings, all identical to the reigning Miss Pitsbury. There was a poster reminding any who had forgotten that Quik-Potato had also subsidized the performance by the Polish State Brass Ensemble in the Queen's School hall, and given a grant towards the Pitsbury Players' production of Monteverdi's *Il ritorno d'Ulisse in patria*.

After Cagmag's Butchers the number of people on the pavements thinned out. From there on the High Street was occupied mainly by charity shops. White-haired ladies rooted through the crocheted and chiffon things in the 'special offer' boxes just inside their doors. A party of Japanese tourists was seated at the old sewing-machine tables of the loathsome tea rooms, the inordinate success of which, David decided, could only be due to a situation overlooking the river. It was at the Ebb that the High Street ended. Here the road forked, crossing the river by means of two bridges. David paused beside the right-hand one, the narrower of the two.

From here you could see on the other side of the bridge, Weaver Street, where David lived. Or rather the renovated part of it. Though the street appeared to terminate at the narrow gap where the road squeezed through the City Wall, it did in fact continue beyond that, into the area of the city called Pitsbury Without.

And Pitsbury Without was the source of most, if not the totality, of David's problems.

It was partly the fault of the river. If it hadn't been for the river, Pitsbury Without wouldn't have existed and David Marsh might not be facing a bleak future. After ducking under the City Wall to the east of Weaver Street the Ebb made a wide, expansive, geography-textbook sort of gesture, throwing out a watery lasso to create, with the City Wall, Pitsbury Without: a large, enclosed, roughly teardrop-shaped expanse of land.

The furthest point of this hemmed-in area – the point at which the river started to loop back towards the city – was perhaps three hundred yards from Weaver Street. At its widest, Pitsbury Without was approximately two hundred yards across. However, by the time the Ebb went under the bridge which actually marked the boundary of Weaver Street, the river was no more than twenty feet from the City Wall again, remaining parallel with it for a while before following the north-westward direction of one of the main roads out of the City.

Yes, David reflected, gazing into the Ebb, it was partly the fault of the river – or of the God who dictated the needlessly erratic qualities of moving water. But it was very much more the fault of Pitsbury Council and their disastrous handling of Pitsbury Without.

What the Council had done with the left-hand side of the section of Weaver Street beyond the City Wall was crass but unproblematic. At the end of the eighties they had pulled down its houses, and those of the streets behind, and made a long, narrow car park, the boundaries of which were the City Wall, Weaver Street, the Ebb and the north-western road. Car parks were what Pitsbury Council created by default when they couldn't think of anything else to do with a site, David had observed. Though why they pursued a policy of demolishing run-down residential areas, purely to create bits of land which they then didn't know what to do with, he couldn't imagine. This particular car park was rarely more than half full. It sporadically flooded.

At the same time as it was flattening the area to the left of

Weaver Street, the Council put into motion its demolition programme for Pitsbury Without. Soon it was a virtual wasteland,
affording views of the buildings on the far bank of the Ebb –
the ancient church of St Friedaswida, Bus Station House, the
garages, warehouses and wholesale outlets of the Elizium Forest
Industrial Estate.

But just before the job was entirely completed, suddenly,
with only one house in Pitsbury Without left standing, the
Council called the project to a halt. The remaining building,
which occupied the entire far end of Weaver Street – those
twenty feet between the bridge where it terminated and the
City Wall – was left completely untouched.

This building was to become Weaver Street's lurking presence;
its festering sore. The fact that it was invisible from the cathedral
end made no difference.

Why in God's name it had been spared no one could begin
to guess. The place looked as if it had been beaten up. It sagged
under the weight of a shattered roof. Walls swelled out or
crumbled inwards. Skewed lintels collapsed onto the gaping
upper front windows which looked out over Weaver Street and
the car park. The lower ones were boarded over. Peeling plaster
exposed powdery wattle and daub. The beams were riddled with
woodworm. A red-bricked chimney, unpointed for at least half
a century, looked about to collapse at any minute. This didn't
stop it from being used, though.

The building had become an enormous squat.

Ironically enough – something David couldn't contemplate
without wishing for a sword to fall upon – the Council-created
wasteland that the squat backed onto was the reason why David
and Fay Marsh had moved to Weaver Street. They had bought
and renovated their house and two shops there in the early
nineties, before the arrival of the squatters. The then Council's
plan had been to complete the demolition programme – namely,
pull this last building down – and to turn the wasteland into a
landscaped park.

Before the strategy could be implemented, however, that
Council was voted out of office and replaced by one which,
according to Mayor Horatio Bullock, could no longer consider
the plan financially viable. Instead of the trees, lawns and

flowerbeds, on the promise of which David and Fay had invested their money, there remained a graveyard of demolished houses and dead gardens; broken metal buckets; shards of willow pattern china; fragments of blue and green glass; tough, fleshy-leaved flowers; flocks of seagulls, picking amongst the debris; earth cicatrized with squares and oblongs of masonry, the remains of what had once been kitchens, sheds, lavatories, sitting-rooms, dining-rooms, bathrooms.

Horatio Bullock, the Mayor who had not seen fit to remedy this situation, was also David's bank manager. He had, in fact, lent most of the money which had been used in the renovation of Weaver Street.

Which David now crossed the river and entered.

The buildings of Pitsbury High Street were a hotchpotch of fifties' and sixties' re-development, Tudorbethan and Mock-Georgian, all muddled in with the odd remaining bits of Medieval and Renaissance. Weaver Street, however, was entirely late sixteenth and early seventeenth century.

There were black beams, white and cream walls, tall, crenellated chimneys, arched front doors with curly locks, intricately carved pieces of woodwork. The occupants of Weaver Street had spared no expense. Their businesses were also their residences – which was partly what made their financial situation so disastrous.

As David walked past the dark grey frontage of Just The Business, with its smoked glass window and minimalist interior, an ambulance shot past in the direction of the cathedral, briefly obscuring the ground floor of the building opposite.

This was an enormous Tudor merchant's residence. A fretwork of unpainted beams, terminating at rooftop level in carved roses and *fleurs de lys*, and gorgeous, faded brickwork, laid out in complicated patterns. It had been divided into two sections; the first proclaiming in restrained gold letters: Henry Pearl Interiors; the other, which took up the majority of the frontage, Marauding Hordes Mongolian Restaurant. In the doorway of Marauding Hordes a beautiful black man, with a shaven head and enough rings in his ears to support a row of curtains, was smoking a cigarette and tossing Refreshers into his mouth, two at a time. This was Colin Rutt, Henry Pearl's boyfriend. At the sight of David, Colin raised a hand crammed with thick silver rings with skulls and eyeballs and called 'Wotcha!'

David gave a quick wave in reply. He was not in the mood for conversation. Now he had come to a bookshop – his bookshop: David Marsh Antiquarian Books. In its window was a display of maps, a yellowed globe, a planisphere, a telescope; volumes lay open to reveal etchings of ships. Though he knew it was pointless, David scanned the window for a 'Pitsbury Festival Window Display Award'. If he had won anything, Fay would have been sure to place it there. There was nothing.

Water was dripping from the hanging baskets which dangled fronds of fern and other leafy things outside Fay's shop, Marsh Meadows – Aromatherapy and Herbs – a name which David had always found intensely irritating, it seeming to combine the maximum of wetness with the maximum of tweeness, along with a cloying overtone of marshmallow. It was galling to think that because his and Fay's shops were part of the same building it would be assumed that he had been involved in the choosing of it.

Through the window of Marsh Meadows, David could see his wife weeping into the box of tansy and snakeroot which she'd informed him needed to be sent off today to the shaman she supplied in Aldershot. No emotional trauma, however great, marred Fay's professional efficiency. Every so often, though, she gave a little sniff and scrubbed at her eyes with her wrists.

The bugger of it, David reflected, with a stab of guilt, was that Fay Marsh was a thoroughly decent person. Worse still, she loved him; loved him with unending, long-suffering patience. And the more patient she was, the more he was irritated by her. The more irritated he was by her, the more he realised what a bastard he was. The more he realised what a bastard he was, the more irritated he became. It was a bit like the endlessly turning cycle of death and regeneration that was described in the leaflets that came with Fay's herb lists.

Unfortunately, the only thing that would make David feel more blameworthy than he currently did would be to leave her. They had been together since they were teenagers. Until recently, she had supported him financially.

Judging from this rainforest of misery, Fay had, indeed,

guessed that he had gone to the cathedral to see the Canadian contingent. Which would mean another deluge of suspicion and insecurity. As David entered, Fay hastily unhooked a length of blonde hair from behind one of her pale ears and, with her back to him, reached up to a scrubbed shelf for a dried ginseng root and her pestle and mortar and started to grind in pained silence.

The house door was open. Fay had recently polished the banisters; the scent of beeswax emanated from the rich, dark staircase and mingled with the cold, silver-polish aroma of the flagstones. She had re-filled the Chinese bowl on the oak chest with pot-pourri, but its flowery odour could not drown out a pervading hint of fungus.

'Henry. The Mongolian Evening,' said Fay, in a tone of muffled bravery. 'He phoned to check that we'll be there.'

'Why, are people clamouring for tables?'

Tonight was to be Marauding Hordes' grand opening. In its previous manifestation, Henry Pearl's restaurant had gone under the name of Grandmother's Footsteps and had served nothing that did not contain lentils or have something to do with a goat; dietary combinations that rendered the digestive tract more a cul-de-sac than a conduit and which owed little debt, as far as David could see, to grandmothers in any of the forms in which Colin Rutt, the restaurant's chef, was likely to have encountered them. David's own grand-mere's idea of culinary aplomb had been to put salt in the cabbage water before it went on for its forty-five minute boil.

Henry Pearl looked upon cooking as a heroic act. Colin Rutt was quite willing to go along with this, if it meant that Henry wrote the cheques. You could tell, however, that as a long-term career choice, Colin's heart wasn't really in it. Catering, he'd once told David, was an option that had been foisted on him at college. Should finances dry up, he would probably go back to being a bouncer or modelling for leatherware catalogues, or have another bash at his first love, bricklaying.

Fay's reproachful voice interrupted David's thoughts. 'This is Henry's last chance. He lost so much investing in Grandmother's Footsteps.'

'All of which he made out of us. Henry Pearl's interior

designs, along with Pitsbury Council's Conservation Officer, have conspired between them to ensure that the only absolute certainty on my life's horizon is penury.'

David remembered, with an inner shudder, Henry Pearl darting around the place discussing inevitably expensive 'concepts' and 'features'. There were even visual puns in two of the bedrooms. If Henry Pearl's insistence on creating a career for his bit of rough meant that he would be accompanying them down the road to ruin, David found it hard to be sympathetic.

'I can call back and say we aren't coming,' said Fay. 'But it would be nice to Henry to make an effort. And, anyway, these things are usually fun.' The last word was said with a little quiver.

'You are sufficiently familiar with Mongolian Evenings to be able to generalise?' There was silence. 'No, we might as well go,' said David, 'since you've bought the tickets.' And there would be no possibility of getting the fifty pounds they had cost back from Henry.

Fay turned to face David now. 'We choose our own raw materials and cook them on hot stones.'

'How delightful. Do we also take a bottle of wine for the chef and offer to wash up afterwards?'

David made his way through the house to the bookshop. There seemed little point in turning the sign to Open, but he did so anyway, unlocking the door with the heavy old key. There were first editions in gorgeous mahogany book-cases; delicate mahogany chairs for browsers. His own little desk was exquisite – spindly legs, scrolling; you could imagine the stretched fingers of one hand would be sufficient to lift it. Upon it was a Georgian silver letter-writing set. The paper on the walls was hand-printed.

When he looked at these things now, David conceived a profound longing for an unfurnished cell, in which to flagellate himself.

What had they been thinking about? What the *hell* had they been thinking about?

David sat at the desk and opened the letter from the bank – Horatio Bullock, to be precise: the Mayor, the bank manager.

First of all, he scanned it – far enough away not to be

completely in focus – for general content. The customary words were there (*regret, concerned, immediately*). David felt the usual absurd stab of disappointment. How, at forty, was it possible still to foster the childish hope that, spontaneously, all your problems would vanish – the belief that your own particular story must have a happy ending and that, when things got rough enough, some anonymous person would step in and bring it about for you?

Next, David read the first and last sentences, word by word, without allowing himself to skip any. He laid the letter down. There was no need to look at the middle. In the hierarchy of threatening letters, this, he calculated, was one – at the most, two – off the one that threatened bankruptcy proceedings.

When atavistic notions had been dominant in Colin Rutt's kitchen, Henry Pearl had taken his Volvo across the Channel once a month and come back with a carful of thick, plastic containers, each of which held fifteen litres of red wine you could have run a tractor on. This he decanted into rough, artisanal jugs he found at car boot sales and sold at around a thousand percent profit to the few customers who ever came to Grandmother's Footsteps. David Marsh had not imagined that anything as disgusting could be deemed contributary to a Mongolian theme, until he was handed the complimentary tiswin that was included in the price of their ticket.

Tiswin proved to be the kind of alcohol that carried the thoughts inevitably in the direction of blindness; gang warfare; illicit stills in wretched backwaters; desperate consumption by natives with nothing left to live for since their tribes had been decimated by smallpox. As such, it was perfectly in tune with David's emotions. Henry Pearl claimed that, though not strictly speaking Mongolian, the drink was all the rage among the gays in Clapham.

Misguided affection, not lack of financial acumen, was Henry Pearl's problem.

A tall, thin, balding man, who always wore a waistcoat, and was so impeccably attired he gave the impression of having been cut out of a magazine with sharp scissors, he was frequently called upon to give his judgements on style by those who had none in places such as Chelsea and Hampstead. He positively *adored* women. Well, actually, he positively adored *every*body. He was fond of gossip. The London socialites loved his company. Marauding Hordes was stuffed to the gills for this, its opening, with people who wouldn't usually touch Pitsbury with a bargepole and who could not be counted on for repeat custom.

'I was just saying to Rick here,' said Henry, refilling David's glass, 'that this time, *this* time, I would be totally confident of success were it not for the neighbours.'

'What I don't get,' said Rick Farr, owner of Just The Business, which was, to everyone's mystification, an Internet shop, 'is why, given that the demolition job had been started, the new council didn't go ahead and finish it – even if they had decided against making a park on the site. Why leave just one building standing?'

Working-class, made good in the eighties, Rick attempted to give off an aura of Wall Street by wearing braces, an effect that was spoilt by his habit of constantly extending his arms to reveal his shirt-cuffs. As he spoke, he tapped the filter end of an unlit cigarette repeatedly on his cigarette packet. Just The Business, as its name implied, was aimed exclusively at the business market. Rick had come to Henry Pearl's opening in order to punt for custom. According to Henry, he owed the bank seventy thousand and was six months behind on his repayments.

'Without the promise of the park, I'd never have bought here. Never never never,' said Henry. 'People were to be enticed to Weaver Street by the thought of a wander among the gypsophila and, instead . . . Well, I've written to the Council, I don't know how many times, begging them to pull the squat down and do something with the site.'

'We've spent money we haven't got,' said Rick. 'We work our behinds off. Only to have potential clients put off by us being slap bang next to a bunch of people who . . .'

'Turn our endeavours to chaff,' Henry finished for him.

'Yes,' said Rick. 'Exactly.' He sought to suggest, by a thumbs-up sign, that this was the way he too would have completed the sentence.

David was silent. He took a gulp from his tumbler. The second glass of tiswin was going down more easily, the first having burnt out most of his tongue's sensory receptors. Sooner or later, all their financial conversations came back to the subject of the Weaver Street squat. Encroaching poverty. Customers were put off by it; felt threatened by the studded, tattooed people who inhabited the decaying building, which seemed to draw into its compass every homeless person who ever fetched up in Pitsbury. Nobody was sure how many dossed down there or how long any of them stayed for. There seemed to be a central nucleus of four or five in constant occupation, but on cold nights the numbers swelled enormously – men, women and children arriving from all directions. They lit fires in rusted metal braziers on the waste-ground. They hung washing lines. When it wasn't raining they mooched about the street. When it was hot they sunbathed on the pavement. The police were constantly hammering and demanding admittance.

One pitied them, of course, but why here? Why in Pitsbury? Why in Weaver Street? David Marsh, Rick Farr, Henry Pearl, had bought into Weaver Street, believing that the houses they had restored, and now lived in and worked from, would be near a park, a minute away from a walk by the river. Instead, they were shoulder to shoulder with displacement and chaos: the death-watch beetle in the woodwork, nightly pounding a coded message on its bongos.

David had taken a risk when he'd borrowed so heavily, but everyone had done that; it was in the nature of things. All you could do was make sure that your risk was well-calculated, build a certain number of eventualities into the picture. The derelict house at the end of Weaver Street being squatted hadn't been one of them. Almost single-handedly it had ruined any chance his business had of making it. People would not come to Weaver Street. He was a cartoon character who had run off the edge of a cliff; air was all he was treading on. Like the cartoon character, he, Rick and Henry had tried, were trying, to move backwards – they'd each made futile gestures in search of financial recovery. Grandmothers were old hat, whereas Mongols were up to the minute; maybe that would make a difference. A prize in the window display competition would bring coverage in the local paper. David had spent hours choosing the perfect volumes to give the perfect impression, to create a window so striking that people would overcome their distaste for the squat and come and look at it. Rick Farr dealt out his business cards as if they predicted good fortune. But all the time, all the time, that battered house undermined everything.

Or so they thought, and they were partly right, probably. A sociologist might have put forward a different explanation, to do with per capita buying patterns, or some such. A psychologist in the service of commerce could have hazarded a theory to do with spatial perceptions. Each in their way might have been correct but, as scapegoats, such abstractions would have lacked the pith of a squatted building falling to pieces beneath one's very eyes.

'Henry!' A heavily subsidised face, which screamed London. 'This' (kiss) 'is just' (kiss) 'too' (kiss) 'too' (kiss) 'gorgeous. Where did you get the idea for the decor?'

'Mona!' (Kiss kiss, kiss kiss). 'Buildings speak to me. They dictate their requirements.'

David poured himself another tumbler of tiswin.

'In that case,' he observed loudly, 'mine must have been particularly garrulous.'

'Do explain the food to us, Henry,' said the woman.

Henry made a graceful gesture with an Aubrey Beardsley finger. 'One piece of advice and then my lips are sealed. I wouldn't deprive you of the chance to make your own discoveries. The trick' – he mouthed this word, as if afraid that others would hear it – 'is in choosing your combination of ingredients.'

The room was becoming rather hazy. 'Trick?' exclaimed David. 'Discoveries?'

But Henry Pearl was clapping his hands and crying 'To table! To table!' People were starting to move in the direction of a central area, where Colin Rutt had laid out platters covered in strips of beef the thickness of tracing paper, a rather more generous quantity of thinly-sliced vegetables and little fingers of raw coley, along with a large number of bowls full of nuts and dips, sauces and shredded relishes. The waiters went round switching the stones on, and people began to seat themselves on the very low benches, at tables for which the optimum height in order to be truly comfortable was four foot three. An ancient man in a corner let up the kind of wail that could only have been produced by somebody who had personally witnessed a massacre, and plucked at a piece of string tied, at each end, to a broom handle. Three dancers appeared, clad in rectangular hats and baggy trousers, and started to execute a dance that consisted mainly of taking a couple of slow footsteps then remaining motionless.

'They cost a fortune,' breathed Henry Pearl in David's ear. 'They've done a Royal Variety.'

'So what's a good read then, David?' said Rick Farr, as they queued for plates.

'Can you fellers give me a comment?' asked an acne-faced sixteen-year-old at David's elbow. In the distance, a faint popping sound could now be made out above the music. The boy quickly turned to the window. 'Sod. Missed it.'

'Who are you?' asked David.

The boy faced them again. 'Local paper. I'm the restaurant critic, but I'm also covering the fireworks because the bloke that was going to do it got put onto the accident.'

'What accident?'

The boy glanced out of the window again. There was a pale green light just tingeing the lower sky. He jotted in his notebook. 'A bit after Duchess Harriet sodded off home. A Canadian. Academic. Walked into something that wasn't there – great story, got a bit of everything, even involved a squatter. And I'm stuck with this one. Anyway, how about a comment? I've interviewed the dignitaries. I only need an overview from the man in the street, then I can bugger off.'

'I daresay you will be able to track down some down-and-outs ferreting among the dustbins.'

'Metaphorically speaking. Literary license.'

'And who are the dignitaries? Don't tell me I have missed the arrival of someone illustrious?'

'Sam Bullock is here.'

'Not *the* Sam Bullock?'

'He is the Mayor's brother,' said the reporter. 'And he owns one of the largest cattle farms in the area.'

'Does he?' asked Rick Farr, who was relatively new to Pitsbury. He peeled a shiny business card off the wad he was holding. 'Which one is he, then?'

'David,' said Fay, approaching now, as he reached for another tumbler of tiswin, 'don't you think you might feel icky in the morning?'

'I have never felt "icky" in my entire life, so I very much doubt it. Sam Bullock is the purple-faced one who looks as if he might be about to explode. Oh, and Rick,' washed over by a wave of empathy, 'I'll take one of your services. You suggest one. Whichever you like.'

'I can do a nice deal on an E-mail box,' said Rick, eagerly. 'Don't suppose you'd use my virtual conference facilities.'

'An E-mail box. I'll have that then.'

David was dimly aware of Fay vanishing, in some state of upset.

Without realising he had done so, he had heaped his plate with a lurid mix of raw, gritty and spiky things that he didn't want, along with masses of herb fronds and chilli flowers – a melange which bore not a little resemblance to one of Fay's hanging baskets. There was nothing to do but look for a stone to cook them on – preferably at a dark table, away from everyone.

But there were no dark spots in Marauding Hordes, in keeping with Henry Pearl's design principles, which were based on the four elements: air, fire, water and earth, in that order. Having financed the unblocking of three chimneys, the creation of two, totally extraneous, bathrooms, not to mention the acquisition of numerous miniature trees in pots, it was a toss-up as to which of the elements had cost David the most. The one that really rankled though was air – windows, lintels, natural light, unexpected views of the cathedral, amusing vistas. Air was supposed to be free, wasn't it?

Anyway, there was nowhere dark and furtive and Henry himself was gesturing in David's direction, pointing at a free bit of bench and rubbing it, chummily, as if to warm it in preparation. There was nothing to do but join him.

'Oh look,' exclaimed one of Henry's cronies as David approached. 'He's put fig sauce with his macadamias.'

'It might work, I've known stranger things,' said another.

Henry Pearl rose to his feet. He handed David a little wooden-handled paintbrush. 'Put a soupçon of oil on the stone, to stop your coley sticking,' he said. 'I'm going to see if we can tempt Colin out of the kitchen so we can fête him.'

The room had started to spin.

'I'm a broken man, Henry,' said David. Out of the corner of his eye he spotted Fay emerging from the Ladies, sniffing courageously. 'I'm going to go bankrupt.'

'At least you've got your health,' Henry Pearl replied.

It was at this moment that David attempted to punch him, missed and went crashing to the ground in a shower of meat, fish and vegetables.

As he lay there, watching people's reactions, it struck him as ironic that the worst thing about the situation was not the humiliation, nor would it be the hangover. It was the fact that Fay, who he did not love, would forgive him.

Clementine Dee, who he did, would have bawled him out. But Clementine Dee, unlike Fay, would have understood what was causing his behaviour. She would have seen that the fabric of his existence was unshredding and that, alone, he had no idea how to hold it together.

Clementine Dee would never return to Pitsbury now and, all in all, David was not making a very good job of having to live his life without her.

3 ∫

The Quik-Potato Fellowship

Clementine Dee was a North American, a bastardised text. There was virtually nothing she wasn't a bit of. She scooped up culture like jelly-beans. She'd been born into a place that was the rag-rug of Europe. History to her was no dignified grey thing, but a matted jumble of human voices; a roaring magpie world-pot; an unstratified amalgam of presents and presences.

Clementine lectured in Renaissance literature at Pitsbury College, Canada. With her colleague, Ruth Carpini, and the other feminist academics of the P.C.C. English Department, she had been largely responsible for the rediscovery and reinstatement of Renaissance playwright, Hermia Mowbray – most of whose manuscripts had somehow found their way across the Atlantic and into Pitsbury College, Canada's gargantuan library. Slow to gain recognition in her own country, Hermia Mowbray had, at last, been fully instated in the British literary canon. Yesterday, in Pitsbury Cathedral U.K., they'd unveiled a plaque to her memory. Clementine Dee and Ruth Carpini were currently working on the first ever edition of Mowbray's complete works, for Amazon Press; Clementine from the Canadian end, Ruth from the British one.

The best laid frigging plans of mice and men.

Clementine took a large bite of salmon and cream cheese bagel, followed by a swallow of coffee, still looking at the E-mail.

It had all been so perfect.

The Quik-Potato Visiting Fellowship had provided Ruth with funding to spend this year in England, doing vital Mowbray research. She would be based at the English Department of the University of Pitsbury, U.K.

The Quik-Potato Fellowship stipulated that the visiting academic should reside in the house of an absent British colleague. Tony Gilbert, of the Department of English and Media Studies – who Clementine had met in the summer – was shortly due to leave for Provence, where he was to spend the year. He'd lent Ruth his cottage in the Ebb Valley, outside Pitsbury, and his car. Ruth had been hoping to track down any remaining unpublished Mowbray manuscripts. Already an ad in the Times Literary Supplement had borne exciting fruit – some Mowbray fragments, hitherto unknown to them, had come to light. They were held in a building called Bus Station House, just outside the centre of Pitsbury. Ruth had even been able to time things so she could travel over to Britain as part of the contingent from P.C.C. that had been invited for the unveiling of the Mowbray plaque in the cathedral. This had saved money and had conveniently enabled Clementine herself to decline the invitation, with the excuse that she was needed to hold the fort this side of the Atlantic.

Just too frigging convenient.

And now . . .

Clementine sighed. She read again the fateful E-mail which she'd found waiting for her when she'd arrived in her office this morning.

To: Dr Clementine Dee, Eng. Dept., P.C.C.
From: Dr Tony Gilbert, Dept. Eng. & Media Studs,
Univ. of Pitsbury, U.K.
Re: Quik-Potato Visiting Fellowship

i write in haste in the light of Dr R Carpini's accident. must join film director Zucchini & the Cannings (Immie and Rupert) in provence tomorrow at latest. Quik-Potato funding contingent upon consistent academic productivity – any break in continuity could result in cessation of backing.

please confirm you will immediately deal with the situation.
this 11th hour upset is not what I needed.

Tony Gilbert, Clementine had been told, had no friends himself, which presumably was why it had not occurred to him
that Clementine could possibly view a colleague's accident as
anything other than a nuisance. It had taken several, desperate
telephone calls to ascertain that Ruth wasn't badly hurt and to
get the full story.

Which was a bizarre one.

After a display of Renaissance dancing, Dr Ruth Carpini had
been presented to Harriet, Duchess of Pitsbury. In anticipation
of which, and notwithstanding the fact that the Duchess's royal
status was shortly to be curtailed by divorce, Ruth had not worn
her glasses, without which she was as blind as a bat. Curtsy
performed and Duchess having left, Ruth had set off, with
her colleagues, to seek tea in Pitsbury High Street. Enroute,
and before her fellow academics could intervene to prevent
it, Dr Carpini had mistaken a trompe l'oeil landscape painted
on a wall for the real thing and, in response to a last minute
realisation of her error, had fallen heavily sideways and broken
her right arm in several places. Which meant she could not
drive. Which meant she could not live at Tony Gilbert's house,
out in the sticks. Which meant that, unless another member of
the University of Pitsbury English Department was out of town
– one who lived in Pitsbury itself – and was willing to lend
Dr Carpini their house for the year, the Quik-Potato funding
stipulation would not be met.

Enquiries revealing no other appropriate person on sabbatical,
there was now just a single, obvious, yet totally unacceptable,
course of action. A course of action that could not be taken
because of what had happened to Clementine when she had
visited Pitsbury, U.K., earlier in the year. Or, rather, it could
be, but unequivocally would not.

It had been balmy weather, Clementine remembered, the day
she had met David Marsh. The end of April.

A rough, tugging breeze puffed clouds about the sky and made
the frothy pink blossom bob on the loaded branches. Clementine

had heard Evensong in Pitsbury Cathedral's fridgey interior. She recognised some of the Lay clerks as they came into the pub for their after-service pints.

The door of the Cock and Hen was open. The sky was taking on the pale blue of a spring evening. New leaves were touched with lime-green sunlight. Clementine could see the Ebb, thick from recent rain, tumbling down the weir, where a watermill had once stood, in a gleaming ribbon the colour of videotape. There was a pint of bitter in front of her. A fire burned in the pub's fireplace. Two weeks in Pitsbury lay ahead, part research, part holiday. She'd take a look at the University of Pitsbury's Mowbray holdings, make a few notes, touch base with some other Mowbray scholars and attend one or two English Department events; check things out a bit for Ruth Carpini's arrival in the early autumn. Otherwise, she'd just drink the place in. Who knew whether the stones her toes rested on might not owe their unevenness, in part, to Hermia Mowbray's footsteps?

It would all have been perfect, if it hadn't been for Tony Gilbert.

Tony Gilbert was the colour of peanut butter. His brown leather jacket was draped over the chair next to him. His mobile phone was on the table. He was holding a small newspaper on which was written the headline, 'PALACE DENIES DIVORCE RUMOUR', pointing, not at this, but at a colour photograph of Immie and Rupert Canning, the *chouchoux* of the film and theatre worlds of Britain and America.

At seventeen, Rupert Canning had founded a theatre company, so that people like him could get a chance to play the major roles. Immie first pierced public consciousness in a fifty-seven part TV drama about World Wars One and Two. Thence, they hit woods Pine and Holly, in that order. Immie dramatised and starred in and wrote the score to George Eliot's *Romola*. Rupert's rendition of Mercutio stole the film version of *Romeo and Juliet*, which he also directed. Now they had turned their thoughts to Hermia Mowbray. Hence the pleasing news of the availability of Tony Gilbert's house to Ruth Carpini during the next academic year. Gilbert was full of his role as literary advisor for the Cannings' screen version of Mowbray's comedy, *A Right Wonderful Error* – the planet's amazement that Immie and Roo had managed to persuade Zucchini to direct it; the anticipated pleasures of filming in France in the early autumn.

'It was bloody, choosing the location,' Gilbert was saying now. 'Absolutely bloody. Immie favoured Tinos, but Roo had been there when he was doing a shoot with Sir Len, back in the eighties. He wanted Barbados but, of course, Immie spent a summer there before university. God knows what would have happened if the Comte hadn't put his chateau at their disposal. Chateau, I say, but it's more a glorified mansion. Still, there'll be room for the entire cast, as long as the crew don't mind roughing it a bit in the stable block.'

'With the horses?'

'Horses?'

'Are there horses in the stable block?'

'Lord. Don't know. Never crossed my mind to ask. Though it's probably crossed Roo's; almost everything does and the things that don't, Immie reminds him of. They're a team. But they always have time for other people. That's the wonderful thing about Roo and Immie: they have time for other people. When Julian had his breakdown, they positively rushed to Hawaii to talk it through with him.'

'They sound all heart.'

'Yes. Yes indeed. I'd love you to meet them. Then there was the trauma as to which third of *A Right Wonderful Error* to cut. Immie was in shreds. Even I, as advisor, was coming completely unravelled.'

'If you're going to hack a third out of a play, do you have any choice but to make it the middle one?'

'Funnily enough, that was exactly the conclusion we eventually came to, but it was a near thing, I'm telling you, bloody close. Lord knows where we'd have been if Roo hadn't kept descending and dragging us out for dim sum.'

Tony Gilbert had been assigned to Clementine by the University. His plan, it appeared, was to spend much of the next two weeks forcing her to do things that he assumed she thought were typically English. Already he had made her eat a cream tea – the cheap kind, with jelly in tiny, plastic containers and aerated cream – at the café attached to Domicile Department Store. He had mentioned going to see some Morris Dancing. There was even talk of a Medieval Banquet. Somehow, she had got to shake him off, though this was not going to be easy since he knew where she was staying: The Cathedral Inn, an old-fashioned, dampish establishment backing onto the precinct with few bathrooms and, everywhere, faded notices about putting lights off and leaving things as you hoped to find them.

Now Gilbert picked up Clementine's hand and stroked it in a way that could be interpreted as avuncular.

'I thought, tomorrow, if it's fine, a picnic by the river. Ginger beer and scotch eggs.'

'Tony?'

Clementine looked up.

The pint of bitter nearly slipped from her hand.

It felt like one of the legs of the chair she was sitting on had fallen off.

It took all her concentration to keep from landing up on the floor on her butt in a fizzing pool of beer bubbles.

She hadn't realised they made them like that here! She'd assumed the British male version of sexy was the coffee commercial type that Tony Gilbert tried for. But this guy looked like he'd really been round the block. The face was rugged, good-looking, intelligent. There was a sardonic curve to the lips. She could imagine witty, satirical comments coming from them.

Clementine took a big gulp of beer, swilled it around her mouth, took it down in one big swallow. She'd never got hit this suddenly this bad before. Here was a man she wanted to argue with. Here was a man she'd like to get a rise out of. Here was a man she could see herself . . .

'David! Join us. Can I get you a top-up?'

'I'm all right,' said David, sitting. 'I just wanted to tell you I've tracked down some of that troubadour stuff you wanted.'

Troubadour stuff! Better and better!

Gilbert turned back to Clementine. 'Immie thought it would be fun to, as it were, underscore the song in *A Right Wonderful*

Error with an earlier burden. David Marsh is a bookseller, and I asked him to look out for any collections – especially in Old French. Sort of thing that was popular in the nineteenth century. But,' looking again at David, 'left hand not knowing what right hand's doing it turns out that, quite without telling us, Roo – consequence of a boozy evening – has asked Mark Casey to convert the whole thing to accoustic guitar and to do a cameo as the jester. Which he's agreed to. The treatment will be most startling, I think. But you can turn over any books you've found specially, can't you?'

'Of course, Tony. People are always crying out for nineteenth-century editions of Provençal poetry in Old French.'

Yup, satirical humour.

'Well that's all right then.' Gilbert's mobile phone rang. 'Good Lord! Talk of the Devil . . . No I was, I'm not just saying it, I really was, there are people here who would vouch for it . . . Yes, I really was, everyone's nodding. But I thought you were in . . . Zucchini! And Veronique's hoping to be there too? Well, it would take me a couple of hours . . . No, nothing I can't get out of probably . . . No, wait, I wouldn't dream of not being there. Wait.'

Gilbert cupped his hand over the mouthpiece. 'Clementine, Zucchini's flown into London, quite unexpectedly, and Immie and Roo are organising a gathering of the team at Harpo's. Would you mind awfully if . . . ?'

An evening at the famous Harpo's, even with the Cannings and Zucchini, would be infinitely preferable to the evening alone with Tony Gilbert that had been scheduled. 'Sure, that's fine by me. You were saying you'd like me to meet them.'

David Marsh still hadn't thrown a single look in her direction.

'Oh. Oh no.' Gilbert looked extremely grave all of a sudden. 'I don't think that would be possible. You see, Roo and Immie are immensely private people.'

Clementine realised her mistake. Looked like this was her lucky day. 'That's okay. You go to London. I'll be fine.'

'You're sure? Yes, Immie, I've managed to get out of it . . . Say nine-thirty . . . No, you're the lovely one. Yes you are, really.'

Within minutes Gilbert had stashed his phone, swung his jacket over his shoulder, reiterated apologies and made his exit, promising to be in touch the next day about the picnic.

Which meant he was tomorrow's problem. Clementine decided that before it got dark she'd walk by the river, let the place in her head where Tony Gilbert had been strutting and fretting fill with space and silence. For now she took another gulp of beer and waited. Outside a bird sang a raw, piercing, almost unbearably poignant note. David Marsh was obviously disinclined for conversation. Clementine put her glass down noisily to remind him of her presence.

It did the trick.

At last he looked at her square on.

'Whoever you are, I am unimpressed by your choice of friends,' he said.

Clementine forced herself to keep from smiling. No way was this man going to turn out to be the kind she usually fetched up with: guys who were nice enough and bright enough but ultimately boring, drawn to her intellect but lacking the imagination to challenge it. Clementine guessed that David Marsh was often bored too, for similar reasons. Her reply was going to have to hit home or she'd lose him.

'Contiguity is not the same as friendship. And if that comment's inspired by your lost sale, since it's up for discussion I could just as easily say I am unimpressed by your choice of customers.'

She'd got him interested. David looked startled.

'Doubtless you yourself dabble in the realms of abstract thought,' he replied. 'My pursuits are more of the concrete variety and beggars can't be choosers.'

'But you don't beg, do you?' Clementine responded quickly. 'You sell books. Unsuccessfully, I suppose. Though in order to be a paid-up member of the I-can-act-like-an-asshole-because-life's-treated-me-so-rough club, you'll need to walk down Skid Row a whole lot further.'

Their eyes met. She held his gaze, her eyebrows arched. Clearly, she'd thrown him right off balance. Clearly, he was liking it.

What followed was why there was no way Clementine Dee

was going to get on a plane and fly over to replace Ruth Carpini as Quik-Potato Visiting Fellow at the University of Pitsbury.

4

Loving Wisely Well

There was a loud banging coming from the wasteland the morning after Henry Pearl's Mongolian Evening: the unlikely herald of dramatic changes in the lives of the people of Weaver Street.

Fay Marsh did not really notice it, however. She was thinking of the clandestine business she was hoping to achieve at Rick Farr's Internet shop before David woke, and, with a view to assessing how deeply he slept, giving him little pokes with a finger as he lay beneath the patchwork quilt – the one that Henry Pearl had advised Fay to commission on that fateful morning at the beginning of May, when she had found out about David and the Canadian.

'Every quilt pattern means something,' Henry had said. 'But your American friend could tell you more about that than I can.'

'I don't have an American friend.'

'Well not exactly American. Canadian. The one who was over here last month, while Colin and I were at Lake Geneva convalescing from the trauma of having to break the news about Grandmother's Footsteps to the goat farmer. What *was* her name? Tony Gilbert did mention it. He was quite miffed you dominated the woman so much, by the way. He was the one who thought he'd scored the hit, but once she'd struck up an acquaintance with you and David, apparently there was no getting a look in.'

Breathe in, one two. Breathe out, one two. Camomile. Ginger. Peppermint foot-rub. Marsh Meadows. Marsh Meadows.

'Clementine. Clementine Something,' said Henry. 'Clementine Dee. That's it!'

'When was this?' In a voice that wasn't much more than a whisper.

'That Tony mentioned her? Oh look at that, Fay, it just screams to be stripped down to see what's underneath. It was when Tony was thinking he might need me to advise on what sort of wall-hangings would best complement Zucchini's interpretation of sixteenth-century Florence, for a film he's making. A meeting was to be set up and everything, but it all fell through at the last minute. Not that anyone bothered to inform Yours Truly. The first I knew of it was when I received a postcard from Cannes.'

It was becoming clear to Fay why the tea-rose essence that she had been secretly adding to her compotes had failed to improve David's humour.

Most people, when asked to pinpoint the worst moment in their lives, would take a while to choose. For Fay there was no question – a lack of ambivalence for which she supposed she should be grateful.

After Henry had gone, she shut herself in the priest's hole with a mug of slippery elm and some sugared violets and wept for two and a half hours. What struck her most was the utter unfairness. She had earned the right to David's loyalty; she had worked for it, both literally and psychologically. She had soaked up his moodiness and sarcasm at the same time as she had supported him financially. The only return she had ever wanted was that he should belong only to her.

Love can easily become a kind of imposition. Ironically, it was precisely because Fay had given so much of herself that David's sentiments had worn threadbare. By means of the tacit communication which is so often the currency of married life, it had come to be understood between them – without a word on the topic ever being uttered – that, in the light of her disproportionate input into their life together, Fay might now demand as a right the love that hitherto she had merely requested.

Though David was not entirely blameless either, and perhaps their relationship would have reached this flimsy state anyway. Fay had never been considered David's intellectual equal, but she had possessed the tubercular style of looks and the rather hopeless insouciance that were highly fashionable at the time when they met each other. She was worth the winning and David – not considering that making a gorgeous pair on arriving at a party might be less important at forty than at eighteen – won her. Now, though Fay was not, actually, bereft of intelligence, David found it harder than he originally had to live with somebody whose intellectual world view allowed them to be of the opinion that the strength of a herbal potion increased in direct proportion to how greatly it was diluted, or that sniffing a buttercup was an antidote to financially-inspired angst. Even though there was an ever-increasing number of people who thought the same.

Their union had not been aided by the fact that Fay had supported them both throughout David's university degree, working her way up from the cash desk to the not-badly-paid post of Fragrance Consultant at Pitsbury's branch of Langley The Chemist. Actually, Fay had been chief earner throughout their life together. When David graduated, with Fay's agreement he got a job at a secondhand bookshop in one of the coastal towns. It was an abysmal salary, and the daily train-fare was expensive, but the owner knew everything there was to know about the book trade and, not long off retirement, was willing to teach David the ins-and-outs of it. The situation, anyway, was not envisaged as permanent – David's elderly and ailing parents who, though affluent, had endeavoured to school their son in financial self-sufficiency during their lifetimes, would have little option but to leave him to his own moral devices upon their deaths.

Which was what eventually transpired – though the time the whole scenario took to unfold was far greater than any, except those who have ever pinned their hopes on an otherwise uncooperative relative (let alone two) shuffling off this mortal coil when most reasonable in them to do so, would have deemed possible.

By then, Fay had had her Road to Damascus. Caused by the

fact that the marketing department of Langley The Chemist – which, for a century or so, had been toddling along checking its concoctions out on rabbits and putting the okayed results into fake cut-glass bottles – had been forced to the conclusion that the only answer to its declining sales was to become eco-friendly. Overnight, its products underwent a transformation. Now they were made of natural things, like sustainable seaweed; tested only on human beings; sold in recyclable, refillable plastic containers. Nor did they simply clean you or make you smell nice, they fulfilled a therapeutic purpose as well. Off Fay went to Epsom, to be informed of the beneficial qualities of herbs and fragrances.

How often students surpass their tutors! Hence Fay quitting Langley's, hence Marsh Meadows as well as David Marsh Antiquarian Books. Now that David was in a position, for the first time, to put down a sum large enough to permit them to borrow sufficient to make a substantial property investment (that would both provide a sumptuous home and bring in good money) Fay had decided that she, too, wanted her own business.

Much, though not all, of this was what Fay Marsh thought about as she considered the handsome, haggard face of her sleeping husband. A hefty proportion of it was what she had strongly hinted at when David found her sobbing in the priest's hole – as priest's holes went, it was not a particularly well-designed one if, indeed, it was one at all. Though Henry Pearl insisted to the contrary, David remained convinced that it was just a cupboard; as supporting evidence for his theory he would have been able to cite the ease with which, on this occasion, he discovered his wife's whereabouts, had it not been for the fact that the racket she was making would have been unlikely in a prelate.

The scene which had ensued lasted not hours or days or even weeks but became, instead, a constant of their marriage; a sleeping poltergeist, liable to be disturbed by lesser cosmic ripples than the visit of a group of academics from the very Canadian college . . .

There is only one consolation in psychological disruption and, depending upon the disruption, as a compensation it might not seem terribly great: distress is not boring. It could even be argued that, sometimes, distress, consciously or otherwise, is sought out as an antidote to *ennui*. And, conversely, *ennui* – or, in its best clothes, *stability* – as a protection against psychological disruption, and the changes that might result from it.

Both approaches to existence are worth a try. Neither is reliable.

Bang, bang, bang.

David stirred at the noise from the wasteland, and at Fay's exploratory finger, but did not look like regaining consciousness. Fay hastily looped her cloth bag over her shoulder and scuttled from the room, reckoning she had at least an hour to achieve what she wanted to at Just The Business.

She was correct. David was in the heavy, clogged sleep of one who has got utterly plastered the night before. In his brain, memory was at that moment a scrambled mass of dislodged pieces; the banging from the wasteland entering his mind subliminally and causing it to play out a portion of the past. The one, as it happened, that was also uppermost in his wife's mind: the time he had spent with Clementine.

When David knocked on the door of Clementine's hotel room on that day in April of which he now dreamed, she was just on the point of leaving via the window.

Clementine did not seem surprised to see him. She stood in the open doorway, a half smile on her face, waiting for him to speak. The lights in the room were off. Behind her was a large, cool oblong of night sky. The room smelled of damp and daffodils. There was a patch of moonlight on the tufty carpet. David remained on the threshold, in the forty-watt corridor, his eyes adjusting to the darkness of the interior. Clementine was wearing jeans and a loose sweater. Her hair was in a long plait. She had a large canvas bag over her arm.

'Is this some kind of convent?' David asked testily; it was not what he had meant to say but he was unable to stop himself. 'Your self-styled guardian at reception insisted on checking my credentials in Yellow Pages before she'd let me up here. God knows, I would have thought they would welcome with open arms anyone willing to set foot in this mausoleum.'

'You don't care for my taste in hotels either?'

'You chose it? I'd assumed that the University had billeted you here in order to save money.'

'Yeah, I chose it. I was here last time I visited Pitsbury.'

Clementine invited him in with a gesture that had some sarcasm to it. David entered. Clementine closed the door behind him but did not put a light on.

'I like the wardrobe,' she continued. 'It's the crazy, typically British, coffin type that's not tall enough to keep the hems of your dresses from having to drape along the bottom. I like the stained wallpaper and the candlewick bedspread and the ancient TV. Most of all, though, I like this.' She pointed to the open window.

'Are you referring to the sky or to the fire-escape? I cannot believe that, even in the event of a lightning strike, this building would be likely to do much more than smoulder, and that sky is available to all who live in Pitsbury. My section of it came particularly pricey but there are areas where it can be had for nothing.'

He did not see so much as feel her smile.

'I mean the fire-escape.'

'You are particularly neurotic about fire?'

'I am not "particularly neurotic" about anything.'

'Why, then?'

Clementine did not reply but, instead, climbed out of the window onto the rusty metal platform. She popped her head back in. 'Coming?'

In a moment, and without thinking, David was standing beside her, gazing at the surfaces of the cathedral and the precinct, which the moonlight had transformed according to their texture. The stone saints, angels, carved decorations were piped icing sugar. The paved areas were squares of glass. The grass was white, Jamaican sand. David had never seen it so beautiful.

'You came to apologise, right?' asked Clementine.

David was thrown. Firstly, because she had guessed his reason for coming. Secondly, because it was not how he, himself, would have expressed his intention. Apologies did not figure in his relationship with Fay; or rather, not as simple words which could be spoken and dispensed with.

'I came to say that you are not to blame for the actions of Tony Gilbert.'

'How did you track me down?'

'With great difficulty. Tony obviously knew your whereabouts but, since he has no friends, it was hard to think of anyone who might know his mobile phone number – of course he's ex-directory. Eventually I remembered that he used to appear in the Cock and Hen with a young woman, who was rumoured to be one of his undergraduates. The landlord asked the Lay clerks and one of them knew her name and I found her in the phone directory. She'd moved but her ex-flatmate gave me her new number. She was at home, but inclined to be hostile, until I reassured her that Tony and I only know one another through work – guilt by association . . .'

'Contiguity.'

A pause. 'If you like. Anyway, Gilbert was in that wretched restaurant and would not divulge your location until he had broken off conversation enough times to be totally sure I knew that he was actually in the company of Rupert and Immie Canning, and some French starlet, and some foreign film director . . .'

'Zucchini.'

'Yes. He also informed me that Zucchini's had the preposterous idea of indicating the polyglot nature of Renaissance Florence . . .'

'Though they're filming in Provence, *A Right Wonderful Error* is set in Madrid.'

'Be that as it may, the polyglot nature of Renaissance Florence is to be indicated by using actors of all different nationalities and language groups, including Chinese. Gilbert said it would be interesting to have the immediate reaction of a member of the public to Zucchini's casting plan. I said I thought it was wonderful and, as a consequence, he told me where you were.'

There was a silence.

Clementine said, 'You went to a lot of trouble.'

A statement of fact, yet it hit David like an express train. He now realised that he had been motivated by a strangely frantic compulsion.

Clementine started to make her way down the fire-escape and into the locked precinct. David followed her.

'Being able to get into the precinct when it's out of bounds is why I came back to this hotel,' she said, as they set off round the cathedral towards the Roman ruins, accompanied by their two charcoal shadows. 'If you hear footsteps, scoot behind something; once I got caught by the night-watchman. Search me what damage he thought I was planning on doing, but he was none too friendly. Though another time I met a tall cleric, in a long black cloak, who simply nodded at me.'

'That will have been one of the Canons.'

The ruins had an osseous look. Standing or fallen upon tightly-mown lawn, they could have been remains of the rib-cage of an extinct creature. Normally empty, they were filled, at one end, with raked, outdoor seating. A performance area was surrounded by ground-level spotlights; other spots hung from the arches. A scaffolding platform had been erected behind what had once been a great oval window. There was a smell of grass.

Beyond the adjacent cloisters the Queen's School was an advent calendar of lights.

'Listen,' said Clementine.

To what specifically, David didn't know. If asked, he would have said that the precinct was silent. Now he heard, however, the low sound of two clear boys' voices from one of the dormitories; from somewhere came a rustling; there were distant shouts from the direction of the road that led up to the university; a pigeon cooed; there was the pop of a champagne cork.

David turned, incredulous. It seemed to him almost unbelievable that a person could be so content, so untrammelled, as to be able to plan their pleasures in this way. Clementine Dee must have bought the bottle, persuaded the witch at reception to chill it for her and carefully packed it into her canvas bag, along with the smoked salmon sandwiches she now produced. She had spread an old wool shawl on the ground and seated herself upon it.

Suddenly David wanted to know everything there was to know about this woman, with her perceptive eyes, and lips that twitched with amusement.

'Were you expecting me?' he asked, as she brought out two plastic cups.

'Huh? Oh.' There was a pause. Then, 'Call it superstition,' Clementine said. 'Call it North American prudence, or perhaps just the sheer, gluttonous pleasure of knowing you've got enough and more. But name me a religion or mythology that doesn't advise one to be ready to share with strangers.'

'Or else.'

'Or else. Well, I guess I've always been a utilitarian.' Clementine poured the champagne, handed David a cup and gestured to him to come and sit beside her. 'Tell me about the books you sell.'

'The books I sell.' David lowered himself onto the shawl. He felt his being relax, his voice unbuckle. 'You'll have to come and see them. Or rather see them, feel them and smell them – antiquarian books aren't just or even mainly about their subject-matter. You wouldn't like that, I suppose? Gilbert told me you lecture in English.'

'I also work with manuscripts. Go on with what you're saying.'

'If you work with manuscripts then you'll probably understand what I mean when I talk about the volumes' resonances, the thought of the hands that might have touched them – of course it's even better when they've been signed by the author. But as well it's the way books of the past seem to have been designed in order to give the reader sensual pleasures as well as intellectual ones.' David put his cup down and stretched out full length now, supporting the back of his head with his hands. 'There's something about handling thick paper,' he continued. 'And many of the typefaces and page layouts strike me as intensely appealing. Then there's the scent of the leather bindings.'

He stopped. He heard Clementine swallow.

'Are you going to this play?' she asked.

'To what?' David was confused by the sudden change of topic. He wondered if he had been boring.

'The Queen's School's Francis Partington Day production of Mowbray's *Loving Wisely Well*. The performance they've got the rig here for.'

'I hadn't thought. I don't usually attend Queen's School events.'

'Have you read the play?'

'I haven't.'

'But you're familiar with the plot I guess?'

'Not of that one.'

'You *are* a typical bookseller. Books are about their subject-matter, too, you know.' Clementine paused, waited. Then, when he did not respond, 'Defend yourself, David Marsh,' she said, 'or else you'll hate me again. You know you're capable of it.'

David sat up. He could see in the moonlight Clementine's taunting, amused expression.

'If you mean you think I'm capable of defending my ignorance I hope you are mistaken,' he replied slowly. 'If you mean you believe me capable of hating you, Clementine Dee, I assure you you are wrong.'

There was a long silence. Clementine poured more champagne into their cups.

'Tell me about your wife,' she said.

It did not seem strange that she had guessed he was married.

David attempted to keep his tone light. 'She needs me.'

'That's arrogant.'

'It might sound so perhaps, and I don't doubt that I am arrogant at times. In this case, though, I'm making a simple statement of fact. We have been together since the very beginning, you see. Why don't you tell me about your husband?'

'I have no husband. I have never yet met anyone I considered worth sharing my life with.'

'Now that strikes me as arrogant.'

'I don't see it. Where to place your love is in part a decision like any other. Don't you think it's sentimental to pretend it isn't? That's what you seem to be saying.'

She was staring at him. David's heart began to pound so hard he could barely breathe. 'No,' he began, 'that's not . . .'

There was a sound of footsteps.

'This way,' said Clementine. She scooped the things back into her canvas bag.

They hurried from shadow to shadow until they reached

the cloisters. The footsteps passed them and disappeared. As his eyes dark adapted, David began to make out the shapes of costumes, scenery and props for the Queen's School performance of Mowbray – shoes, hats, tapestries, rugs, jackets, musical instruments, tambours, banners, backdrops – stacked on or resting against the stone bench which ran the length and breadth of the cloisters. Clementine gave a laugh of pure pleasure.

'Athens, Istanbul, Alexandria – it's like that here, don't you think? The present is only the thinnest of strata and everything people have experienced is lying right under our feet, just beneath the surface. Can't you feel that it might all suddenly burst out, like some gigantic volcano?'

David could.

'I don't suppose you can tell me the whereabouts of Dr Dee?' said Tony Gilbert, in a voice riddled with irritation.

'Indeed I can. She is here.'

There are better ways of suggesting that you have nothing to hide than by hiding nothing. Gilbert's tone, irritating David in his turn, evoked an honest response where a discreet one might have been wiser – something that was vaguely to occur to David as soon as he put the phone down, only to be followed by a hot, inner defence along the lines that nothing had taken place between himself and Clementine. The sexual act is still the stamp of authentication, without which love is deemed invalid. In this respect its absence is a useful get-out clause.

The truth of the matter was that David had fallen crazily in love with Clementine Dee.

The almost ceaseless conversation of the ten days which followed their initial encounter had been one extended sword fight. Dazzling, stunning, invigorating, it had taken place beside the river, across tables – stained with rings from beer mugs, white-clothed, with arrays of gleaming wine-glasses – in the main streets of Pitsbury and along narrow back-alleys. Skirmishes, sorties and sallies, pounces, challenges. David barely felt he needed sleep. Though he himself shied away from the obvious parallel, getting involved with Fay had been a soporific sort of experience, entailing each of them feeling sorrier and sorrier for the other until this thorough appreciation of the true awfulness of their mutual adolescent lives was possible to mistake for accord which, in its turn, could be mistaken for love. Falling in love with Clementine was like waking up; it did not drain his energy but increased it. In later weeks, after it was all over, David was to remember how, during that time, his darkening financial situation had not seemed inexorable, on the rare occasions he had thought about it; and to reflect that, with Clementine at his side, he might have had the imaginative strength to come up with some means to extricate himself from the quagmire of debt in which he now flailed.

'I've been calling and calling at the Cathedral Inn,' Gilbert continued. 'Immie and Roo were completely bloody exhausted by the evening with Zucchini. Well, we all were, but them principally, so when Zucchini said he was heading straight on to L.A., it seemed the sensible thing for them to go with him and try and catch up with some rest in Santa Barbara. I hoped to be able to join them, of course, but . . . Anyway, I've had absolutely nothing to do and no one to do it with. Put Dr Dee on the line, will you? There's a reading of English verse by Dame Julie at Splatters this evening and I'll run her out to it.'

'Dr Dee is in the shower and we're going to see *Loving Wisely Well* tonight.'

There was a silence.

'In the shower?' said Gilbert.

'There is no shower at the Cathedral Inn. North Americans cannot survive long without them, Clementine informs me.'

There was another silence.

'And how is Fay?' asked Gilbert. 'It must be pleasant for her to have made a new acquaintance.'

'Fay is in Devon studying kelp.'

'Kelp?' Gilbert evidently imagined an actor-manager.

'Seaweed.'

'To what end?' asked Gilbert, seeming to take offence.

'The teleology of Fay's endeavours escapes me.'

There was a pause. Then, 'Dr Dee is an extraordinarily beautiful woman,' said Gilbert, huffily, apparently suddenly realising this and peeved that he had not done so earlier.

Now, too late, David did lie. 'Is she? I hadn't noticed.'

'Intelligent, too. I daresay you'll have a stimulating evening. If it isn't too cold.'

Gilbert's concluding bitchiness was well chosen. The Queen's School's Francis Partington Day event was, like most British outdoor arts activities, the brainchild of the same kind of mentality that believes that, though climbing a mountain is good, climbing it during the most inclement season without oxygen is even better. Much of the blame for this could be laid at the door of the Queen's School's founder, Francis Partington, himself.

The monarch of his day might graciously have permitted the school to be named after her but Partington stomped up the cash. He therefore felt justified in exacting his own pound of flesh, in the shape of the Francis Partington Decree, which laid down that, henceforth, on his birthday in April, an outdoor 'frolic' should take place in his memory. Either the definition of a 'frolic' was broader than the Queen's School headmasters now permitted, or the climate had taken a decided downturn since the sixteenth century, or Francis Partington was simply bloody-minded. Nevertheless, the Queen's School was inordinately proud of the occasion and, since much of Pitsbury felt it took a reflected gloss from the distinguished school, members of the public, too, believed that they were doing something glamorous when they set off for the performance of *Loving Wisely Well* carrying duvets and thermoses. A crack team from the St John's Ambulance was on hand in case of hypothermia.

David had argued against attending the performance – *Thalia*, Hermia Mowbray's greatest tragedy, was showing in London and he'd offered to book tickets – but Clementine had been particularly insistent. Extremes of climate held no fears for her, she said. *Loving Wisely Well* was the Mowbray she wanted him to see in particular. It was important that he go along with her wishes on this, her penultimate night in England.

A particularly chilly one. Great would have been the possibilities for complaint, had the cold not rendered it perfectly natural for David to place his arm around Clementine's shoulders – the first time they had touched. David felt not just the sexual excitement which had been crackling in the air ever since they had met, but also a sudden complete trust. His personality might dare to strip naked in Clementine's presence.

The performance began.

Numbers being among the school's few trump cards, it was exploited wherever possible. There was the inevitable, waning fanfare, and a Duke and his massive retinue entered and sat and witnessed an awfully long dance, involving a lot of people, before so much as a couplet was uttered.

There then followed a rather shouty scene, the gist of which appeared to be that the Duke's daughter must, today, make a choice between suitors, or she would be banished to the Forest of Elizium, with, for company, only three faithful friends and a philosophising Fool who – though the Duke and his retinue (and a few of the Pitsbury artsy set) made semblance to find rip-roaringly amusing – David felt could quickly become tedious.

The wayward daughter was brought in and, just so she (and, presumably, the audience) would know what her choice was, so – rather tactlessly, it seemed to David – were both the suitors. Now, somewhat improbably, the heroine was given a few minutes to think things over. She and her ladies took up their tapestries. The ever-present Fool strummed on a musical instrument that looked a bit like half an onion. The Duke and his lords waved goblets around, without spilling anything, and laughed silently. In the foreground, the two suitors got into surprisingly friendly conversation. It transpired that, should the wayward daughter fail to decide, for various tortuous reasons they were to be banished to Elizium also; each to their own particular patch of it.

Another dance began.

David's breathing felt cramped, his mind preternaturally alert. His heart was pounding, as if something terrible were about to or had just happened. Could it be that Clementine was using Mowbray's play as a means of raising the question as to whether there existed the possibility of a future in which the two of them might be together?

'Are you asking me to leave my wife?' It tumbled out of him before he could stop it.

'Are you saying you would if I were?' She was looking straight ahead. Her expression was unreadable.

'Are you saying you are?' Maybe she wasn't.

'Are you saying you would?'

He felt weak. Overwhelmed. Daunted. Too much. Not now. One day, perhaps. One day, yes. But, for the moment, it was just . . .

'No, I'm not. Look, Clementine, it isn't that I haven't . . . and me and Fay, it isn't as if it's . . . but . . . the enormity of it and, quite frankly, the risk . . .'

But had she actually asked? Maybe she hadn't. He petered out, still unable to read her, though her lips rose in a little smile.

'Don't go on,' she said. 'Crossed purposes.'

Now all the stage-lighting was extinguished. There was a long, long pause. The audience coughed, sneezed, shivered, rubbed their frozen hands together, succumbed to attacks of asthma, sipped brandy and Scotch broth and wondered how long it was before the interval. Not any old Forest of Elizium but a mysterious, misty one had been fixed on by the English teacher, who, in his youth, had auditioned for RADA. The idea was that, when the lights eventually went up again, there would be the lovely brume of an autumn morning. The smoke machine wouldn't work at first, however, and then, having at last managed to get it going, Special Effects over-compensated. The smoke belched out as from a factory chimney, making a thick fog which obliterated the ruins, obliterated the stage area, obliterated the front rows, where Mayor Horatio Bullock and other dignitaries had been trying to look as if they were enjoying themselves, then spread to the rest of the seating.

When at last it cleared, Clementine Dee had vanished.

It was better, of course, than the prolonged soul-searching and recriminations customary on such occasions. Nor need David feel, in that respect, cheated of his emotional moment: he got these and more from Fay when he found her in the supposed priest's hole. Clementine, he reflected, had done the wise thing in making her exit when she did – before anything really happened. David did the wise thing in not returning to the Cathedral Inn until he was fairly sure she must have departed for Canada.

Questions remained, however. Henry Pearl did not have a malicious bone in his body, but the same could not be said for

Tony Gilbert: had he deliberately mentioned Clementine's visit to Henry, purposely omitting the crucial detail of Fay's studying kelp at the time, with a view to the information getting back to her? And what had been the nature of Clementine's feelings for David? – something that he longed to know ever more fervently as the months passed and his own affections did not diminish.

On the contrary.

Ironic, in the light of his financial recklessness, that, emotionally, he had been so destructively cautious: a thought that David's subconscious admitted – though his conscious argued that he had had no choice but to be loyal to his marriage – as noise and voices now began to drag him, through levels of awareness, out of sleep.

To a situation which since the day before had changed quite radically. Due, in large part, to Harriet, Duchess of Pitsbury.

5

The Duchess has a Good Idea

Although she resided only fifteen miles or so outside it, Duchess Harriet very rarely visited the city from which she took her title. There was the dull yearly meeting at the headquarters of the Royal Society for the Help of the Homeless, which was in one of the buildings surrounding the cathedral precinct, and there was the odd thing, like yesterday's plaque, to unveil – which had been dull also, Duchess Harriet not being much of a reader. There was also the yearly All Souls Eve service in the cathedral, because it was really called All Souls Cathedral, Pitsbury (though since no one referred to it as that, it might just as well not be, which would mean they wouldn't have to bother with the service, or the midnight lighting of the traditional Hallowe'en Bonfire afterwards). By and large, however, the Duchess managed to avoid Pitsbury and its duties.

Not that that meant she lacked occupation. In fact, the Duchess rarely had a spare minute. There were holidays to plan and her stories to talk over with the girl from the publisher's, who helped her get her ideas down on paper. Then, most nights, there was bopping at Riddle's and Mosley's with her new boyfriend, an utterly dishy Venezuelan who was also a billionaire magnate. And, of course, there were the egg-and-spoon races to take part in at the boarding schools of her two daughters. Not to mention the round of visits to her ever-more-grumpy in-laws. And as if all that weren't

enough, there was also, at the moment, the divorce to nego-
tiate.

Duchess Harriet laid down her copy of *Vogue* and contemplated the events of the day before. Again, it struck her how
jolly unfair the Archbishop had been to give her those dirty
looks throughout the unveiling ceremony. Especially when she
really really *had* meant to obey her hubby forever and ever,
and it had been the Archbishop's own choice to make such a
long-winded sermon about it. Also, it did seem extra mean, and
sort of unarchbishoplike, to take such a downer on her when
he must know what a horrid time she was having, due to the
awful muddle she'd got into with her finances.

Now Duchess Harriet turned her head to look out of the
window of her beloved ranch-house style, split-level mansion,
architect-designed for her and the Duke in the happier early
days of their marriage. As she did so, she caught sight of herself
in the lovely big mirror with gold surround, and had another
quick practice at looking up from under her eyelashes, like her
sister-in-law had shown her.

Deer were grazing in the parkland beyond the garden, which
had been landscaped by Guy Dylan who was now on breakfast
telly, giving phone-in tips, and who had bought Duchess Harriet
a double snowball with a cherry on top the night he'd dared
her and Miffy Mitre, the gin heiress, to hide their chauffeurs'
car-keys.

Happy memories. Yesterday's rainbow. Oh, to have the promise of medals and titles at one's disposal again – such a good way
of dealing with financial shortfalls. It was proving increasingly
difficult to persuade those who were now clamouring for their
dosh to be a bit patient and understanding, and wait and *see* if
her cut of her husband's dough would cover the debts, rather
than just assuming that it wouldn't. Up until yesterday, it had
been far from certain that Duchess Harriet would be able to pay
for the ranch-house's upkeep, even if the divorce settlement let
her continue to live in it.

Just as well she was a person who could rely on her own
initiative to bale her out of a sticky situation.

Duchess Harriet gave a sigh of relief and plunged a hand
into the silver-plated sweetie-box, inscribed with her initials,

bringing out a vanilla fudge, part of a Souvenir Of St Ives Presentation Pack sent by royal command from Cornwall. (Probably that sort of thing would dry up as well, once they'd taken away her title.) Thank goodness for the totally brilliant idea she had had yesterday during the drive round Pitsbury with that creepy Mayor-person, Horatio Bullock.

It had come about, really, because she'd been asking about bombs. *Just* like her grandmother-in-law had told her she should, incidentally – which was jolly well one in the eye for those who said Duchess Harriet wasn't caring enough.

An area of wasteland was what had prompted the question. Duchess Harriet had spotted it as the official Roller was leaving Pitsbury.

'Bombs?' she'd said. Even the intonation was perfect.

'I beg your pardon, Ma'am?' The Mayor hadn't followed.

'This area was bombed, I take it?'

The Mayor latched on.

'Actually not, Ma'am. Very run-down, however. The last council had all but completed the demolition programme when they were voted out of office. The idea was to make a park on the site, but the present council found the scheme somewhat profligate.'

'I can appreciate that.' Duchess Harriet surveyed the littered carcass of land. It would have been an awful waste to make such a well-situated chunk of real-estate into somewhere just used for walking in and growing flowers. Especially when she thought what her Venezuelan boyfriend, Giorgio, would do with it.

Yes, especially when she thought that.

'Is any project for the site currently being considered?' she inquired.

For someone not very bright, the Mayor, it had to be said, did cotton on pretty speedily.

After a moment's pause, he replied, 'None, at present.' This was followed by a short silence, after which he added, 'The wisest course might be for the council simply to sell it, should a suitable buyer materialise.'

'If that happened, do you think planning permission would be forthcoming?' asked Duchess Harriet, in her best casual chit-chat voice.

'I can be very confident that it would,' answered the Mayor.

Though she'd always been a twit at mental arith, Duchess Harriet did some surprisingly agile sums, to do with percentages, in her head.

'I suppose,' she said, 'that, once this sort of thing gets going, everything can happen rather quickly?'

'*Very* quickly,' agreed Mayor Bullock.

'And the park idea?'

'The present council has different priorities.'

Neither the Mayor, nor the Duchess spoke for a little.

Then, 'Most of Weaver Street, which we have just passed through, came up in the early nineties,' the Mayor observed. 'The people who bought and renovated the properties there got their fingers burned quite badly when the park didn't happen. Which was regrettable. But there are not many of them and, anyway, having presumably accepted the park's non-viability, they are urging Pitsbury Council to do something with the wasteland site. They would not therefore be in a position to object, whatever was put there, and whatever the effect on themselves might be. It is the way of life, anyway,' he added, 'that these things happen.'

'Indeed it is,' said Duchess Harriet, thinking that she'd found her way to a cash-stash that might mean she could stay on at the ranch-house indefinitely.

6

Virtual Reality

There were people in the bedroom. There was a smell of smoke. A mallet-beaked creature was trying to smash its way out of David Marsh's skull. His stomach was a cement-mixer full of sulphuric acid. David opened his eyes in time to catch the burst of muddy light that vomited into the room as Henry Pearl drew back the curtains.

Henry smelled of shaving soap. He wore a little bowtie, an orange and yellow waistcoat under his tailored jacket and a pocket-watch. He positively gleamed with well-being. Colin Rutt, earringed as usual, was puffing on a fag and eating from a packet of Cheesy Wotsits.

'We have come to kiss and make up,' Henry announced, 'and I'm trying to persuade Colin to cook you a Mongolian breakfast. We also bring exciting news.'

'Whatever Mongolians eat for breakfast,' said David, his tongue feeling like a boxing glove, 'I don't want it.'

Colin Rutt opened the window and chucked his fag-end out.

'Too right,' he said. 'Like what I was saying. You got a 'angover, you want' – he counted them off on his fingers – 'bacon, fried bread, black pud, sausages, eggs, fried tomato, mushies and lots and lotsa ketchup, with PG for your lost fluids.'

'What is the exciting news, Henry?' asked David.

In reply, Henry placed a hand behind one of his ears.

'Can you hear something?'

'I was of the opinion that that banging noise was inside my head.'

'Absolutely not. When you get dressed you can come with us and be enlightened.'

'I am happy to be enlightened from where I am and I would be most grateful for the PG aspect of your menu, Colin. Where's Fay?'

'Dunno. Out,' said Colin, lighting another fag. 'But PG won't do you no good without the rest. I'll put the kettle on and go down Cagmag's, buy some meat items. Got a fiver, Henry?'

'Only a ten pound note.'

'That'll do. Back in a mo.' And Colin was off.

Henry sighed. 'He'll fritter half of it on Maltesers.'

'What's the banging, Henry?'

Henry brightened again. 'Guess.'

'I'm sorry about last night, Henry, but if you do not simply tell me what is going on I shall be inclined to attempt a repeat performance.'

'Watch my lips, then,' said Henry, unperturbed. 'SITE FOR REDEVELOPMENT.'

There was a pause.

'The wasteland?' said David.

'The very same. All morning they've been putting up boards, at various points along the perimeter, advertising it. That's what the hammering is. They've nearly finished.'

'What will it become?'

'Who can predict? All possibility is there. At last my pleas have borne fruit. The site will be re-developed.'

David was silent, taking the news in. Of course, it might be some months before the site was bought but, with the property market still depressed, now that Pitsbury Council had decided to sell, it would probably go sooner rather than later. Whoever could afford to develop the area would be likely to be getting a bargain. The consequence for Weaver Street would be financial regeneration, disaster averted. David could continue to borrow on the strength of the projected development.

In the whirl of emotions that attended this unbelievable,

totally unexpected reprieve, there was one which was quite absurdly anomalous and which David was at a complete loss to explain to himself: it was disappointment.

'I have a vision of the future,' Henry said. 'Here it is. Listen. I see numerous luxury homes, inhabited by cultured, aesthetic, restaurant-going individuals. I see a French-style market. Craft shops. Institutes of higher-learning, absolutely stuffed with people wanting your volumes and Rick Farr's . . . communications expertise. Holistic clinics desirous of Fay's beauty products and carminatives. I see a landscaped place where there are no homeless . . .'

Henry continued in this vein for some time, while David lay back on his pillow, his eyeballs throbbing, wondering where the tea had got to and thinking about oases, springs, spas, waterfalls, fountains, pools, rivulets. The door slammed. There was the distant sound of Colin Rutt booting up Fay's kitchen, which was a complex melange of high-tech and cosy. The smell of dripping – the extractor fan could have swallowed a pygmy hippo, so Colin couldn't be using it – wafted up the stairs. At last Colin appeared with a sprigged mug of almost black tea.

'Get that down your throat,' he said to David. Henry he handed a porcelain cup of Earl Grey. He rubbed his nose with a knuckle and gave a big sniff. 'Site's sold,' he said, 'so the rumour goes. Bloke in Cagmag knows someone's been talking to Bullock.'

'The Mayor Bullock?' asked Henry, ceasing mid sip.

'Mayor's brother.'

'That was quick.'

'It's not signed and sealed yet, but all the boards are just to make it look like it's been out on the open market. Truth is, so the rumour goes, the deal'll go through in the next few days. Council had a secret meeting last night, down the Duke Of Pitsbury's.'

'But that's wonderful,' Henry Pearl exclaimed.

'Not so fast.' Colin produced a *Gitane*, lit it and blew out a large puff of smoke. David wondered whether he was going to throw up. 'You haven't heard what it's going to be yet. Only the second in the country. Other one's just off the M25.'

'What is it going to be, Colin?' asked David impatiently.

Colin spoke a number of largely incomprehensible words.

'A *what*?' burst out David.

'It may be better than it sounds,' said Henry.

'One way of finding out,' said Colin.

There was the blast of a horn. Fay jumped, guiltily. Henry Pearl was gesturing to her from the driving seat of his Volvo. Next to him, huddled and ashen-faced, was David. In the back, Colin Rutt was eating a bap.

'Where have you been?' asked David, irritably, as she got in beside Colin. 'I've put up Closed signs in both the shops, in the unlikely event that anyone comes wanting to buy anything. I also left a note, in case we didn't see you.'

'Looking for herbs and wild flowers on the waste ground,' said Fay, which was untrue, though she sometimes did. Herbs and wild flowers being the streetwise of the botanical world, the waste ground was a good place to find them. Among the crumbling remains of human habitation they flourished and prevailed.

'Then you'll have seen the billboards,' said Henry, pulling out with his usual extreme caution.

'Oh,' said Fay.

'Explain all, Colin,' commanded Henry.

Through mouthfuls of bap, Colin did just that as the Volvo crawled towards the Pitsbury ring-road and thence in the direction of the M25.

When Colin had finished speaking, the four subsided into silence. By the time they reached the motorway, the mist had become a thick fog the colour of barley water. Runic signs, put there by the Department of Transport, issued speed warnings. All light was diffused; it seemed to leave imprints on the moist air.

Fay gave a little sigh. Her visit to Just The Business had not got her what she wanted and she had had to wait around while Rick Farr, in his Brut and cufflinks mode, twitching like mad, dealt with Sam Bullock, the Mayor's brother.

Rick's sales talk at the Mongolian Evening had been successful. As far as Fay could tell, Sam Bullock was making a substantial investment in Just The Business's Internet facilities.

These consisted of a row of monitors and keyboards, placed on black, rectangular tables, in front of each of which was a small, black leather swivel chair. The walls were pale grey. There were no pictures. On one of the monitors was a swirling, black, white and grey design, which reminded Fay of those chiffon scarf-type jellyfish she'd seen in Florida. Another seemed to be leapfrogging between the stockmarkets of the world. Another kept up a constant tickertape of financial news bulletins: premiums, profits, trusts, securities.

'Now let me get this right,' Bullock was saying. 'If I want a conference between, for example, South America, Holland and Pitsbury, there's no need for anyone to actually be seen to be present?'

Rick plucked a menthol cigarette and a lighter out of his jacket pocket. He didn't light the cigarette but fiddled with it between thumb and forefinger.

'That's the beauty of the Net,' he said, nodding vigorously. 'You have a virtual room where you have your virtual conference. You may not be there – in all probability you won't – neither may anyone else. Certainly not at the same time. Like I say, that's the beauty of the Net: nothing, inverted commas, "real" needs to happen at any point.'

Sam Bullock had stiff little white hairs in his ears. His hands were large and red, his eyes watery. He wore a tweed jacket that smelled as if it had hung, for a very long time, in a vestibule above unused Wellingtons.

'Take the transfer of money, for instance,' said Rick, rushing on nervously. 'We're all familiar with how that works. You sell me a concept – shares, let's say, for the sake of argument. I borrow in order to buy them. The bank is allowed to lend more money than it's got. What happens?' Rick glanced at Sam Bullock, willing him to complete the scenario.

There was silence. Fay noticed a sad little line of text, edging across one of the computer screens: 'this is jez cybercaff romford is phil there coz he owes me a 5er?'

'What happens?' Rick continued. 'The bank lends me money it doesn't have so that I can buy something that doesn't exist. The figures pass through my account and into someone else's. The shares end up in my imaginary portfolio. Oh yes, I could cash them in at some point. More likely, though, I'll simply sell them on. Same sort of thing with the Net, except you're dealing with invisible people as well as invisible money.'

'Hold up,' said Sam Bullock. 'Are you trying to tell me there needn't be anything real anywhere?'

Rick Farr looked relieved. He lit his cigarette. 'In theory there does, in practice there often isn't,' he said, blowing smoke out swiftly. 'Things can be bought and sold so fast that it ceases to matter whether they exist or not. Even as we converse, imaginary products are travelling across the planet in fictional means of transport. It's what the markets call confidence. Ditto invisible companies. This here,' tapping the jellyfish-displaying computer screen familiarly, 'just lets you see what isn't happening and talk about it. Which is useful. No, vital.'

'Cows exist, lad,' said Sam Bullock, still an unwitting Cartesian, 'as you'd know if you'd had to feed them over a winter, but I can see that this whatchamucallit can have its uses. Like a sort of long-distance telephone plus tape-recorder. And cheaper.'

Fay looked back at the monitor with Jez on. He was persisting: 'coz i need that 5er & he said hed get it posted 5 days ago. is phil there?'

Unable to resist, Fay touched the 'n' and the 'o' on the computer keyboard. Jez apparently vanished.

Rick was looking pleased that he had made a sale, but a bit deflated. 'I can do you a virtual cow,' he said, stubbing out his cigarette and tossing his lighter from hand to hand. 'It'll perform every function a cow could be expected to perform, but you need never feed it or have a field to put it in. You can watch it be born, grow old and die.'

'You can't eat it, though,' said Fay.

Sam Bullock was the type of man who didn't notice women. Rick had no choice but to ignore her or risk losing momentum.

'Virtual conference facilities, E-mail box, anything else?' he asked.

'Privacy,' said Bullock. 'Send me an invoice. Good day to yer.'

'David's E-mail box,' said Fay, as the door closed behind

him. 'The one he took last night, at the Mongolian Evening? I suppose, since there's never going to be anything really in it, from abroad, for example, I could check it whenever I wanted to?'

'What?' Rick's mind was still on his sale.

'David's E-mail box.' Fay suddenly felt like crying. 'Since there'll never be anything truly in there, I may as well be able to check that there isn't?'

'Old sod,' said Rick. 'Bastard's right, of course: an ace telephone. But there's nothing wrong with that.'

'So I might as well have access to David's E-mail box, just in case someone . . . real-ish tries to contact him – so that I would know about it – though we know they won't.'

'Yeah,' said Rick. 'As long as David gives me the okay.'

'Would that be necessary in the case of something so . . . virtual?'

'Netiquette,' said Rick.

Which hadn't seemed to have any answer at the time. Now, however, travelling glumly through a cave of whiteness, it occurred to Fay that netiquette must, by virtue of its recentness, be an evolving concept. She would simply have to return, perhaps when Rick was less preoccupied, and put it to him that, Net-wise, all was still fluid. She simply couldn't bear the thought of being unable to check that David really truly wasn't having contact with the Canadian.

'Are you sure this is the M25?' said Henry Pearl to David, who was reading the map.

'I can't think why you doubt it, since we have been driving for the best part of an hour without sight of any human traces, unless you count the service station, which I don't.'

'Can't be far now,' said Colin Rutt. 'Fog's lifting.'

'It's doing nothing of the kind,' said David. 'If anything, it's increasing.'

'I want to wee,' said Fay.

'There will shortly,' cried Henry, 'be ample opportunity for weeing. I spy something on the horizon.'

'Henry, there *is* no horizon,' said David.

'Nevertheless, I spy something.'

'Flipping heck!' said Colin Rutt, now spying it too.

'Oh!' said Fay.

'Dear, dear, dear,' said Henry Pearl.

David shut his eyes and let out a groan. It was a fifty-foot-high cowboy, holding a hammer. Next to it, in fifty-foot letters, pasted on the fog, was a sign which read: BARG-MART GINORMOUS DIME-O-STORE.

There was no need, really, having seen the BARG-MART GINORMOUS DIME-O-STORE exterior, to venture inside, except in search of a toilet (of which, incidentally, there were dozens, covered with blue plastic symbols, depicting and suggesting most of the things you might want to do in them). Nevertheless, propelled by stunned horror, Henry Pearl found a place in Car Park Yellow/A, Row 66R, a mere half mile's walk from one of the main Entrances, and they all got out.

Here, to one way of thinking, every basic human need was catered for. The BARG-MART GINORMOUS DIME-O-STORE was the commercial equivalent of a life support machine; provided you were able to keep spending, there was no need ever to leave: you could stop over at the BARG-MART MOTEL; the store and its two DIME-O-STORE restaurants, four SNAX areas, interior playgrounds and creches, were open round the clock.

As soon as the automatic doors closed behind you, you were blasted with hot, bread-smelling air, specially designed to entice you to buy one of the seven dozen different varieties of loaf on offer. These ranged from the worthy, 'made from organic, hand-crushed, coarse-ground seed-casings' through to the fancy 'stuffed with peach preserve and glazed with apricot-icing, lovely spread with butter for breakfast, or warmed in the microwave for a teatime treat'. There were numerous unleavened varieties, of the kind that had caused the civilisations that had originated them to yelp for joy when they discovered yeast and proper ovens. Worst of all, though, were the Mediterranean assortments – oval after oval of yellowish dough, perspiring into their plastic wrapping, studded with dry, black olives, pasted with uncooked onion or bejewelled with sun-dried tomatoes.

'Least there's a bookshop section, Dave. It'll bring readers in your direction,' said Colin Rutt, pointing to twenty-five feet or so of shelving.

'I scarcely think,' David replied, 'that carrying the top ten bestselling titles, albeit five hundred copies of each, justifies the appellation, "bookshop", Colin. Especially since there is not one volume there that is less than four inches thick or without bullet holes on the cover.' He gazed around him, remembering the one time he had taken acid.

Next to the books section were the magazines and news-papers. Square after oblong after rectangle of them, all depicting Harriet, Duchess of Pitsbury, in an unwisely cut and coloured frock and conveying, in their differing ways, the same seman-tic content: 'PALACE AT ODDS OVER DIVORCE SETTLE-MENT'; 'F-OFF MA'AM!'; 'CONTROVERSY CONTINUES TO DOG ROYAL COUPLE'; 'THANKS FOR NUFFINK'. Many of the dailies also ran a smaller photograph of Roo and Immie Canning, all smiles and suntans, accompanied by a cross, Latinate-looking man: 'CANNINGS DENY RUCTION RUMOUR'.

Past great, humming wedges of refrigerator, the height of a Massai, David, Fay, Colin and Henry walked; through souks of tins and hectares of identical vegetables, catacombs of dead cheeses, ranks of prepacked meats leaking dye into their poly-styrene patens.

'You could read a letter by that,' said Henry, pointing at a slab of day-glo haddock.

There was gleaming hair-gel with suspended, glutinous bubbles in it, a choice of toothpastes beyond the dreams of avarice, an enormous selection of knobbly, hairy, hard, soft, spiky exotic fruits that no one knew the use of, accompanied by FREE recipe cards: *Tree Tomato Stir-Fry; Steamed Hog Plum Pudding With Mangosteen Coulis*. David recalled reading once a probably apocryphal story about a tribe of gypsies condemned to be shot by some regime somewhere. As the guns were aimed, so the story went, the gypsies ripped their clothes off and made love until their bodies were nothing but holey knitting. Banal though it seemed in comparison, David suddenly experienced a similar, vital, defiant need to defend everything that was human – Fay's watery nature, Henry Pearl's waistcoats, Colin Rutt's cigarette smoke; every stench, stink, squelch of the sweating, excreting, loving mortal frame. Even the mild affection he felt for his wife was mighty, held up against prickly pears and the 'DAY "N" NITE HOT DO-NUT PANTRY'.

Far from being the answer to their problems, this was the ultimate nail in the financial coffin; the last, inevitable piece in a disastrous jig-saw. The good citizens of Pitsbury who rejoiced in Burger-Fish and Can-Do Computers would welcome, with open-arms, a BARG-MART GINORMOUS DIME-O-STORE with a car park the size of Middlesex. Now no one need ever again enter the city centre – the High Street businesses would be peeved, of course, but they would simply relocate; one place was much the same to them as another. No one need see, let alone go into, Henry's restaurant or any of the shops in Weaver Street.

Compared to the BARG-MART GINORMOUS DIME-O-STORE, the Weaver Street squat now seemed suddenly of small importance. Whatever its role in their financial downfall, it had never possessed the engulfing power to stop things getting better, ever; to obliterate completely any possibility of regeneration. The BARG-MART was a mighty enemy, a solid culprit; it must be challenged. David realised that as he stared into its temperature-controlled face. And, strangely, not just for financial reasons. If he and others were to be pushed to the margins, it was suddenly vitally important that it be kicking and screaming.

At this most terrible of moments, David began to feel a growing energy, animation and, yes, excitement.

There was not only a Car Park Yellow/A, Row 66R, there was also a Car Park Yellow, Row 66R, and a Row 66R Car Park A; the divisions between each notional rather than actual, it being virtually impossible to figure the limits of the billboards' denotations. Not only that, the fog was still as dense as when they had entered. It took nearly an hour to find the car. Then Henry followed 'Exit' signs for ten minutes, only to discover, at the end of that time, that they were back where they had started. They set out again, following different 'Exit' signs, which eventually shunted them into the SERVICE STATION AREA, where people were slotting credit cards into a regiment of petrol pumps. Henry couldn't back out, because there was another car behind him. They had to sit for twenty minutes, while the cars in front served themselves to petrol, and then to convince the person at the one NON-AUTOMATIC PAYMENT EXIT (which Henry unwittingly got funnelled into) that they hadn't bought any petrol. After that they managed to find a promising perimeter road, still inside the car park but looking as if it might lead to a way out. It did, but not before circling very nearly the whole site. By the time they reached an 'Exit' – on the opposite side to the one they had come in by, thus necessitating a vast detour in order to get back to the right bit of motorway – Henry Pearl was in the throes of a panic attack like the one he'd had when he got into the wrong lane at Rouen and was forced to cross the bridge and the French lorry driver yelled something nasty about British agricultural policy at him. In a rare bit of reckless driving, Henry shot onto the M25, cutting in on a car already on the motorway and causing it to have to swerve to miss him. The sound of a pissed-off horn ploughed its way back to them through the obscurity. Colin unwrapped a Fox's glacier mint and slotted it between Henry's lips. For a few miles there was silence.

Then, 'The irony,' proclaimed Henry, still shaking, 'the biggest irony, is that now, at long last, they will have to demolish the squat.'

'Yes,' said Fay, thinking of the Ebb filling up with milk cartons and freshly-squeezed flavour orange juice tetra-packs. 'They'll have to be able to get in and out.'

'Least,' said Colin Rutt, 'there'll only be one entrance and exit. No place to put another.'

There was a long, breathless pause.

'Essentially,' said David, slowly, 'access to the site – the thing that renders the site usable – can only come from the demolition of the squat. There's no other way in or out. Even Pitsbury Council couldn't get away with letting the supermarket knock down the city wall and, except for where the squat is, the rest of the area is completely hemmed in by the river, on the other side of which is St Friedaswida's and Bus Station House and the Elizium Forest Industrial Estate.'

Now there was another silence as the four took in the full implication of what they were all thinking.

7

A Debt to Guinea-pigs

Bus Station House, on the edge of the Elizium Forest Industrial Estate, was an unlovely building. Nevertheless Clementine Dee, who did not believe in jet-lag, was glad to be there early the following morning.

This was what she'd come to Britain to do: to work. She'd agreed with Ruth Carpini to take over the Quik-Potato Fellowship because that had seemed, to both of them, the wisest course of action: the only course of action, in fact. Right about now, Ruth should be landing back in Canada, ready to take up Clementine's teaching schedule that she'd had to drop so precipitately. And here Clementine was, at Bus Station House, all set to look at the Mowbray manuscripts which, unlikely though it was, had fetched up here. She'd left the hire car she'd used yesterday to get from the airport to Pitsbury at the rental agency, which, luckily, was on the Industrial Estate. Later in the day she'd get a taxi back to Tony Gilbert's cottage. The whole mess had been dealt with by taking the only professional option.

It was beautiful weather.

Autumn ran wild among the woodlands outside Pitsbury, Canada; here it was more restrained and understated – more English. Out of the none-too-clean upper window of Bus Station House, Clementine had a view of the Ebb, some waste ground, the city wall and, of course, Pitsbury Cathedral – a great, melting, ivory candle in the morning light. The river was cocoa-coloured, criss-crossed with ancient, narrow little grey-stoned bridges. The trees along it were turning rust. On the waste ground, a small, berried holly bush dipped in the slight breeze.

Quite a contrast with the fog of the day before. On the freeway, it had been like driving through milk. Some idiot nearly cut her off the road just by the BARG-MART; though, in all honesty, maybe she'd had a slight lapse in concentration at that point: she just hadn't been able to believe that BARG-MART's were allowed in Britain.

It had been a relief when she'd eventually got to Tony Gilbert's place – a well-preserved cottage down a long, winding lane (though not as long as it had seemed in the fog) which ran along the bottom of the Ebb Valley. She'd had to drive three or four miles past it first, in order to pick up the key from Tony's nearest neighbour.

The cottage had a fussy interior, and there were fussy notes pinned up and scotch-taped in strategic places – windows must be kept open or shut, the fridge left at such-and-such a temperature, certain people given certain messages if they called. The information that the vast tabby would eat only 'Prawn-Flavoured Yum-Yums' – available at only one location in Pitsbury – was written on a piece of paper placed under its bowl; though, patently getting the measure of Clementine as soon as she walked in, the cat gave her a look which suggested it reckoned it could kiss its 'Yum-Yums' good-bye.

Clementine had chucked her cases in the bedroom, put the heating on, made a coffee, and slumped into an armchair in the sitting-room, which was stuffed to the brim with pictures of Tony Gilbert, including a rather terrible black-and-white one of him in stage make-up.

'Well here I am again,' she said out loud, then fell silent, thinking.

People referred to breaks as 'clean'. Did the medical profession, Clementine wondered, use that terminology? Probably, heartless bastards. Anyway, the person experiencing the break sure as hell never did. Her exit, in April, had been quick but agonising; Pitsbury had seemed to let out an awful groan around her, like Milton's Creation when they ate the apple.

But she hadn't eaten the apple, had she?

Clementine sighed. What would have been the good of sticking around, though, after she'd had her answer? How could her pride sit there waiting for judgement to be passed upon her suitability? Wasn't what she could have offered David so obviously preferable to his supposedly noble self-sacrificing marriage? Could his wife, Fay, really be happy gleaning what was left of his affections? But then, Clementine had observed often enough how bad marriages have their own kind of stability: a jaundiced world-view is unlikely to encounter many existential challenges; to settle for second best is to make a fairly safe working agreement with Fate. (Had Fay Marsh also come to that conclusion? Clementine had a hunch that she had.)

That was the best case. The worst was that David had felt only a passing fancy for her and that, now, she was quite forgotten. The fact that he didn't appear to love Fay any more didn't necessarily mean he had ever loved Clementine Dee. She could have misread the indications.

Anyway, Clementine wasn't planning on finding out either way. David had chosen his option. Marriages were made, not in heaven (or hell), but in a foreign land, with its own incomprehensible language. Clementine Dee was not in the business of building justifications which would allow her to try to bust up another woman's relationship. It should be easy enough, in a town as large as Pitsbury, to avoid running into David. She would have to make sure she spent the majority of her time either in the university library, or Bus Station House, or back at Tony Gilbert's cottage.

Brave resolutions, which she reiterated to herself this morning, looking out over Pitsbury.

The door opened. Clementine turned back to the dismal little office, with its solid, metal desk that had no space where your legs could go. A little man with a shiny head entered, carrying an old, yellowed cardboard box.

'Bus Station House is something of a centrepiece,' he observed, placing the box on the desk. 'Which is how come the manuscripts are here, Dr Dee.'

'Good,' said Clementine, briskly, attempting to inject into her voice a note of grateful dismissal.

But the man continued. 'Back in the 1960's, the Pitsbury branch of the then nationalised bus service invested in paintings, *objets d'art*, manuscripts, for its pension schemes. When the system was privatised, Red Buses took on board the pension scheme holdings. As the nerve centre for the whole of the South East Red Bus Service, Bus Station House became the repository of the artistic investments – though Red Bus did away with the pension schemes in favour of more personalised initiatives. You must not think, either, Dr Dee – as you well might, being a Canadian – that the new Red Bus Service has anything to do with the old red buses. Red Bus Service spent 100K with a Colour Recognition Consultancy, in order to ensure that the difference is immediately discernible to the naked eye.'

'And these manuscripts represent the entirety of your Mowbray holdings?'

'The entirety. They were bought at auction, under advisement. At that time, I believe, Mowbray was a little-known writer; still, even minor dramatists apparently have a certain street value. These proved to be a particularly astute buy, as we expect to see evidenced when they go under the hammer again, later in the year.'

Who in Bus Station House, or among the administration of the Red Bus Service, read the *Times Literary Supplement*, Clementine wondered. Someone must, in order to have responded to Ruth's request for information about any, possibly unknown, Mowbray manuscripts.

'Who saw Dr Carpini's advertisement in the TLS?' she asked.

'Pardon me?'

'The *Times Literary Supplement*. Who saw the ad in it?'

The man gave a little tremor of pride. 'My wife, as it happens; she knew about the Mowbray holdings because I had been inventorying all Bus Station's art investments prior to their being auctioned. She has an arrangement with the newsagent. She buys off him, cheap, once a week, a pile of the papers that haven't sold.'

'For what?'

'She shreds them to make nesting material for the guinea-pigs. You'd be amazed at what you pay in a pet shop, though it may not mean a lot to you, being a Canadian.'

Did Canadians have money to fritter on guinea-pig bedding, or did they just not understand the exchange rate? Clementine did not inquire. Shortly, though reluctantly, the man left and Clementine Dee and Hermia Mowbray were alone together.

They had met many times before, of course, and in more congenial surroundings, but never with such intensity. As she carefully went through the manuscripts, Clementine felt as if she were laying out a beloved body; smoothing an old wedding dress; listening to a familiar voice. She was travelling in another place, where love-in-idleness grew on the banks of the Ebb and – on the site of Bus Station House, across the Elizium Forest Industrial Estate, over the patch of sward on which Tony Gilbert's cottage would be built – ragged, smocked wild flowers frolicked among the grasses.

The manuscripts consisted of fragments mainly. A piece of dialogue, similar to that found in Act II of *Thalia*. Disjointed parts of an apparently longer poem. The two last scenes of a drama entitled Repossession. A playlet, entire but obviously very early. A sonnet.

Today, Clementine would just familiarise herself with what was here. Later, she would go through the texts in detail, checking which of the pieces were versions of already known Mowbray manuscripts and which were unique.

'We have a canteen, if you want some lunch, Dr Dee,' said a secretary.

'Thanks, no. I'll get some coffee later.'

The sonnet was of particular interest. The only extant version, Clementine was sure, and in Mowbray's own handwriting. She could not resist lingering over it.

It went as follows:

If timbers carved, like faces, with my rhyme –
Those oaken beames which saw my lyfes first day –
If well that suckled me from birth to pryme
Could utter words, my history might they say.
But tree and spring and carving fine are dumb,
Save to the eye that hath the skil to reade
And heart to heart is all too often numb,
The ear of lyfe closed to a corpses need.

So will I whisper through anothers voice,
And echo in this playce when I am gone,
That here my infant rime may still make noise,
Existence keep abode, though I have none.
    Though I be dust, yet household shal I keepe,
    Though tongueless, talke, rest watchful, though I sleepe.

Clementine smiled: Hermia tickled semantics as if they were fat trout lazing in the unpolluted shallows of an unpolluted Ebb. Not unusual. Nor were the references to that Renaissance obsession: decay.

And yet, there was something about this particular poem which made Clementine keep coming back to it.

'Can I get you some tea, Dr Dee?'

'Thanks. Milk. No sugar.'

Hermia Mowbray usually hid behind one mask after another. Her changing voice was her authenticity. She danced a dance of many steps. She wore a robe of varying fabrics. But here, along with the Renaissance struggle to construct a permanent dwelling out of language so true, so human, that it could contain the past, give flesh immortality, there seemed to be references to a most specific place.

Clementine had the bizarre sensation that she was being sent a message. Was Hermia talking about her nascent art, or could it be more literal than that? As she puzzled over the sonnet, outside, the landscape dissolved into the blue darkness of an autumn evening.

The door opened.

'I'm afraid the cleaners are going to need to come in here, Dr Dee. If you'll replace the manuscripts in the box, I will return shortly and take them to the vault for safe-keeping.'

Clementine looked up. There was a mug full of cold tea beside her. The clock on the wall said a quarter past six.

The man disappeared. Clementine rose, stiffly, and started to gather the papers together.

When she was done, she stood at the window, unable to see much but her own reflection.

She was suddenly hungry and very tired and overcome by an inhabitual depression. Yes, life was so short, said the eyes looking back at her out of the weary face. Bus Station House, a cube of strip-lighting, most certain of its role in the scheme of things, would soon be merely a dull, compressed stratum, a little sliver of history.

In which case . . .

Snatch the moment. Gather ye rosebuds. Eat, drink and be merry.

Clementine Dee could trust herself in most things and she had a repertoire of comforts to stare life down with (tonight it would be a large Dry Martini and a peanut butter sandwich). But could she rely on tomorrow to bring fresh resolve, to make her sensible, when Hermia Mowbray's lovely, dead voice would always be whispering in her ear: 'As you are now, so, once, was I'? Could she really trust herself not to try to see David, to stick with the wise decision?

Wasn't that why she had fought against returning to Pitsbury?

8

The Wrong Sort of Charity

'As the Bible says,' concluded Horatio Bullock down the telephone, 'the poor are always with us. *If* – and I neither deny nor confirm – the site is to be developed and the squat – which has always been condemned, remember – is to be demolished, it is because Pitsbury Council believes in egalitarian principles: the poor have been much more with Weaver Street than with the High Street; we wish to redress the balance by ensuring that they are with neither.'

David was silent. Then, 'Though it is many years since I last read the Bible,' he said, 'I think that Christ was suggesting one help the poor, rather than simply move them around.'

'Possibly,' said Bullock. 'Nevertheless, Mr Marsh, I am somewhat surprised that, as soon as the council does what Weaver Street requests – I have numerous letters from Mr Pearl, in which he claims to be speaking for all of you when he demands that the squat be demolished – you suddenly phone me up to express concern about what will happen to the homeless when we bulldoze the illegal dwelling in Pitsbury Without.'

There was a pause. Bullock was right, David admitted to himself: he was a hypocrite.

So was Bullock, though he certainly experienced no pricking of conscience. Had it not now become commercially delightful to him to do otherwise, he would have taxed Weaver Street's Christian sentiments till Kingdom Come – the location of the squat had always been pleasing to the High Street in that it tended to keep the homeless outside the city centre.

David was different, though. Already, the Weaver Street decision to champion the rights of the homeless – albeit in order to prevent the supermarket development – was re-kindling the spirit which had made a brief entrance and exit with the visit of Clementine. He felt as if his intellect had taken on a furious sorting task and was classifying everything into piles labelled *desirable* and *undesirable* (with reasons) along with *avoidable* and *unavoidable*.

This new sense of purpose was also having ramifications on his relationship with Fay. A few weeks earlier, he had put the television on for the news and caught the end of a terrible beach drama. A man and a woman, who looked as if they rarely ventured far beyond the reaches of a sun-lamp, bobbed in a choppy ocean, kicking like mad in order to prevent sharks from eating them (sharks, David gathered, did not like people kicking). At such a moment there was no time for mutual recrimination – or admitting that it was you who had accidentally set fire to the locker-room, for that matter, which was what one of the lifeguards had done; still, up to that point, the metaphor was pertinent. Besides, though an understanding of the properties of kelp in relation to inner and outer beauty was not, to David's way of thinking, terribly important in the scheme of things, Fay had, in a fashion, preceded him in the rejection of the unnatural.

'You are aware, of course,' David now said to Bullock, 'that we have been completely betrayed. Given the amount of money that most of us have borrowed, the supermarket signifies the end of us financially.'

'I cannot discuss individual cases,' said Bullock. 'That is a matter between you and your bank manager.'

'You *are* my bank manager.'

'At present I am speaking from the Council Offices. You are addressing me in my Mayoral capacity. The squatters are resident illegally, which cannot be tolerated.'

'It has been tolerated quite happily up to now.'

There was a silence.

Then, 'We must be willing to make sacrifices, Mr Marsh,' said Horatio Bullock.

David snapped. '*Who* must make sacrifices?' he asked, his voice raised. 'Can we define exactly who it is we are talking about? Not people who can afford to buy their homes outright, for instance? Or those with jobs that allow them to service their mortgages? Not the parents of the children who go to the Queen's School? No, I think that we are, rather, talking about myself and my wife, Fay, and Rick Farr and Colin Rutt and Henry Pearl and, of course, the poor bloody . . .'

He paused. 'The poor bloody squatters,' he finished, and put the phone down.

It rang again five minutes later.

'Yes?'

'Mr Marsh?'

It was Horatio Bullock again.

'You have something to add, I take it?' said David.

'Yes and no. It *is* Horatio Bullock, but I am now calling as your bank manager.'

There was a silence.

'You teleported to the High Street, did you?' asked David.

'No. I am, at present, just leaving the Pitsbury Council Offices' car park, but I am driving in the direction of the bank.'

'And your role has changed accordingly?'

'Precisely.'

'It relies on which way you are pointing?'

'That is a factor. Anyway, Mr Marsh, I am phoning you because I am surprised by the lack of a response to my last letter, in which I outlined the extreme gravity of your present financial situation. Although I am unable to discuss them, rumours are now reaching me of a development in the vicinity of your property which, while desirable in itself, might not be of the kind to help your property to realise its true value, should it have to be auctioned.'

'So you confirm the supermarket development?'

'Mr Marsh, we are only talking rumours. Besides, my point holds good whatever happens: you must, immediately, inject some funds into your account with us.'

'And where are these funds to come from? Especially since Pitsbury Council seems determined to render my home and business completely worthless.'

There was a pause.

Then, 'That I cannot discuss, Mr Marsh. You will have to take it up with the Mayor,' said Horatio Bullock.

'We aren't really that sort of charity, David,' said Ms Court. They had never met before, but she had called him by his first name ten times in the last five minutes.

Ms Court was seated at the sort of desk that crops up in television programmes about antiques. The view from the window was of the Roman ruins and the Queen's School Quad ('Partington's Acre'), a perfect square of perfect lawn, around which were the headmaster's house, the medieval hall and classrooms and the sixth-formers' studies. On the wall behind Ms Court was a large, framed photograph of Harriet, Duchess of Pitsbury, patron of the R.S.H.H., The Royal Society for the Help of the Homeless.

'Indeed? What sort of charity are you, then?'

'David, it would be so easy simply to give the homeless money and accommodation, but that wouldn't actually be a solution.'

'It might be a fairly useful starting place.'

Ms Court shook her head emphatically.

'I know what you mean, David, but it wouldn't foster self-reliance.'

David began to be angry.

'It seems to me,' he observed, 'that people who sleep in doorways, on park benches and in condemned buildings already indicate a fair degree of self-reliance.'

'But David, they don't need hand-outs, they need employment.'

'And if the employment doesn't exist?'

'Then they need training, David.'

'So what you are saying is that you will not attempt to prevent the demolition of the squat in Pitsbury Without, even though it gives shelter to any number of homeless people?'

A bell sounded. Ms Court, who evidently lacked a sense of dramatic irony, looked out of the window. The flagstoned pathways around the Quad started to fill with Queen's School pupils on the way to their next lesson.

'I can show you a formerly homeless family who are now

renting a perfectly decent house on what used to be the Elizium Forest Council Estate,' she said. 'Through an R.S.H.H. initiative, we were able to help the mother to find a cleaning job at Bus Station House – which means she can walk home to make her children's lunch – and the father is now a food preparer at Burger-Fish. This, I think, represents a tremendous achievement, David.'

'You are saying that you will not intervene to try to prevent the demolition of the squat in Pitsbury Without?'

'David, it is not the business of the R.S.H.H. to get involved in political issues.'

Since that was apparently that, David bid a curt good morning and descended the elegant chestnut staircase and exited by the slim, Georgian front door. Standing beside the R.S.H.H.'s brass plaque and original doorbell, he experienced a wave of resentment that was not entirely selfishly motivated. His attention was caught by some activity in the area around the cathedral's north tower. There was little point in rushing back to Weaver Street purely to deliver the news that he had achieved nothing, so David went to investigate.

Clearly something architectural was taking place. Pitsbury's Conservation Officer, Brian Baffle – in hard-hat and suit looking rather like an electoral candidate doing the obligatory building-site visit – was standing beneath a network of scaffolding, looking up at the sky and shielding his eyes against the light as he conversed with someone in overalls.

One of the more imaginative columns in the Sunday papers, which Fay always read over her morning cup of lime juice and hot water, was an unchanging list of questions, to which somebody one should have heard of gave their answers. The most interesting of these, to David's way of thinking, was 'Which living person do you most despise?' When he could not sleep, due to compound interest, David fantasised about having that question put to him. There was only one possible answer: Brian Baffle.

Though Henry Pearl and Fay's combined ideas for the house and shops had been ruinously expensive, their inspiration had, at least, been aesthetic. Brian Baffle, on the other hand, who had made regular inspections, had his own absolutely rigid notions about historical authenticity, to which everything must adhere absolutely, whether The Beautiful would be served thereby, or whether it would not.

In vain had David argued that, surely, when an eighteenth-century householder discovered a rotten beam, he did not hike all the way over to Suffolk to fetch one of identical age to the rotten one, to replace it with. Baffle would not be gainsaid. His revenge for insubordination was instant and deadly. He had as many gradations of masonry-colour in his visual repertoire as Eskimos are supposed to have words for snow. He discovered that, at some stage, a chimney had been repaired using the wrong shade of brick – scarcely visible to the naked eye but, still, horrendously out-of-keeping with the rest of the building.

When not actually visiting a site, Baffle cruised Pitsbury, undercover, in search of anachronisms.

Today, however, Baffle looked what he referred to as 'satisfied' by the hue of the statue that was evidently about to be hoisted up to an empty niche at the very top of the north tower. The statue proved to be of the previous Archbishop, Nimrod Struther.

As head of the Queen's School, Struther had been involved in the kind of incident that is not uncommon in such institutions. As Archbishop, he had entered the women priests debate with gusto. To the country at large – the press, of course, excepted – women priests were, for the most part, neither here nor there, but they were a hot issue around Pitsbury. It wasn't until Struther had gone (it must be presumed, for the sake of argument) to meet his Maker that a few musty, yellow-tinged ladies with support stockings were, in a manner of speaking, welcomed into the priesthood. (You saw them sometimes, wandering somewhat aimlessly around the cloisters, neither one thing nor the other.) It was probably, therefore, not for the rectitude of his opinions, but the vehemence with which he had held them, that Struther was about to get his spot on the cathedral.

The choir was there. And the Archbishop, of course, and the current Queen's School headmaster, along with a hand-picked group of pupils: some boy-soldiers from the school's O.T.C., a few prefects, two or three sixth-form girls and all the first year. Horatio Bullock was represented by his wife, the Lady

Mayoress, Gloria Bullock, a great balloon of a woman who looked as if she might float away on a thermal of civic pride, but who *some* remembered from when she was a meat-chopper at Cagmag's. On the scaffolding were members of the cathedral's masonry department. David spotted the journalist who'd been at Marauding Hordes' grand opening. There were also, as usual, a number of bewildered tourists, trying to fathom what was happening. The Archbishop embarrassedly splashed a bit of holy water over Struther's image and said a hasty prayer. Glad to have got that over with, those not involved in a practical capacity now watched as the masons hauled on the rope and Struther ascended. High above, in the stone niche where he was to be put, four men waited to catch him and guide him into position. If his eyes had not been made of stone, on a clear day Struther would have been able to see as far as the motorway.

The statue neared its pedestal. A cheer burst forth from the bystanders. The cross-faced choirmaster, clearly totally uninter-ested in whatever ceremony his music might be accompanying, raised both his hands and gave a slight nod. The trebles' voices struck up *Jerusalem*. Struther dangled opposite his ledge now, almost motionless. Arms reached out to pull him into place. Slowly, he approached his lodging.

Then, something happened. There was a cry from above. On the ground there were screams. The Queen's School Head scanned his charges nervously, fearing post-accident trauma. There were yells of 'Hang on! Hang on!' One of the masons trawling in the Archbishop had lost his balance and hung, suspended, seven feet below where Struther's effigy teetered ominously.

In a moment it was over. The statue was steadied. The mason, who had been harnessed, was pulled back up to the ledge by his colleagues. 'He's all right,' one of them yelled down to the supervisor.

David heard a voice in his ear. It was the acne-faced teenage journalist.

'It's happened again,' he said. 'Bang goes my story. Why couldn't that bloody Struther have gone flying?'

David looked at the boy with distaste. 'There is no story in a man narrowly escaping a nasty accident?'

The journalist shrugged. 'Escaping? No. Even if he'd fallen . . . Nasty accidents are mundane. You'd still need a twist to it. Something that would get people interested.'

Now David became genuinely curious; the conversation suddenly seemed relevant to the problem of getting anyone to weigh in on the side of the squatters.

'People are not interested in human suffering?' he queried.

The journalist rubbed his acne. 'Are you? Like I say: without a quirk, it's not news. It's everywhere. You don't need to read about it in the papers.'

'But if the statue had fallen? That would have been something people would have been concerned about?'

'In a manner of speaking.' The boy gave David the look the young reserve for the naive middle-aged, which was maddening, but David forced himself to continue to listen. 'You see, with accidents, famines, wars, etc., etc., etc., people don't know where they fit into the picture,' the journalist went on. 'They think they ought to do something, but they don't know what, or it'd take too much effort. They get to feeling guilty and guilt makes them resentful and they stop reading your papers. But if you give them something they know where they are with . . . Well, architecture's a winner every time. Long as it's old enough, it's an undisputable good thing – "benefit", we call it; they like the word "benefit". If it's modern, then all you've got to ask is if it serves the needs of the community. If it does: bingo! People know where they are with architecture.'

David looked up at the tower. Struther was in place and would probably remain there for the best part of a millennium. Pitsbury Cathedral had been repaired, patched and restored throughout its entire history. You could even argue, so consistently had it been reconstructed, that it was no longer the building that had initially been placed there: just the original cathedral's stone facsimile.

The odious youth was right: people did know where they were with architecture. A building was one thing; what occupied it, quite another. Which was why there was no point in arguing on behalf of the squatters, any more than there was a point in talking ethics to a bank manager.

David started to walk quickly in the direction of Weaver Street. He had found the answer to his problem.

9

Pitsbury Without

It was like when the gunfighters enter the little Mexican village.

Washing was hastily grabbed off the ruined walls and bushes where it had been drying. Infants were scooped up, dogs dragged inside by their collars. People clambered in through the downstairs windows or shinned up to the first floor ones, aided by crumbling footholds and ropes, which were then speedily hauled in. Wooden boards appeared in all the windows not already blocked, with the exception of a small attic one. There was the sound of something enormously heavy being dragged against the front door.

By the time the five of them were standing outside it, the squat had become a fortress.

A face popped out of the high, unboarded window: a cornered, contorted woman's face, feral and spitting. She had a ring through her eyebrow, two through her nose, one through her upper lip. Her head was shaven and tattooed, except for a short Mohican bristle of ginger hair. Her emaciated arms were smeared with coloured chalk. She was wearing tatters of painted gauze. She made David think of paintings of Victorian circus-performers.

'Fuck off,' she yelled. It was a desperate, animal sound.

'What on earth is going on?' said Henry Pearl, turning to David. 'What can we have done to offend the woman?' A bucket of something liquid was emptied out of the window. It missed them by inches.

The woman disappeared, to be replaced by a round, mild-looking, saggy male, with folds of chin and soft rolls of stomach.

'We've got provisions,' the man called down, waving, in illustration, what looked like a doughnut. 'We can sit it out as long as we have to.' Then he too disappeared.

'Do they think we're besieging them?' said Henry.

'I knew it wouldn't work,' said Rick Farr. He plucked a cigarette from an inner pocket, put it in his mouth but didn't light it.

'I certainly never dreamed they would be quite this antisocial,' said Henry Pearl.

They were silent for a few moments.

Then, 'They must think we're bailiffs, Henry,' said David. It hadn't occurred to him previously, but now he realised that probably no one in ordinary clothes ever came to the squat with benign intentions.

'Bailiffs?' Henry Pearl took the idea in, aghast. 'That is to say, all of us?'

It took a great deal to discomfit Henry Pearl. David was puzzled.

'I don't imagine they differentiate between us, Henry,' he replied, it striking him at that moment that, in as much as they had imposed themselves upon his notice, he had never differentiated between the squatters.

The woman reappeared now, and so did the man, perhaps to assess whether the five on the ground were giving any signs of leaving. Henry Pearl took a few steps backwards, in order, David assumed, to see them better.

He was wrong. It was in order better to be seen.

'Do you think *I* am a bailiff?' Henry called upwards.

From above there was silence. The big, mild-faced man took a bite of doughnut and started to chew, rhythmically. The woman had apple-slice shadows under each of her hollow eyes.

'Look at me,' Henry continued. 'Look at my waistcoat. Look at my jacket. Do I really strike you as the kind of person who wears a polo-neck on his days off and purchases his clothing from shops that go under names such as "Beau Brummel" and "Mr Coathanger"?'

The silence thickened. David was suddenly aware of not just two pairs of ears listening but, perhaps, dozens.

'*He* looks like a bailiff,' yelled the pierced woman suddenly, pointing at Colin Rutt, who was eating a Kit-Kat. 'And so does he,' pointing at Rick Farr.

The comment didn't matter in the case of Colin, but in the case of Rick – given his social aspirations – it was embarrassing. Now he, too, took offence. He raised his left arm. Round his wrist was a thick gold watch.

'You think a bailiff would wear something like this, then?' he shouted.

'Yeah,' yelled the woman, without hesitation.

'They might wear a *copy*,' Rick countered, after a most uncomfortable moment, 'but this is the real thing I'm wearing.'

'A bailiff would wear the real thing,' yelled the woman, beginning to sound bemused, her rasped voice thinning.

'It's true, Rick. I'm sorry, but it is,' said Henry, with a consoling pat. Then, calling upwards, 'I want an absolute assurance, however, that whatever Rick here looks like, you now realise that, where I am concerned, you are mistaken.'

Rick turned on Henry. 'One more word about my Rolex and I'm leaving you to it.'

In the light of the sympathy he had offered, Henry was offended. 'Do,' he retorted, with uncustomary pique. 'You're scarcely necessary to the proceedings anyway.'

Rick exploded, his accent wandering in the direction of home. 'And you are? Can there be anyone more unnecessary on the face of the effing planet than an interior designer?'

'Unless, perhaps, it's an Internet Shop owner.'

'I, unlike some, provide a necessary service,' said Rick.

'Wotchit. Wotchit,' said Colin Rutt, chucking down his Kit-Kat wrapper.

'Well at least my clients are real people,' retorted Henry.

'In a manner of speaking,' replied Rick.

'Please don't be rude to each other,' said Fay. 'Everyone's looking.'

David, who was only half listening to the argument, glanced

up at the windows. It would be easy enough to calm Rick and Henry down; harder was to know how to proceed with the squatters, which was what he had been considering. Fay was right: boards had been pulled aside, just enough to permit the squatters to watch the performance, just enough to reveal more faces. David looked at them, puzzled; they were not bystanders so much as . . . the word came to him . . . *witnesses* – quintessential spectators; not called upon to participate. And, if you did that for long enough, the expressions on the watching faces told him, the likely and unlikely, the possible and impossible – even, perhaps, the interesting and uninteresting – merged into a unique *Given*, an anthropological *Big Bang: Potential*.

'I don't know how you can do it. I don't know how you can stand there and insult my calling,' Henry was crying.

'Henry,' said David, spurred into intervention by the outrageous terminology, 'you are an interior designer, not a prophet.'

'I flatter myself I am a harbinger of good things, a zealot on the side of good taste, a proselytiser for *the lovely*.'

'I don't know how you can claim that and still wear that waistcoat.' Rick had lit his cigarette and was puffing on it ardently.

'What is wrong with my waistcoat? Can someone tell me what is wrong with my waistcoat?' Appealing to David.

'I have nothing to say about your waistcoat, Henry. I am merely observing that your language is absurdly grandiose.'

'I suppose *you* would like to be called a shopkeeper?'

Fay, who could produce an impressive volume in relation to her build, now let out a piercing scream. Unnoticed in the heat of the discussion, the heavy object blocking the doorway of the squat had been rolled aside. A tall, grubby man was standing a few feet from them. He had a long face with a hooked nose, long legs, long, straight hair. He wore a black woolly hat, jeans, a holey jacket over a khaki sweater. He smelled of stale sweat, smoke and mildew. With a smug expression that also had a whiff of schizophrenia in it, he appeared to be awaiting silence.

When it fell, 'I've been expecting you,' he said, looking from face to face, in a manner that David could only assume was supposed to indicate he could see the soul within.

*   *   *

A pallid man was turning the handle of a duplicator. Several people were clustered around it, apparently sniffing the air in the vicinity. At first David assumed this must be in an attempt to drown out the other stenches. He thought of Fay's pomanders which were bought by ladies at Christmas to give to people they didn't particularly like; swinging incense-burners; strewn herbs and meadow-grasses. Now he could see that they probably really had once had a practical purpose. Poverty stank. There were no two ways about it. A hideous, subtle, invasive stink which sat on the stomach and made one feel in danger of heaving.

'Gary found some herbal teabags,' said the duplicator man as they entered. 'Tea?'

'Herbal? Yes,' said Fay.

Found turned out to be a word which, in this context, did not operate in the 'Where did you find this little wine?' sense. Gary, who proved to be the round-faced man who'd appeared at the upper window, was now stirring a big pot of baked beans that hung from a hook over a fire, crouched on a mound of copies of *The Big Issue*. He produced a soggy box of teabags, still bearing vestiges of what looked like potato peelings, and, bending his head to the smouldering logs, blew on them until they began to crackle. A cloud of black, acrid smoke billowed into the room. It settled in the back of David's throat and irritated the membranes in his nostrils. Gary poured water from a scummy plastic bottle into a saucepan.

'It'll take about twenty minutes,' he observed, taking a fossilised half sandwich from a pocket.

'Sit,' said the tall, long-faced man with the slightly mad expression, pointing at the littered, grime-caked floorboards. Dishearteningly, he appeared to be viewed by the other squatters as some sort of leader. 'I am Merlyn Orb,' he added, a piece of news that David also found discouraging.

Gingerly, the five visitors lowered themselves into varying degrees of hovering position.

'It has been given to me, alone, to understand that you are not literal bailiffs,' said Merlyn Orb.

'We are not, as it happens, figurative bailiffs either,' said David.

'Absolutely not,' Henry Pearl concurred.

'It was given to me, alone, to understand this,' Orb continued, oblivious, 'due to a vision of the Hanged Man, yesterday, which told me I should engage more closely with my subconscious and read the augurs.'

'You mean the statue of Archbishop Struther?' said David, after a baffled pause, realising that this must be what the man was on about. It occurred to him that, neither in life nor in death, would Struther be likely to approve of anybody having even a nodding acquaintance with their subconscious.

'I know nothing of archbishops,' said Orb.

'Be that as it may, it seems to me,' said David, unable to stop himself, 'that esoteric insight was unnecessary in order for it to occur to one who has, presumably, seen bailiffs in action, that they are generally not quite so lacking in unity of purpose.'

'Nevertheless, it was vouchsafed to me alone,' Orb persisted.

'Don't be nasty, David,' said Fay.

'I am not being "nasty", I am merely pointing out that one does not need messages from the spirit of Archbishop Struther or, indeed, any of the other powers of earth or air, in order to realise that Henry Pearl would not make even a tolerable bailiff.'

'Nor to see that he doesn't dress like one,' Henry Pearl added.

'You believe in logic,' said Merlyn Orb, looking at David accusingly. The duplicator wheel stopped turning, the pallid man was looking warily in David's direction. The woman in gauze and chalk was staring at him. David felt, at once, alien and intensely irritated that a belief in logic should cause him to experience this sensation. He fell silent.

After a pause, 'I respect what my soul understands you to be saying,' said Orb. The tension broke. The duplicator started up again. Gary checked the pot of water.

'Well that's just as well,' said Henry.

'You are a hierophant. You preach *the lovely*,' said Orb now, looking at Pearl. 'It was your words that told me why you are come. It is that our dues might be exacted from the Commonweal.'

'Indeed I am. Indeed I do,' Henry replied, looking pleased.

'Oh really . . .' David began, but Colin Rutt intervened.

'Don't knock it,' he muttered.

David looked at him. Colin shrugged. David took the point, which was a good one: if Merlyn Orb's belief in this mystical nonsense was going to further their purpose, they might as well humour it. Observing that there were, as yet, no bubbles in the pan of water for the tea, David ceased to listen and looked, instead, at his surroundings.

When he and Fay purchased their house in Weaver Street the market was buoyant – or had seemed so; there were signs that might have been read, even then. They had bought a building, the restoration of which had reached a certain state of completion. It had been gutted, old wiring taken out, bath-tiles hacked off, wallpaper shaved away. It smelled of dust. The beams were grey. It was not squalid, just in need of finishing: decoration, wood-treatment, re-wiring, plumbing, new floors, a damp course, a new roof. It also needed 'opening up', as Henry had called it. Successive generations had divided the massive Tudor rooms into ever-smaller compartments. For a time, the building had evidently been let out to students; there was a plastic skylight in the attic.

The overall impression, however, had not been unpleasant. Sunlight slotted through cluttered segments of window and made neat oblongs on the uneven floorboards. At parties in London gardens, sipping white wine from heavy glasses bought at the Reject Shop, Fay and David would speak to friends and strangers of having 'a hell of a lot to do', and friends and strangers would reveal themselves to be in similar situations. The entire English middle-class, it seemed, was 'camped out in tents in the garden, living on sausages – the children love it; you can imagine,' or 'taking a house in Brittany for the summer while the builders deal with the dry-rot'. Open a Sunday newspaper and the journalists were indulging in the same project abroad, laughingly admitting to writing beneath neglected tangles of bougainvillea, while *maçons* struggled into their villas with rescued marble fireplaces and their husband or wife made friends with the local *boulanger* or *viticulteur*, or *patron* of the local restaurant, who served marvels for mere sous and who, inevitably, took the couple under his wing, revealing to them, and them alone, where you could get the best tapas, champignons, tortellini.

One mystery went unexplored, however, one question unanswered: why had such incipient loveliness been discarded by those who had previously owned it? Someone had left, in order that David and his like might occupy these half-done sets; every one described, orally or in print, was at roughly the same stage of incompletion. The answer had been delivered to David gradually, from a source which, at first glance, appeared unlikely: the bank manager.

Now as he looked around the squat David saw, made visible, the empty stage – his own house two bankruptcies ago; the peasant *fermette* before the sinking of the *fosse septique*; the airy warehouse, filled with nothing; the barn. At this initial point – a few scenes previous to the one at which David had entered the action – it was not so much a question of what you had to add (that would come later), but what you would have to take away.

The squat had been choked by modernisation. It was as if, back in the fifties, the idea had been to construct a dwelling with every possible mod-con inside the old, inconvenient, external structure. Ceilings had been lowered, forty years of damp had turned them into sagging udders; a kitchen had been fitted, razor sharp and tinny; beams been boxed in; fireplaces blocked off – the squatters had taken an axe to the hardboard to get at the one they used for cooking. And yet somehow, struggling to be revealed, David's own, Henry Pearl's, Rick Farr's house was in there. Their beautiful properties had once been in this state also.

It was this that David had realised when the averted fall of Archbishop Struther had galvanised the awful young journalist into being informative – something manifestly at odds with the tendency of his occupation. It was to this insight that he had had to steer Henry Pearl and the others the previous evening.

Pitsbury could not be constrained to get hot under the collar about poverty; if Jesus Christ had meant the ubiquitous poor to be an unquenchable source of possibilities for virtue for the fortunate, the idea had backfired – as Horatio Bullock illustrated, one could easily grow used to the needy. But Pitsbury was largely of the opinion that it did care greatly about architecture. Though here it was still in need of guidance. The word *slum* could be waved, like a magic wand, over a building, and the majority of Pitsbury would will it to vanish – even if it be the Neanderthal form of their own window-boxed property. If the squat in Pitsbury Without was to rally people to its defence, it must clearly reveal its architectural merits. Untapped potential had absolutely no future. David was going to have to instigate the squat's renovation: renovated, there would be a public outcry against its demolition.

This was the plan he had outlined at Marauding Hordes the night before, the place deserted except for a couple of confused tourists and a lab-assistant, vaguely known to Henry, apparently on a computer date. One of the cooking stones had fused earlier in the evening, taking all the others down with it. Henry and Colin had been bickering. Henry had cracked open a bottle of tiswin and was drinking it on the rocks. Colin was smoking an azure cigarette, from a box of all different colours, and licking the chocolate off a Fry's Turkish Delight.

'Munny,' he said, when David had finished.

'Yup,' agreed Rick Farr, picking wax off one of the candle-sticks.

'The idea is we do the work ourselves,' said David. 'Judging from the I.Q.'s of the people who did the job on my property, it can't be that difficult.'

'Mentally, they were unnecessary,' said Henry. 'What they furnished was brawn. Some of them had physiques I would die for.'

'Can't we provide the brawn?' asked Fay, who found it a struggle to lift a nutmeg.

'Watch my lips,' said Henry. 'Watch my lips. I am smiling ruefully.'

'I'm sure the squatters will want to join in,' said David. 'Once they understand what we are doing.'

At the time, it had seemed that a renovation project would be the easiest of concepts for the squatters to internalise. Even the builder who'd prepared the cement for the roofing work on David and Fay's might have been able to grasp the rudiments of it. Now, becoming once more aware of Merlyn Orb, it dawned on David that, yes, he would definitely want to join in – to an extent that could speedily become undesirable – but also that his, and via his unfortunate influence, the rest of the squatters' understanding of what they were setting out to achieve was likely to be, at best, lateral.

Because the ground floor windows of the squat were boarded up and anyway the room was full of smoke, though it was broad daylight outside, the interior was decidedly murky. Candlelight juddered in jam jars. Sudden draughts hammered the flames horizontal. There were several torches, propped in unsteady containers, lurching at angles, dripping wax and shedding the odd spark on mounds of two- or three-day-old newspapers, most of which sported crumpled, orangey photographs of the jolly face of Harriet, Duchess of Pitsbury, topped with headlines such as 'I LUV HIM EVEN THOUGH HE'S A DAGO'. (David imagined a sudden conflagration, the report of it on the six o'clock news: a weary fire-chief standing in what the reporter referred to as 'a burnt-out shell'; 'it was a time-bomb waiting to explode,' he was saying.) On the walls of the squat were drooping, blu-tacked posters for past events ('*Loving Wisely Well* by Hermia Mowbray, the Queen's School Francis Partington Day Frolic'; 'Could You Be The New Reigning Miss Pitsbury? Come to Langley The Chemist for Entry Details'; 'Kandy Lam will be reading from *Supermodels* HERE, tonight, sponsored by Quik-Potato'; 'Twelfth Annual Wise Lady Free Festival'; 'Vote Babcock'; 'Pitsbury Hallowe'en Bonfire Procession'). Ranged beneath them on the floor, a fresco of bodies silently took in the action. The duplicator churned. Nothing in the whole scenario appeared deliberate and yet now, unexpectedly, Merlyn Orb grabbed one of the torches, with considerable dexterity, and cried, 'See! See! We make our own beauty.'

'Fucking Ada,' said Colin Rutt.

Rick Farr threw down a half-stubbed cigarette end.

The duplicator ceased.

'*See! See! We make our own beauty,*' said the duplicator man. He was writing.

'No, Al. No,' said Merlyn Orb, noticing. 'It's not a poem. Or, rather, it's the poem that is all of us. Not just mine, but *Snew?*'s.'

'Bless you,' said Fay.

'Not me. Us all. Bless us all.'

'If Tiny Tim would cease for a moment,' said David, tiring of the nonsense, 'perhaps we could take some measurements and start to assess how much adversity we are going to be required to triumph over.'

'*Snew?* is a newspaper,' said Al, the duplicator man, ignoring David and addressing Fay. 'Ideas, grass-roots, word on the street, poetry – Merlyn's mainly. Merlyn is a poet.'

A poet. Of course. David was struck by the relentless inevitability of it. He wondered whether the planet had ever produced a deranged visionary who wasn't also a poet.

'Look! Look!' cried Orb. He raised the torch, held it up to the wall, as if to illuminate cave-paintings. The squatters' bodies, shapeless under clothes and blankets, formed dark shadows, not like those of people, but like sagging tents, straw huts, teepees. Behind them, there was a garden, adobes, people dancing. It took up the shadow pictures as a backdrop takes up the scenery. And now, for a moment, David lost his detachment.

He remembered stepping out of a window onto an escape with Clementine, the transformation of known locality into exotic location. He thought of *The Nutcracker*, when the clock strikes and the Christmas tree grows and its baubles fall away and it is only one among others in a snowy forest. Again, he thought of the word: *Potential*.

'You are saying,' he said, slowly, meaning the posters, meaning the *trompe l'oeil* painting he was staring at, 'that this is deliberate? It is not a coincidence?'

'Nothing is a coincidence, my friend,' said Merlyn Orb, with a cat-that-got-the-cream expression so unbearable that the spell was broken.

'Oh my,' cried Henry Pearl. 'Who is author of this delightful oeuvre?'

'Me.' It was the pierced, shaved, tattooed, gauzed, chalk-smeared woman. Her body looked, to David, as if lots of different things had been tried out on it.

'And you are?' said Henry, with the tone of reverence he reserved for when in the presence of the goddess, Art.

'Becs,' defensively. 'I'm a street-artist, but I also juggle, busk and fire-eat.'

'Fire *eat*,' wailed Fay.

'But Gary, too, is no less than the least among us,' said Merlyn Orb, raising an arm, and indicating Gary, who had just taken the water off the flames, and was dunking one herbal tea-bag into two mugs of water, then squeezing it out and setting it to dry on a stone by the fire. One mug he handed to his left, the other to his right. People took a sip and passed it on. David's brain dumped a surprisingly sizeable delivery of information about infectious diseases into his consciousness, with a sub-section for those specifically communicable by saliva.

'Here,' said Gary, looking at Colin, who he had evidently taken a shine to. He handed him a piece of chocolate, white with age.

'Thanks mate,' said Colin, popping it into his mouth without hesitation.

There was a pause. The imbibing, even of tea, was, David saw, too precious to be interrupted by anything as extraneous as conversation. When his turn came with a mug, he took the smallest sip possible, still enough for him to register quite how gritty the rim of it was. The tea itself didn't taste greatly different from any of the ones Fay sold, however, which was to say, as if somebody had wandered within a mile of something flowering, carrying a cup of hot water.

'We are all part,' said Merlyn Orb, eventually, 'of a millennial project. You have come to us for that reason.'

'No,' said David, feeling that whatever the consequences, he really must clarify the situation. 'We have come to renovate the squat – subject to your agreement – in an attempt to prevent its demolition. We are greatly opposed to the supermarket development which is proposed for the wasteland site behind the squat, and stopping the squat being demolished is the best way that we can think of to make the development impossible.'

'You are on the side of hope and beauty.'

'Not specifically.'

'Oh, I am,' said Henry.

'Me too,' said Fay.

'Yeah,' said Colin.

'Have you ever seen a computer go haywire?' asked Rick, fidgeting with his shirt-sleeves. 'It looks a bit like you lot sound.'

'I have,' said Al, the duplicator man. 'I used to be in computers.'

As one, Fay, David, Colin, Rick and Henry turned to stare at him. David felt run down his body the chill which he knew the others were also experiencing. Blue eyes. A chipped front tooth. That keen expression. Clean Al's face and it was strip-light pale: office pallor. It was Rick Farr. It was Rick Farr, the squatter. His eyes shot to Becs, a colander of a person, in nineteenth-century circus-acrobat gauze: a street-artist, a creator of interiors. Gary, the cook, who was decanting the remains of the water into a thermos. Merlyn Orb. Then, the sweating walls, collapsing ceiling, peeling plaster, rotting boards: his own house. His. David's. Strip it bare and there it was. Remove a layer, find another layer beneath it, right back to the beginning. Tear away an inch and a half of pulpy wallpaper and sodden paint and you had a Neapolitan of all the colours that had ever been there, right back to the first, thin pigment, applied to the first, new plaster.

It was no coincidence that poverty had created the palimpsest.

10

Martini and Sandwiches

The weather had changed from crisp to soggy. There was a pungent smell on the air. When Clementine took her solitary morning walks, the dew on the banks of the Ebb soaked through her shoes. A guerrilla damp had infiltrated the heartland and made regular, unexpected appearances, much as the Vikings must have done among the Anglo-Saxons: Clementine found one morning an intricate mould growing up the back door, which had not been there the night before; the trees in Tony Gilbert's garden were covered in semi-circular slices of velvety fungus.

Autumn and winter were a great icy whoosh where Clementine came from. People rushed out and met them with zest – waxed toboggan runnels coated their lips with thick white sun-screen. Here, it seemed more a case of succumbing to the new season. There was a meeting in the English Department staff common-room at the university to mark the beginning of the semester. A third of the lecturers were absent: some had still failed to recover from their end-of-year nervous breakdowns, in spite of a summer in which to rally; others had fallen to a flu epidemic – early, but, apparently, as predictable as the wave of suicide attempts among the first years (finding it hard to cope with leaving their stay-at-home boyfriends and girlfriends, it was explained to Clementine, who, coming from a country of massive distances, would once have been at a loss to understand how one could pine so greatly for someone who lived only two or three hours away). Of those who made it to the staff meeting – and an atmosphere of heroism was not entirely absent – a third were hacking and sneezing. As they waited for the Department Head to arrive, they hunched in cardigans, reading copies of *The Times Higher Education Supplement* left over from June, their noses buried in wet handkerchiefs, sipping coffee from the vending machine. At Pitsbury College, Canada, colds were treated with blusher, bright sweatshirts and leggings, vitamin 'C' pills and yogurt and honey.

Clementine offered to do some stand-in 'Introduction to the Renaissance' lectures and to take some undergraduate and post-graduate tutorials until it was ascertained who among the absent staff were going to be lost, this year, to advertising and industry – these being the customary directions taken by those who could no longer hack it in academia. In addition, as part of the Quik-Potato Visiting Fellowship, she was required to do a special lecture on Mowbray in which, the terms of the Fellowship stipulated, 'potatoes should be referred to'. This, apparently, was a clause in all of Quik-Potato's arts sponsorship and no one appeared to be willing to say that it was a pretty tall order; in some cases, a virtually impossible one. Although lost time had more than been made up for, the potato wasn't eaten in quantity in England until a good century after Hermia Mowbray's death.

'Maybe we could sell what you call crisps outside the lecture hall,' said Clementine.

A facetious suggestion which, to her surprise, was taken up. The discussion which followed revealed considerable departmental in-fighting. The idea was eventually rejected on the grounds that people might not make the connection between a crisp and a potato, particularly not a baked one.

On the departmental noticeboard, along with the private-sector job ads, were a few sad postcards with pictures of seaside donkeys with straw hats on, or 1950's beaches, with 'Greetings from Bournemouth' in curly white letters. Among them, glossy and recent and clearly slumming it, was the same sunset over Provence that Tony Gilbert had sent to Clementine. In this case, as in hers, she suspected, not so much to send salutations as to rub in the fact that Gilbert was in Provence and everyone else wasn't. Though, reading between the lines, all was not quite as idyllic as Tony attempted to render it. Roo and Immie Canning had had a most unwelcome shock, namely autumn, which they had not realised took place in the Mediterranean. Roo – Gilbert tried for a tone which might have fooled one who had not schooled year after year of undergrads in ambiguity – had taken to sitting in the warm, cosy, well-heated local bar with its big, wood-burning, heat-belting stove, and chatting (in dialect – typically, Roo now had it virtually like a native) with the *paysans*. It was part of getting a feel for the place, which was Roo all over. He was learning a tremendous amount from these humble folk, he'd told Tony, as, stumblingly, they sought the words in which to confide their hopes and fears. Meanwhile, their host, the Comte, was wintering in Guadeloupe. Could Clementine, by the way, post off Tony's cable-knit sweater from Mull?

She found it in Tony's fitted wardrobe. It smelled of garden twine and shitakes.

The university was stuck out on its own on a windy hill, overlooking the city. It had spawned a small cluster of businesses: an insurance company, a sub post-office, a couple of banks, one of which sported a banner that read 'FREE BOOK TOKEN WITH YOUR SPECIAL-RATE STUDENT LOAN', the other, 'FREE CD TOKEN WITH YOUR LOAN'. From this vantage-point, you could see that the Ebb had determined Pitsbury, just as the Nile had determined Egypt.

In general, the further away they were from the river, the younger the buildings, except for where war-time bombing, Clementine guessed, had necessitated redevelopment. In that respect, Weaver Street had been lucky. It was the loveliest street in the town, really. Clementine tried to imagine what it would be like to live in a house – like David's, say – from which you could look out and see ivied walls, a twisty green river, a network of other windows and rooftops, the odd, glimpsed patch of garden, roses clambering up the ancient stone of old convent and monastery buildings. She thought of how she'd raised the bathroom's sash-window to dry her hair in the spring sunlight, and had heard the cathedral bell chiming for Evensong.

On the days she didn't have stuff to do on campus, and quite often when she did, Clementine worked obsessively at Bus Station House. There was barely time to look out the grubby window, across the wasteland, to where the city wall prevented you seeing much but the rooftops of Weaver Street.

It wasn't work everyone would have enjoyed, but Clementine found it mercifully absorbing. It was the linguistic equivalent of an archaeologist clearing each layer of a site with a little brush, inch by inch, examining every minute detail.

Handwriting, for instance, must be painstakingly gone over. The piece of dialogue similar to that in Act II of *Thalia*, really was very similar. *Thalia* had come down to the present through two manuscript versions – now in P.C.C.'s library – both in the hand of Percy Glyde, a sleazy type who'd made a living copying down plays as they were being performed, and selling them off to rival companies. With his eye only to a fast buck, Glyde hadn't been overly concerned with accuracy. Much more accurate was Glyde's colleague, name unknown, referred to as O. Clementine reckoned the Bus Station House version of Act II of *Thalia* was in O's handwriting; in which case, it was more likely to be what Mowbray had originally written. Clementine went through, word by word, looking at the variations between the Glyde and the O texts.

The last two scenes of the drama entitled *Repossession* might not be by Mowbray at all, but by someone else, Clementine decided, after three days spent studying it, checking the dates of the first known uses of certain words and the number of times, if any, that they occurred in Mowbray's other writing. The playlet seemed more certainly authentic. And the sonnet! The sonnet was, beyond any doubt, Mowbray. The sonnet could be described as totally new – though, in another sense, it was four hundred years old. Clementine wished there were someone she could share it with. She'd typed it up and sent it to Ruth Carpini, of course, and Ruth had called, late one night – Clementine had had to dash out of the shower in a towel – and they'd discussed it. Ruth was wild with excitement. But it wasn't the same as having someone beside you, able to touch the paper, the way you could.

The level went down on the peanut butter jar and on the

gin and vermouth bottles. Clementine went to a supermarket to replace them, and to get some more bread and cat food. She bought a copy of a fat novel, entitled *Supermodels*, by someone called Kandy Lam. She read it in the evenings, lying on the sofa in a baggy sweatsuit and a pair of socks, a single lamp on, eating peanut butter sandwiches and drinking Martini.

One night the phone rang, late. Clementine grabbed it. There was silence, and then the sound of what seemed to be someone picking up an extension. Clementine's throat tightened. Her pulse started to race.

'Hello? Hello?'

It was just Tony Gilbert.

'Hi Tony.'

'Please wait a minute.' Tony sounded irritated, as if Clementine had called him. 'There seems to be a cross-line.'

Now a famous voice spoke from the extension.

Gilbert's tone changed immediately.

'No, Immie, it's only me. I don't know where Roo is. I haven't seen him since he set off for Nice after lunch ... Yes, that's where he said he was going. But, look, Immie, if you need to make a call, this really doesn't matter, I can do it later ... That is so so kind of you. It won't take long, I promise.'

The extension was put down. Clementine took a gulp of Martini.

'They're such a team,' observed Gilbert. 'Immie worries when she doesn't know what Rupert's doing. I think it's the thought of him on those narrow roads in the Ferrari.'

'Why did you call, Tony?'

Now, inexplicably, appearing to remember some forgotten purpose, Gilbert turned on the charm.

'I phoned to see how my favourite Canadian is coping with life in the Motherland.'

'You have numerous Canadians among your acquaintance-ship, whom you rate in order of preference?'

Gilbert laughed for some minutes. 'But, seriously, Clementine, are you comfortable? Did you manage to get Oliver's prawn-flavoured Yum-Yum's?'

'Yeah. No problem.'

From the leather armchair, Oliver, his stomach full of Top-Value Tibbles, gave Clementine a doleful look.

'And you're keeping busy in your ivory tower?'

'Yeah, I'm keeping busy. There's a lot to do on Mowbray.'

'Good. Good. How's David?'

Again, Clementine's heart speeded up. 'David Marsh, you mean?' She attempted to keep her voice light. 'Why? Did you speak with him?'

'No. No, I haven't. I just thought you probably had.'

'No.'

'Ah.' There was a pause. 'Clementine, much as I'm enjoying our conversation,' said Tony, 'I really must let Immie use the phone now. She's probably going to try to contact Zucchini in L.A. – he had to jet off there suddenly. Gives us all a breather, of course, and we bloody need one. So I'll say good-bye, but I will phone again soon, I promise. You haven't changed the refrigerator temperature, have you?'

Funny how until you talked with someone, you could get away without realising that you were slightly drunk and feeling low and cussed.

With the exception of the cleaner at Bus Station House, Clementine hadn't exchanged a word with a living soul all day. Tony Gilbert's intrusion had accentuated the silence with which she'd surrounded herself and brought out the depression she was fighting against. Face it: in order to deal with being here, Clementine was having to work her ass off, place herself in a state of suspended animation, turn into some kind of human robot. Things could not continue like this.

Clementine hauled herself to her feet and went into the kitchen to put the kettle on for coffee. It was the uncertainty that was the problem, she decided. If she knew how David Marsh had viewed their encounter and how he felt about it now – if, indeed, he felt anything whatever – then she could cope with the consequences.

Maybe, after all, it would be best to see David, Clementine reflected – for purely practical reasons. It would clarify the situation, one way or the other, and then she could forget about it. Maybe it would also be a good idea to get out of this frigging sweatsuit and buy something new to wear –

go into Pitsbury, have lunch at the Cock and Hen, do some shopping, have her hair cut. Why not? Shit, Clementine was in Britain, for God's sake; it was a waste not to enjoy it to the fullest extent. Which wouldn't be possible until she'd got things sorted with David.

The Interior of a Butterfly

Henry Pearl was of the belief that if someone looked like a builder they must necessarily possess the skills of a builder. The early stages of the project reinforced this notion since it mainly involved ripping things out, which most of those squatters who got involved were rather good at.

'We don't want to draw attention to what we're doing,' said David as a metal cabinet, lined with a sticky-backed plastic design of loopy, purple and blue, sixties flowers was dropped from an upstairs window.

'Does anyone attend to the pupa when its interior is mush?' Henry retorted.

'I daresay not, Henry. However, a pupa is the size of a thumb-nail.'

'Two thumb-nails,' said Merlyn Orb. 'But maybe the planet is also.'

'Two, you're right,' said Henry. 'Though I have tapering fingers.'

'One of mine,' said Colin Rutt, cracking his knuckles.

This was the kind of occasion when it occurred to David that it might be easier to go bankrupt, welcome the BARG-MART GINORMOUS DIME-O-STORE, and have done with it.

'We are not,' he said, with forced patience, 'renovating the planet, nor yet are we part of the interior of a butterfly. Relatively speaking, the squat may be a speck of dust in a cosmic immensity.

I am merely pointing out that, if we become too visible, we will be noticed and prevented from proceeding.'

'We will not become too visible,' said Merlyn Orb.

Which proved to be eerily correct. Piles of rubble grew on the wasteland, old cupboards, thick tangles of fifties wiring, the thigh-bone shape of a heavy black telephone receiver. Wardrobes were heaved onto shoulders, oblongs of damp carpet pulled up and rolled into spongy scrolls. But no one stopped to look. No car slowed down, not even conservation officer Brian Baffle's, which David spotted once in the vicinity.

And yet – trying moments notwithstanding – it sometimes seemed to David that, except for during the time he had spent with Clementine, he had never before been so intrinsically a part of the city he inhabited, so intimately involved with all the people that had given it life. He felt this especially when he arrived at the squat early and made his way between snoring, muttering, groaning, unshaven bodies to the warmth of the massive fireplace, where Gary was preparing tea. Or when he and Fay, Colin, Henry and Rick discussed plans at the end of the day, over Fay's rather thin leek and potato soup. Or when he looked out of one of the squat's upper windows at sunset and saw the broken forms of the wasteland turned to golden fish-scales. Then he experienced what Orb, rather terribly, referred to as 'connectedness'. He thought of people sleeping in the Underground during the war. He thought of back-packing across Europe, and how he had often woken on some slow train or chugging ferry to discover that he had fallen asleep against a stranger's shoulder. All those times when he had been truly happy came back to him. It seemed that, in recent years, he had only haunted his existence.

Remove a stratum and you revealed another film of life beneath, life which had used whatever means it had to make its earthly sojourn tenable.

In the basement of the squat the floorboards were soft and crumbly. Taken up, they exposed a mosaic of scattered pieces of broken pottery. A molar of stone was just visible, poking through the earth.

'Medieval,' remarked Henry, looking at the shards. 'And *that* is, almost certainly, the top of a Roman pillar.'

Henry Pearl was in his element. He had rushed out and purchased a buff boiler-suit which he wore over his pin-stripes, and a thing for measuring damp. Some of the squatters helped; these he directed. Some were willing to get out of the way; these he shooed into other parts of the building. Some would not move, or help; these he stepped over.

In this respect, it was hard to classify Merlyn Orb, who did not exactly help and who was eternally present but who could not, unfortunately, be stepped over.

'You sell books,' he remarked to David, leaning against the sill of a large, latticed bedroom window on the warm day which proved to be the last of the year. The old glass, thickened at the bottom of each diamond of pane, was clouded with dust. David's hair was caked with it. Colin, who had taken to wearing a tight string vest and cut-off jeans, the effect of which was to make him look mildly pornographic, had a floury coating over his shaven head. Henry Pearl was protecting himself with a knotted scarf. In her circus gauze in the goldy light, Becs, the street-artist, was a bronze, Degas dancer. There were circles of sweat in the armpits of Rick Farr's t-shirt.

They were removing a false ceiling.

Merlyn Orb had a maddening way of making what should have been a question into a statement.

'I am a bookseller, yes,' said David. Beads of gritty sweat trickled down his cheeks.

A large lump of plaster-board fell to the floor.

'I don't believe in books,' said Orb.

This was no great surprise. David refrained from comment.

'Like the man says,' Orb went on: 'the words of the prophets . . .'

Another lump of board came down.

'Well I can hardly sell subway walls, can I?' said David.

There was a sound like a violent hailstorm: pigeon shit, sand, marbles, coins, blackish debris, shredded paper and fabric, leaves. The air took on the colour of school stew.

An aftershock rained down a pile of twigs.

'Rat's nest,' said Orb. 'Brother Rat.' His knitted hat was ridged with dust. His hooked nose looked as if it had been outlined in charcoal.

Later, at home, David raised his face to the shower-nozzle

and let the water bombard it. Diluted crud poured off his hair, ran along his legs, disappeared down the plug-hole. His muscles ached. He felt the heavy yet floating sensation of one who has spent a long time swimming in the sea.

In stiff, newly laundered jeans and a sweatshirt, David returned to the squat to view the day's achievements. The stripped building, greying in the autumn sunset, had a flimsy look to it, as if it might suddenly fold in upon itself. On the wasteland, Becs was practising her fire-eating, lighting brands from a flaming oil-drum.

In the upstairs room a soft down of dust covered every surface. Particles, floating in the air, thickened the evening sun and shadows. David waded through light. From below, in spasmodic, dense emissions, came the stench of the squatters' supper.

'Look,' said Merlyn Orb.

David started.

Blackened and grimy, Orb was still leaning against the window-sill. He pointed a filthy finger in an upwards direction. Not one, but two – possibly three – ceilings had come down that day: two, possibly three, centuries' layers, along with all the things which had fallen, settled and been stuffed in between them. The rubble remained in great, motionless dunes on the floor. How, David wondered, had the building ever supported the weight of it? He raised his eyes, expecting Orb's thinking to be, as usual, opaque. Perhaps because of this, it took him a while to notice that the beams were not just the usual simply planed tree trunks. Instead, where they met and crossed, they had been fashioned into ovals, circles, thistle-shapes, concentric bands; smooth yet, here and there, pocked, as if other patterns might be hidden beneath the dirt they were still encrusted with.

'Victorian Gothic,' proclaimed Henry Pearl, late the following morning. He lifted a stiff brush and applied it vigorously. Summer had been extinguished overnight. The wasteland gleamed with dew. There was a chill in the room. Henry's breath was visible.

As the dirt fell away, forms emerged.

'There seems to be something along the length of several of the beams, too,' said David.

Henry swept the brush across one of the places that David indicated.

'Runes,' said Merlyn Orb. 'A message in the bottle that is wood.'

'A feature!' cried Henry. 'Terribly Walter Scott. But shall we – why not? – go with it? Shall we succumb and permit ourselves to gild the lily?'

'Meaning what, Henry?'

'Meaning bring the feature out with highlights of varied hue. Yield to its nostalgic Medievalism.'

Becs sneezed. She had a cold. Her uplifted face revealed a crimson nose. She yawned and shivered, then doubled up, coughing.

'I am thinking Mongolian coffee,' said Henry. 'But first, let us monitor the progress of Gary's re-pointing.'

Once the building had reached what Henry referred to as 'tabula rasa stage', he had allocated tasks to everyone who looked even vaguely willing to perform them. Gary's bloated stomach, saggy muscles and saggy jeans had led Henry to deem brickwork his appropriate occupation. Due to this simplistic way of assessing the skills of the squatters, he had not thought to ask whether Gary had the slightest ability in that direction.

Henry dashed nimbly down the stairs and round to the back of the building. David followed more slowly. By the time he got outdoors a scene was ensuing: halfway up the ladder, Henry Pearl was gesticulating as wildly as his position permitted. David looked at the roof with a terrible sense of foreboding, and was relieved to discern that the cause of Henry's upset was not structural. Instead of the floppy bulk of Gary at work on the chimney, his eyes were met by the taut, gleaming form of Colin Rutt.

'*Who* is cutting the coley? *Who*?' Henry was crying.

'Like I sed: Gary.' Colin Rutt's voice floated down. He was perched high up, on a narrow ridge, with no more nervousness than if he had been standing in the middle of a football pitch.

'You have left Marauding Hordes in the charge of a person whose idea of food preparation is hotting up a half-chewed, hose-shaped apple pie which he has scavenged from the tables of Burger-Fish?'

'Doesn't mean that's wot 'e wants to be eating. Gary luvs his nosh.'

Henry Pearl let go of the ladder with one hand and covered an ear.

'Do not use that word in my presence. Just do not use it.'

'Thing is,' said Colin, calmly, turning back to his re-pointing, 'Gary doesn't know squat about brickwork. But he does know about cooking. We did a swap. Made sense.'

'Watch me descending,' said Henry. 'I am going to Marauding Hordes to inspect the damage.'

'Won't be any damage,' said Colin, laying down his tools and following Henry down the ladder.

David decided that he had better be on hand in case he was needed to defuse the situation.

Marauding Hordes was busier than usual. Which was to say that one of the tables was occupied by what looked like a couple of lorry drivers who had probably gone astray in the Pitsbury one-way system, and another by a group of fresh-faced students from the university – first years, judging from the newness of their scarves. The students were tucking into plates of fish and chips, accompanied by large dollops of Mongolian chutney. The lorry drivers were downing cups of tea and doorstep-sized chip butties. The soundtrack of Mongolian music, which Henry had sent off for from an organisation called 'Inner Light Recordings', had been replaced by Radio Pitsbury.

'I am fighting back tears,' said Henry to Colin.

David, on the other hand, surveying the scene – such an animated contrast to the successive attempts at rural and exotic – found it quite extraordinarily appealing.

'It's not so bad,' said Colin.

'Do you, for one moment, believe that Mongols eat chip butties?'

Colin shrugged. 'Probably do now. If they like 'em, why shouldn't they? The planet's a global village. Small is beautiful.'

'Well you've certainly changed your tune,' said Henry with a petulant look, though something in his expression suggested to David that he might have noted the increased number of customers.

Gary appeared from the kitchen in a chef's hat and a large

white apron. A smell of frying wafted out after him. David's mouth watered. He suddenly felt, with a pang, as for an intensity of life lost or forgotten, a desperate desire for coffee and a bacon sandwich.

'What have you done with the coley?' cried Henry. 'Tell me what you've done with it.'

'Coated it in my Gran's batter recipe and deep fried it with some spuds,' said Gary.

'Batter? Batter?'

'Real cuisine grand-mere, Henry,' suggested David, in an attempt to give Henry Pearl a pretext for laying aside his indignation. Now he experienced a poignant need for crisp, slightly sweet, chips, with salt and vinegar, creamy fish, yellow batter. And, along with it, an urge to burst out laughing.

Henry Pearl exploded. '*We* were referring to discerning grandmothers. The kind that cooked lentils and goats and dried their tomatoes, podded peas in the shade of old apple orchards, bottled fruit at the waning of the season. Not ones who dunked fish in dripping and served it up with chips the size of mouse-traps.'

'Do you think, Henry,' David asked, 'that such grandmothers ever existed?'

'Can you make that *two* bacon sarnies?' shouted one of the lorry drivers to Gary. 'And another chip butty with that hot ketchup?'

'Have you got any puddings?' asked a student.

'I can do you a deep-fried Mars Bar,' said Gary.

'I down my pencil,' said Henry. 'I wash my hands of the project. I resign.' He was looking, however, in the direction of the door, which had just opened. Four burly men entered, smoking roll-ups.

'Spotted your rig,' said one of them to the lorry drivers. 'What you doing down here, then? Four all-day breakfasts, mate,' he added to Gary.

The door opened again. A second group of students came in, pulled up chairs and ordered a round of tiswins and six plates of chips, with Mongolian chutney to dip them in.

'I smelled the bacon,' said Rick Farr, entering now. 'A change of concept?'

'Oh, Henry,' said Fay, appearing a second later, 'All the

people! The increased business! I wondered what had happened.'

'Don't ask,' said Henry. 'Gary here has taken over my kitchen. He is, apparently, unable – or unwilling – to work on the rooftop and Colin' – with a dismissive gesture – 'is re-pointing the chimney.'

'I get vertigo,' said Gary.

'Wot I always wanted,' said Colin: 'to be a builder.'

There was a silence.

'Oh, Henry,' Fay repeated, seeming to have taken in the fact that things hung in the balance, 'and you are going to let this continue, for the sake of all of us?'

Some more students entered.

There was a long pause.

Then, 'For all our sakes,' said Henry Pearl, face evidently sufficiently preserved, 'I have decided to comply.'

Fay rushed over and gave him a little kiss. It vaguely occurred to David, watching, that maybe she had been rather clever. Now that he thought about it, Fay *was* quite good at handling people. Though it did not cross his mind that it was living with him that had given her the opportunity to perfect this ability, David was beset with a sudden unease. Admiring his wife was not something he felt at home with.

The disquiet that had overtaken David that day lingered, translating itself into a diffuse insecurity.

The nights lengthened. The renovation continued apace. Many of the supplies for the building work appeared spontaneously, showing up in places where there had been nothing the evening before. Some had to be purchased, however. For these, Rick and Fay and David – and, supposedly, Colin – owed Henry.

Two letters arrived from the bank in quick succession. David left them on his desk, unopened. He was dogged by the lurking consciousness of the failure of the renovation of his own building. It was because certain important things had not been taken into account. Was something vital not being taken into account now? Though he could not say what, David became convinced that there was, indeed, an element that they had overlooked, and equally certain that it constituted a weakness, a flaw, in the structure of what they were attempting to accomplish.

A partition had been removed: David also continued to see Fay Marsh's virtues. Not the spurious, martyred ones, but those which were authentically Fay. This added to his sense of instability. After all their years of marriage, he had assumed he knew where they stood in relation to one another. Had Fay changed, or had he?

There were alarming times, too, when David caught brief glimpses of Merlyn Orb's meanings. Maybe it was simply this that was causing his mental queasiness. Anyone who could come even to a partial comprehension of Merlyn Orb's vision must fear for their sanity, unless, as in the case of Fay, they already had a sympathy for the mystical. Rick Farr thought Orb was a complete nutcase, a viewpoint that David was largely in accord with, and which he found reassuring. Though when the air smelled of bonfires, and woodsmoke drifted vertically from the Pitsbury chimneys into a vanilla sky glimpsed behind great tarpaulins of purple cloud, David did sometimes succumb to millennial sensations. Then it seemed to him that big issues were at stake and that humankind must somehow find a way of reconciling itself with its accumulation of pasts.

What he had learnt about cities with Clementine now came to occupy the foreground of his thinking: how much they were places of shifting perspectives. Material levels shelved, caved in, rose with time, of course, but cities also mimicked this process psychologically. You could live in one all your life and not notice a listing Medieval doorway, a particular stained-glass window; entire buildings, even, could be utterly unremarked until, one day, the kaleidoscope turned and a different city was revealed to you.

In the lovely bedroom, Becs continued the task that Henry had dabbled at. Watched, most of the time, by Merlyn Orb, upon whom the room exerted a particular fascination – which gave everyone else a merciful respite from his presence – Becs carefully cleared each wooden nick, groove, crevice and socket of dust. And then she painted. Gold. Crimson. White. Yellow. The first frost came. Becs wore fingerless gloves, leg-warmers, knitted socks, a skirt, a t-shirt, two sweaters, a faded Queen's

School blazer with a fraying crest. She sniffed and coughed constantly. Her cold did not get better; none of the squatters, in fact, seemed to get over colds or flu, once they had them. The ceiling erupted in an Oz of colour which David knew, with growing desperation, was pointless unless he could locate the origin of his increasingly compelling unease.

Then the storm came. And David discovered the flaw in the structure.

12 ∫

British Flu

David was not the only one to feel that their life had gone all confused and worrisome.

Fay opened various bottles and packets, most of which depicted rising or setting suns or serene, fairy-like women, lying prone upon banks of blossoming flowers. She crammed a pill or capsule from each into her mouth, washed down with spring-water. She nibbled on a rice wafer. This was her lunch, a very late one, it was almost four, but still she had little appetite.

Fay looked out of the window. The sky was a pale, faded blue, combed through with thin wisps of white and grey cloud. It seemed to be hovering, uncertainly, up there. Fay made a decision – the wrong one, it transpired – put on her duffle-coat and Wellingtons, hooked the osier over her arm and left the house.

She must be with Nature: it was one of her means of coping. That, and Marsh Meadows.

She turned right, went under the city wall, and proceeded past the squat and over the bridge. The ancient bulk of St Friedaswida's was a drowned, trailing, grey mass in the Ebb. Fay recalled that, as Abbess, the holy Friedaswida had withstood something undesirable. The thought made her feel flimsy. St Friedaswida would have been a woman who Fay would have had to admire, but been unable to like. She was glad to turn her back on the stalwart building and trace the Ebb along the edge of the car-park then, having crossed a narrow, metal bridge, through a bit of suburb and into the fields. From here, the footpath carried straight on to the Ebb Valley which, if you walked along it for long enough, ended at the sea. To hike its whole length was something everyone in Pitsbury meant to do sometime.

Fay wished she hadn't worn a long skirt. The hem was sodden already. She paused beneath the massive Victorian railway bridge to wring it out a bit. The ruddy bricks seemed to exude optimism and certainty, no less sure of themselves, in their way, than St Friedaswida's had been. In the fields, actual cows with grubby tails and muddy hooves and bony flanks pulled at the grass, making crunchy-munchy noises.

Fay trudged on, making a fairly good job of avoiding thought, unable to refrain from noticing, though – running alongside the grass-edged path that she had taken – a fainter, parallel path, that also followed the river. Perhaps it had come about so that two people could walk next to each other; perhaps because its slight variations had something to recommend them. Anyway, it was an alternative, neatly lying there.

Most things, most of the time, flowed into one another in Fay's experience – days into years, a headline into a back-page mention, miso paste into miso soup – but, occasionally, they gave a great belch and a frog-hop. Like when she'd not only realised but *known* that she could no longer be a Fragrance Consultant. The whole discipline of herbology lay before her: a lifetime, a dozen lifetimes would not be enough to explore it.

The landscape had lost its sharp, summer definition.

Fay thought of the soft-focus photos in *Country Manner* magazine and then how she never remembered to look at the recipes in it before the shops were shut. There'd be a page of pottages or winter puddings, or warm salads, or Mediterranean bakes. She'd decide to make a Mediterranean bake, with new potatoes, fresh tomatoes, basil, black olives, pine-nuts and rosemary oil. She'd look in the cupboards and the fridge. Cashews, not pine-nuts; oil, but not rosemary oil; coriander, no basil; tinned tomatoes; baking potatoes; green olives. You could pretend to yourself it was your own creation, sort of inspired by the magazine, but you knew you were hoping really that the effect would be the same as if you'd started with the right ingredients.

Fay did not dare, even the teensiest bit, to let herself begin to imagine that she could possibly ever think of her marriage that way. All she had ever longed for, strived for – other than Marsh Meadows – was her husband's love and loyalty. Fay blinked her eyes and tried to slam the door shut on all negative feelings, but they seeped out under her resolve anyway. In spite of Nature, she was weepy, icky, listless, scared: generally under the weather.

Fay looked up at the sky. She was not a person who walked with any decisiveness but she frequently discovered that, without realising, she had drifted several miles. So it was now. Empty-osiered, she was in the Ebb Valley. The river had widened and become shallower, the hills bunched together a bit. A flock of plump, white doves scattered out of the dovecote of one of the valley's gorgeous properties. They glowed against the clouds, which were no longer thin veils but big and dark and swelling. A moment ago there had been no wind. Now it was rattling branches, tearing through the undergrowth, clanking the bullrushes against each other, mussing the long grasses. A fat, cold drop of rain plopped onto Fay's face. The clouds seemed to have gathered up the remainder of the day and crushed it into one crack in between them, which showed a strip of concentrated, eye-watering light among the steely grey; the rest of the sky had given in to dusk. Fay raised her left hand and looked at her watch, halfway down her thin arm: five-thirty.

Since she hadn't been going anywhere, there was nowhere to press on to, but home was an hour and a half away. Another drop fell. Another. And then there was a whole, nasty, roaring, cheering crowd of them, gushing around her ears. Fay put up her hood. Every scent, smell, aroma had been activated. The air reeked of mud, leaves, cow-pats, weeds, river water. The path had suddenly got slippy. Fay continued at a dogged pace, but kept having to throw her arms out sideways to keep from losing her balance. A noise she thought was a squirrel tumbling between branches turned out to be a falling branch snagging on others. Fay looked behind her, to reassess heading back where she'd come from, but the landscape had lost its horizontal hold and was only a mass of wavering, slanted silvery lines. From here you should be able to see Pitsbury Cathedral.

A bridge crossed the river. Fay took it, since she was pretty sure that in this direction was a lane whereas, to her right, there was only a seemingly unending stretch of drenched fields. The path after the bridge dipped between trees, which muffled the rain a little. There was a stile, just skimming a massive pin-cushion of whippy brambles. She climbed over it, pausing to detach her hem. Her duffle was covered in a cold sheen, it felt like being inside wet cardboard.

Shelter. Fay was assailed by childhood memories. You could plait live willow, couldn't you? Sometimes the beams in houses, even, began to sprout. It was because they put them in green, so they'd expand as they dried. Or was it contract? The building in Fay's mind moved with her speculations, expanding and contracting – fragile, unstable. Water running down her face, she surveyed the fluid landscape. None of these facts seemed particularly useful.

Clementine Dee's legs still felt like jello. There were still expensive-looking bags by the door. Plastic ones in blue and gold, and thick, restrained paper ones with reinforced cardboard handles. There were a couple of pale green shoe-boxes and some thin, oblong packets containing subtly-coloured hose. Everything was where she'd let it fall. The central heating was up so high the sitting room seemed to be pulsating. Clementine was stretched out on the sofa, huddled under Tony's black duvet, three pillows behind her head, a box of Big Man Paper Tissues on the floor beside her. Nearly two weeks she'd been like this, and now she appreciated that the British flu was a thing not to fight but to cherish.

It'd come on while she was in a hairdresser's called Fringe Benefits, just off Pitsbury High Street. All scrubbed pine and women in black, who picked up and dropped clumps of your hair while they discussed with your reflection what you wanted doing with it. Gone. Lopped. No more scattering pins. A boyish crop. Slightly French, though Clementine guessed that was what you always thought when you had all your hair cut off. Not that she'd had much of a chance to appreciate her new look. She'd ascribed the lightheadedness to less weight on her skull for the first millisecond. Then gravity had doubled, tripled, quadrupled, seemed like it wanted to pull her legs through the floor, her hands down level with the ground. After that the shivering began.

Staggering out of Fringe Benefits with her bags and boxes, Clementine had spotted a health food store called Nature's Way and made a mental list of all the usual things she'd need. But then she was, quite suddenly, quite unexpectedly, washed over by a luscious, warm wave of self-pity, more cathartic than Mowbray's *Thalia*; her eyes watered with big hot tears of sympathy for herself. This did not happen when you got Canadian influenza.

Clementine sidestepped Nature's Way and walked instead to the High Street, where she ducked into a shop called Langley The Chemist. She paused, drunkenly transfixed by an array of balls of scented wood for rubbing dead skin off your feet with, before heading towards the pharmacy, where a mixture of capable-looking women and barely pubescent girls presided over twenty feet of counter, devoted pretty much entirely to cold and flu remedies and accoutrements. In a daze, Clementine purchased two boxes of (recycled) Big Man Paper Tissues, blackcurrant and honey-flavoured throat pastilles, various sips and nurses for night and day, lemon and barley and ('New') pineapple and barley, a selection of soups in cartons – made by well-meaning people, the pastel writing informed her, out of organic ingredients – a tin of cocoa – picked by natives working for enlightened co-operatives – and a fabric-covered hot-water bottle, made to look like a badger in a dressing-gown.

Heading in the direction of the multi-storey, where she'd parked the car, Clementine passed a newsagent-cum-general-store. She bought an over-priced bottle of whiskey, a magazine called *Country Manner*, with a picture of a basket of pumpkins and gourds on the cover, four bags of marshmallows, a novel by a guy called Reggie Bell, entitled *Choc Ice* ('a story of sex, lust and violence, which highlights the ever greater need for censorship') and, to assuage her guilt, a bargain copy of *Hard Times*.

Once inside the front door of Tony Gilbert's, Clementine dropped all the unflu-related objects onto the carpet. Everything else she piled on the table in the kitchen. She made a fire and carried a big store of wood into the cottage, weeping, audibly, for sorrow that there was nobody but her to do it. She burrowed through a chest of drawers until she found one of the nightgowns her mother had bought her – the kind for women who have given up on the idea of sexual intercourse – and put it on in front of the fire.

Then she called the English Department and told the secretary she wouldn't be in until further notice. To her surprise, there was no saying thank-you for the information through pursed lips. No reproach. Just oodles of sympathy, and encouragement to drink plenty of fluids and not to hurry back until she was sure she was over it.

Lastly, Clementine filled the badger hot-water bottle and made herself a cold drink. She collapsed onto the sofa. Oliver, who had watched the proceedings with interest, decided he temporarily liked her and leapt onto her stomach and curled himself up into a heavy, purring ball. Clementine put the TV on, using the remote-control. It was an Australian soap-opera called *Over The Fence*. She watched it, eating marshmallows and sipping her pineapple and barley. She had never been so miserably happy.

It was like a holiday from the tight, wiry, capable Clementine Dee.

For the next ten days she was loose and sloppy. She watched films about brave dogs and snuffled into a Big Man Tissue. She read articles about painters who'd happened upon dilapidated watermills and peat-cutters' cottages and snapped them up and covered them in pale, terracotta-coloured, hand-mixed distemper. She discovered that, with only *Country Manner* to inspire you, you could create a stencilled frieze of shells or seahorses for your bathroom or, taking only an ordinary old wooden box, you could make a showpiece for a child's bedroom by covering it in layers of pictures you'd cut out of magazines and varnishing the result. Why you might have a large, unused wooden box about the place, Clementine lacked the energy to speculate. She dunked toast soldiers in carrot, coriander and butter bean soup and thought of sending off for a gardening apron with usefully roomy pockets and the *Country Manner* logo or, when she was better, travelling north for a sheep-dipping and sausage fair.

Often, she thought of David Marsh. Especially when she woke in the night from swirling, muddled, technicolour dreams, and put the light on and listened to the lovely silence of the Ebb Valley, watching the blue behind the window, shiny with her reflected bedside light, modify from navy to lavender as if someone were changing the filters on a stage spot. Then David's imagined presence had an almost palpable texture. He was a warm being, awake beside her in the buttercup light while every other mortal slept. He was the sound of a kettle being filled, the chinking of a teapot lid being lifted, the click of the kettle being switched off.

Soon now, soon, Clementine would see him.

Canadian influenza was gone one morning. British flu headed off ever so gradually, with several false farewells. On day six, Clementine reckoned she was strong enough to poach an egg and look through some mail. She fell back into bed an hour later, roasting and shivering like she'd got malaria. Day eight, she had to sleep the whole afternoon, due to making a call to the university to keep them in tune with her progress. This evening, she'd looked at her face in the bathroom mirror and felt sorry for it. The new hairstyle, unwashed since Fringe Benefits, was every which way. Her poor little wrists, sticking out the ends of yellow nylon frills, were weak and bony. Her nose was the colour of a tomato.

She returned to the sofa and picked up Reggie Bell's *Choc Ice*, since she was now strong enough to hold it so she could read it. The day had been snuffed out, though it wasn't awfully late. A wind whistled round the building, tried the windows, tugged at the flames in the fireplace. Outdoors was full of thumps and crashes.

Then two things happened, almost together. There was a banging on the door and the house was plunged into darkness, the copy of *Choc Ice* spontaneously illuminated only by firelight.

It took Clementine's flu-befuddled brain a minute to separate the knocking and the blackout and to figure that the one had not actually caused the other. Another bang on the door brought her to her senses. She threw back the duvet, dislodging the slumbering Oliver, and fumbled her way to the door, one of her feet kicking up against something papery. She unlatched it. A blast of night rushed in and bounced madly off the walls and ceiling.

'Oh, Tony,' a voice said. 'Thank goodness you're here. It's Fay. Fay Marsh.'

She stepped into the room. Of its own accord, the door slammed behind her. Hooded and with a basket and a long skirt, she looked Victorian: sweet-faced, frail and awfully pretty.

'Oh! You're not Tony,' she said.

'Nope,' said Clementine, with her red nose, lanky hair and yellow nylon nightgown.

'You're Canadian!' Fay's voice took on a backing away quality. She knew! No, it wasn't anything quite that certain. She knew the facts but suspected there was more to it. 'You're an academic?' she asked, weakly.

'Yup,' said Clementine. 'On an exchange. Borrowing his house from Tony Gilbert. You're an acquaintance of Tony's who got caught in the weather, I guess?' She held out a hand. 'The name's Ruth. Ruth Carpini.'

'They say it could be up to two hours,' Fay told Clementine. 'There's trees fallen across several of the roads and the Ebb's broken its banks in places. Some of the taxis are stranded and most of the drivers haven't been able to get into work. Do you mind if I phone my husband, too? Just to let him know where I am?'

'Go right ahead.'

Fay Marsh hooked her hair behind her ears; Clementine noted the high cheekbones. The walls glistened with rosy firelight; Clementine watched the long shadow, slim even in her own baggy sweatsuit and ski-socks, reach out a Mandarin finger and dial.

'David . . . ?'

Clementine strained to hear, but all she could make out was the usual, muffled murmur that might have been anyone.

'Oh he *is* in Provence . . . Ruth, Ruth Carpini. She's an academic. From Canada, actually . . . Yes, I suppose she must be . . .' Fay lowered the receiver a little. Clementine held her breath.

'You broke your arm, David says. It was in the paper . . .'

There was a pause.

'I heal quick,' said Clementine. 'And . . . uh . . . anyway, it wasn't exactly broken. The newspaper exaggerated.'

Fay returned to David. 'Yes, that's who it is . . . No, she didn't: the paper got it all wrong . . . I don't really know . . . It could be as much as two hours . . . I know it was silly. There's a mushroom consommé – made of those ink-caps and ceps I gathered. It just needs heating up. And stir in some coriander.'

She put down the phone and, 'Oh!' she exclaimed, catching sight of Clementine.

Clementine blew her nose with a Big Man Tissue. 'These stoopid handkerchiefs.' She pointed at the packet and tried to laugh. 'Do you reckon men are supposed to have bigger noses than us, or is it that they get worse colds?'

'They certainly make more fuss about them,' said Fay.

'Tell me about it!' Clementine wiped her cheeks and tried to laugh again, very aware that Fay was watching her. 'It's nothing,' she said. 'Only the thought of mushroom consommé.'

David Marsh was married to a woman who gathered wild mushrooms and made soup out of them – a woman like those frugal, resourceful, massively English sophisticates in *Country Manner*. No wonder he hadn't wanted to leave her.

'Oh!' cried Fay. 'You're ill and in a foreign country and there's nobody to cook for you. That would make *me* sniffly too.'

'Do you want a drink?' asked Clementine, trying to pull herself together. 'I've got gin and vermouth and some lousy whiskey.'

'How about a mulled wine? That would do you so much good,' said Fay. 'But you're not to move. I'll make it. I can put things in it that I know will clear your sinuses.'

'I don't have any wine.'

'But Tony will, he's the kind of man who loves words like "Shiraz" and "Napa Valley".'

Clementine smiled. 'You're right.' Then, struck by the thought that maybe Tony Gilbert did have friends after all, and that maybe Fay was one of them, in which case she was bound to discover the truth about Clementine's identity, 'You know Tony well, I guess?' she called croakily in the direction of the kitchen, into which Fay had vanished.

'No,' said Fay, returning with a bottle of red wine, a saucepan and various jars from the spice-rack. 'I'll have to heat it on the fire since it's an electric cooker. I've only met Tony once, actually. He had a drinks party, one Sunday in . . . um . . . May, just before I went off to study kelp . . .'

'Uh uh.' Clementine shook her head.

'What?'

Clementine realised what she had done. 'I mean, that can't have been much fun.'

'The kelp? No, it was wonderful. That kind of thing is what I like best.'

'The drinks party.'

'No, it wasn't, though it was quite kind of him to ask us. I don't know why he did. I suppose he wanted a sort of gathering of people in the arts – David has a bookshop. But, thinking about it, it must have been earlier, because I learnt about kelp in April . . .' Fay's voice trailed away. 'I suppose you know someone called Clementine Dee?' she asked tremulously.

'P.C.C.'s a big college.'

'But you're in the English Department?'

'And Media Studies. Not quite the same thing.' Clementine thought of the horror with which Ruth, who was a purist through and through, would have met the doppleganger she was creating for her.

'Well, that drinks party was the only time I've ever met Tony Gilbert,' Fay resumed. 'He was wearing white trousers and a shirt with puffy sleeves, and carrying a bottle to fill people's glasses with and trying to look . . .'

'Rakish bachelor with interesting young girlfriend who, for some reason, couldn't make it.'

'Yes. And he was talking a lot about a film he was going to be involved with. Though none of the actors were there.'

'*A Right Wonderful Error.*'

'Probably. He asked David to find a book of poetry for him – Provençal, I think it was – and David did, but in the end Tony didn't want it.'

'No,' said Clementine. 'I mean, I guess not.'

'Are you keeping your strength up?' asked Fay, after a pause. The wine was heating on the fire. She'd put cloves, a cinnamon stick and a star-shaped seed in it. 'What are you eating?'

'Soup, mainly.'

'Can I make you something?'

'A fried peanut butter and jam sandwich,' said Clementine, with a touch of malice, remembering what David had told her about his wife's interests. She waited for Fay's reaction.

'Do you know?' said Fay, slowly, 'I think we have something in common.'

'What's that?' asked Clementine, with a sudden intake of breath.

'I like peanut butter when I'm feeling poorly, or whatever. Especially with bacon – though I avoid meaty things the rest of the time; and impurities and toxins. Do you have any bacon?'

'There's some in the refrigerator.'

'Shall I feed the cat?' asked Fay, noticing Oliver bounding after her as she got up to go to the kitchen to look, leaving Clementine alone and feeling she'd behaved shabbily. Fay Marsh was really a lovely person. A bit dippy in some areas, perhaps, but effortlessly kind and with a core of common sense. She returned a few minutes later with a tray on which was a ladle, two wine glasses, a slab of bacon, butter, plates, bowls, knives, forks and spoons, mango chutney, a pepper grinder, bread, jars of cherry, raspberry and apricot jam and a tub of Haagen Dazs. Under her arm was a frying pan.

'I guess I'd like peanut butter and bacon, too,' said Clementine as Fay took the saucepan off the flames to dole out the mulled wine, and replaced it with the frying pan in which she'd put a big knob of the butter.

'They're super with mango chutney,' Fay said. 'But we can start with bacon and chutney, then have jam, if you like, and then the ice-cream, which should have softened a bit.'

The two women took a sip of the wine. The warmth, taste and aroma of it flooded Clementine's senses in a heady blast.

'You've got this month's *Country Manner*,' said Fay. 'I read it, too. But I don't know why: it always makes me feel so . . . inadequate. As if I should . . .'

'Gather mushrooms?' Clementine's expression was mischievous.

'Oh, that,' said Fay, catching her meaning. 'But the people in *Country Manner* don't just gather mushrooms, they gather mushrooms with . . .'

'Zeal.'

'Yes. Zeal. A sense of *pur*pose.'

'They gather them pre-meditatedly. And I'll bet they don't eat fried peanut butter sandwiches.'

'Not unless they've ground the peanuts . . .'

'And, ideally, grown and harvested them . . .'

'And made the bread. And it wouldn't be in butter . . .'

'It could be in unsalted *Normandy* butter.'

'Yes it might. But it would probably be walnut oil. Anyway, here's your sandwich. I didn't butcher the pig, or ripen the mangoes, I'm afraid . . .'

'Nor bottle the chutney . . .'

'No. And we're not overlooking my orange orchard in Tuscany.'

Clementine bit into the offered sandwich. Crisp. Buttery. Creamy. Salty. Sweet. She drained her glass of mulled wine and accepted a refill.

The ticking of Tony's clock sounded like it was tutting them repeatedly. It would be typical of Tony to have a clock which noted how much you'd been eating and drinking. Yet Clementine's brain was clear-ish and her forehead was clammy, but cooler than it had been in days.

'. . . cross and grumpy and sarcastic,' Fay was saying. It was a long while later. Her clothes had dried out and she was back in them.

'So why'd you put up with it?'

'Um. Well, he's always been like that – to some extent – and he was unhappy.'

'Which doesn't give him a right to be a pain in the ass. What was he unhappy about, anyway?' A sharp little pulse began pounding in Clementine's neck.

Fay thought a moment, her head cocked to one side.

'Financial things . . . Though there *was* something else. I spent a lot of time in the priest's hole, eating sugared violets.'

'Back up there. The priest's hole? Sugared violets?'

'They're not as good as peanut butter and bacon sandwiches, but they would probably have made it smell. And, besides, I was too depressed to get out the frying pan.' There was a silence. 'I suppose the priests ate bland things which wouldn't give them away,' said Fay. 'But recently things have started to get so much better. I think he's found a sense of purpose and . . . he sort of appreciates me more. It's as if – as if there's a stage he's been through. Only . . .'

'Only what?'

'I still find it hard to trust him.' Fay's voice faltered. 'He has an E-mail box, you see.'

'And?'

'And I wonder whether there could possibly be a person he's writing to.'

'I see.'

There was a long, hollow pause during which the elements shrieked, sobbed and bawled.

Something landed Clementine the psychological equivalent of a hard kick on the shin. Spontaneously, she thought of the portrayals she'd seen of Mowbray's Thalia – the tragic queen who gave up her kingdom for the greater good. She'd been a monarch in jeans, black tunic, Medieval red and gold, full Tudor. She'd gabbled, declaimed, just plain spoken. Some of the actresses had understood what they were saying, others hadn't had the first idea: they'd left words dangling that should have been carried on; they'd gathered in phrases that should have been left behind. Not one of them had managed to completely kill it, though. Not a single one. Wise, acute, intact: Mowbray endured, beneath whatever overlay.

A *kingdom*. A whole frigging kingdom. And here you are, Clementine Dee, making a song and dance over . . .

'You know, Fay,' said Clementine. 'I'd guess that David *is* faithful to you.'

'What makes you think that?' Fay looked curious.

'Just, there's nothing on the planet that can keep a person if they properly decide they don't want to be someplace.'

'You think I shouldn't try to check the E-mail box, then?'

Clementine paused a moment before answering. 'No, do,' she said. 'I think you should, if that's what it takes to reassure you. You'll find nothing, I'm willing to guarantee. But then, think no more about it: *be* sure, and let yourself be happy.' She swallowed. 'He sounds basically a . . . a great guy.'

'He is – really.'

Clementine stood. Outside, it was pitch black. Rain was bucketing against the windows. The wind had grabbed the house and was shaking it by the shoulders. Clementine rubbed her hands down the sides of her face. She felt chipped round the edges but the flu, she somehow knew, wasn't coming back now. By morning she'd be well enough to gather up the clothes she'd bought and put them on coat-hangers. Take a shower. Wash her hair. Phone the university and tell them to expect her back. Soon she would be sitting in Bus Station House again with the Mowbray manuscripts. She would eat salad lunches and not hanker after things that were not available to her. In the evenings she would read good books or watch dramas and documentaries. She might hit London and do the theatres and the museums. She and David Marsh would not cross paths again.

A horn hooted. Fay jumped to her feet.

'That's the taxi. Goodness! How can I thank you? You've been so nice. Perhaps we could meet up – for lunch or something?'

Clementine shook her head. 'I won't be around much. Busy life.'

The horn hooted again. Fay opened the door and waved out. 'Good-bye,' she said to Clementine, pulling on her duffle-coat, half into the night already. 'Go back in. You'll get cold.'

Clementine returned to the sofa. The sound of the taxi moving off was drowned by the swirling storm. A ruckus in the heavens. Wouldn't it have been great to have been able to believe that you had somehow caused it?

The electricity came on for a minute, then went off again.

'You've still got me,' said Hermia Mowbray.

'Yeah,' said Clementine, 'I've still got you. But you're dead: it makes a difference.'

'Not very dead,' said Hermia Mowbray. 'Not a very big difference. You'll see.'

13 ∫

A Troubled Spirit

Throughout the night the storm increased in momentum: roared through the undergrowth of the Ebb Valley, rattled past the windows of Tony Gilbert's property where Clementine slept, splayed out under the black duvet. Heard only by security, it galloped across the parkland and gardens of the ranch house-style mansion of Harriet, Duchess of Pitsbury – Duchess Harriet was dossing down with a pal in South Ken.

In Pitsbury High Street water dribbled onto cardboard boxes, big-value packs of toilet rolls, soap and paper-towels, stored in the empty flat above Burger-Fish. It seeped under the door of Quik-Potato and across the easy-clean floor; filled an oniony dustbin that foxes had dragged the top off, out the back of Bigga-Burgers.

High speed confluents rushed and scurried through underground networks and hurtled, whitely, from gurgling gutters and from the spitting gargoyles of Pitsbury Cathedral.

The wasteland became a mass of streams, rivulets and rock-pools. The Ebb rose in a tarry gloss, up the eroding flank of St Friedaswida's, flooded the perimeter road of the Elizium Forest Industrial Estate, choked and gagged in buried wells and Victorian sewers.

The wind threw playing-card packs of ridged, paw-marked, moss-covered roof-tiles into the air. They scattered and crashed to the ground in fragments, shards, powder. A water-main burst.

Shiny red fire-engines and ivory, blue-topped ambulances left V-shaped wakes of light on the shiny roads. Windows wrenched open and smashed their panes. Haemorrhaging clouds poured rain through tablets of air onto attic floors and rafters; squeezed it, as slow drips, between invisible cracks into pinging buckets. Roofs became clattering, lifting canopies; doors flew open, admitting soaking gusts.

At the mouth of the Ebb, fresh water throttled with grasses, blown hay, cow parsley, sodden beige rose-petals, plunged into the listing, furious sea where small boats bobbed and clanked, made skipping ropes of their moorings. The twisting gale scooped up sand and saltwater, carrying it inland to Pitsbury so that, when light eventually came, the air was thinly saffron. Grainy deposits lay in the crevices of windows and teary puddles flooded sills.

Near daybreak the wind faltered, the storm caught its foot on the Channel, which slowed it down and sapped its energy. By morning it was only thick, fertile, drenching rain falling softly upon the emerald pastures, brown and white cows and skew-whiff farmhouses of France. Late the next night, it pattered on the shutters of Provence, briefly disturbing Tony Gilbert.

Porous.

'We should work out where it's coming in,' said Fay.

She was, untypically, sipping a coffee.

'It seems to me that what we should do is work out if there is anywhere it *isn't* coming in and construct a new dwelling, outwards from that point.' David looked bitterly at the bedroom ceiling. It was covered in light brown stains. The floor was a mass of bowls, pails and pudding basins. 'I'll have to get up in the roof,' he said, not because that would tell him anything he didn't already know, but because it was what one did at such moments. It gave the illusion of a measure of control. Though the control didn't lie in the hands of David; it lay in the hands of Conservation Officer Brian Baffle, whose despotic powers seemed to be such that, had he decreed the roofs of Pitsbury be tiled with doilies, there would have been no recourse against it.

'The books are all right,' said Fay. 'I checked.'

'I'm sure the letters from the bank are dry as a bone.'

'Some of my seeds have sprouted.'

'That doesn't surprise me. Judging from the fungal odour permeating everything, I would not be startled to discover that new forms of life had evolved overnight in the primeval soup that is my residence – or, rather, the bank's residence. In which case, I say good luck to them. I hope they make a bloody better job of it than we have.' David reached out and took his wife's free hand. He held it tight. There was something reassuring in its familiarity. How had they stopped being teenagers and become adults, with problems and obsessions? When had time played that terrible practical joke on them?

David looked out of the window. To add insult to injury the sun burst through at that very moment, burnt off the mist, seemingly in seconds, and revealed a naked, new sky.

'The gods are angry,' said Merlyn Orb.

Fay gave a little gasp. David swung round.

'What are you doing in my bedroom?' he asked.

'The gods are angry,' Orb repeated. 'Do you have any cereal?'

'Well I'm none too thrilled myself,' said David. 'And may I repeat my question?'

Fay said, 'Muesli?'

'No Coco Pops?' asked Merlyn.

'I'm awfully sorry.'

'Fay, I really feel there is no call to apologise to somebody, who has entered our house uninvited, for the fact that we do not have in stock whatever loathsome brand of cereal it is that they favour.'

'Rice Krispies?' said Orb.

'Is there a purpose to this visit, Merlyn? Other than cereal? For, if not, as you might have noticed, my home is leaking in a hundred or so different places and, perhaps unreasonably, I feel a certain urge to address the situation.'

'Don't be nasty, David,' said Fay.

Orb said, 'There's a Troubled Spirit at the squat.'

'There's a troubled spirit everywhere.'

'He's questioning our repairs.'

'*He*?' David's simmering, generalised anger leapt to attention, becoming honed and specific. 'Who's questioning our repairs? Describe him.' Though there was no doubt in David's mind as to who Merlyn had encountered.

'His spirit?'

'No, not his spirit. His face. His car. His unctuous expression. His smug voice. I am accurate, am I not?'

'Which repairs, Merlyn?' asked Fay.

'The ones I did this morning.'

It was strange and unfortunate that, having shown only an idiosyncratic and unpractical interest in the renovation and restoration process up to now, Merlyn Orb, upon opening his eyes to the not unfamiliar sight of clouds had, today, taken it upon himself to remedy the damage that the storm had wreaked upon the roof of the squat.

Outside, the air had a bubbly, throaty, spring-like quality. The people on the pavements – officials of various sorts, mainly – radiated that jollity that is evoked in the British only by terrible disaster.

As David followed Orb up Weaver Street, he had cause to think that it was an ill wind that didn't blow Henry Pearl any good. The windows of Marauding Hordes were a steamy fug. On one of them Henry – in the French-style white paint that he'd used for writing the menu there when it was Grandmother's Footsteps – had inscribed 'Two Sarnies For The Price Of One For All Our Brave Emergency Services'. As a result, the interior was stuffed with firemen, police and ambulance people, downing mugs of tea and sandwiches.

The pavements gleamed. The road sizzled when a car went past. The wasteland was a great glasshouse of reflections. On the polished, bloated surface of the Ebb floated thick, upturned bridges. What would once have been the garden of the squat was ridges of chocolatey mud, interspersed with molten pools of light.

Conservation Officer Brian Baffle, thin and shapeless in a belted, mustard-coloured raincoat was surveying the roof of the squat with an expression of disbelief on his face. David did likewise. His jaw dropped. The tiles that the wind had ripped away had been replaced by a pocket-shaped patch, large and surprisingly tidy and bright green.

'I suppose this is someone's idea of a joke,' said Brian Baffle in nasal tones. He was only about thirty but had the knack of conveying the impression that, while the rest of the human race remained juvenile, he alone had attained maturity.

Green. Green tiles such as were found only on the most desperate of modern bungalows – ones with frilled net curtains and striped, symmetrical flowers, conifers, automatically opening garages. Throughout Pitsbury, middle-class men and women lost sleep over nuances of roof pigment, the likelihood of being caught converting their attics into spare bedrooms, the fear that their walls weren't high enough to obscure the progress of clandestine windows. They rehearsed arguments, pleas and justifications, appealing to the canons of taste and appropriateness. And here, among the uniformity of Pitsbury's obedient rooftops, was a patch of livid green. David experienced a reluctant wave of admiration for Merlyn Orb – felt a sudden inclination to rush to the nearest supermarket and buy him whatever cereal he desired. Why, in this no-win situation, be found wanting with the ever-so-slightly wrong shade of red? Why not yellow or blue, an Indian temple of the wrong colour?

'The roofs of Pitsbury are not green,' said Brian Baffle.

'I found the tiles,' said Merlyn Orb.

'They are green,' persisted Baffle.

'So are the trees,' said Merlyn Orb.

'The trees are in keeping with one another,' said Baffle. 'They match.'

'Not in autumn,' said Merlyn.

'I think, Mr Baffle,' said David, hastily, 'that, in the circumstances, it was vital that some kind of temporary cover be put on the roof to make it weatherproof.'

'Maybe,' suggested Orb, 'since there'll be a lot of repairs because of the storm, you could encourage other people to use green tiles so they'd be in keeping with us?'

There was a horrified silence.

Then, 'Nobody,' breathed Baffle, 'uses tiles in any colour other than ferruginous. They never have. They never shall.'

'Can I, perhaps, reiterate my point here?' said David.

'They do in Dijon,' said Merlyn Orb.

'There are fines and penalties,' said Brian Baffle, his voice carrying an inescapable tone of regret that these paltry punishments were deemed sufficient for such heinous crimes. David glimpsed wistful images of incarceration in narrow oubliettes, flogging, crucifixion, slow torture.

'I think,' he said, 'that there was an immediate problem that had to be dealt with using the only available building materials.' Perhaps it was because of his sudden, nasty insight into Baffle's thoughts, but the unease, the haunting, headachy insecurity that had so long throbbed at the back of David's brain now set up a loud, tom-tom beat. He experienced the ghastly inevitability that you feel when you know, beyond any doubt, that you are going to be sick.

'Mr Marsh.' Baffle turned his glimmering, Gestapo eyes upon David. 'You, and everyone else in Pitsbury, are well aware that Pitsbury Council keeps a stockpile of traditional, ferruginous tiles which may be purchased from themselves between ten and three-thirty every day of the week except Tuesdays and alternate Fridays.'

David's patience snapped. He had the dizzy sense that he was thrashing wildly, drowning in a torrent of miscalculated circumstance: something hadn't been taken into account.

'I know that those tiles are extortionately priced and that they are also porous,' he said.

'They are red,' said Baffle, '*that* is their purpose.'

'Their purpose, surely,' David protested, 'is to keep rain off people's heads and possessions.'

'They must be removed instantly,' said Brian Baffle. 'They are an abomination to this city. They are a blot, a scar, a gaping wound.' He looked at David and Merlyn Orb as if gaping wounds would not have been unwelcome in their proper place.

'What if it rains?' David asked.

'They must be removed and replaced with the tiles which have always been there . . .'

'Until recently, the building was falling down. In many places there weren't any tiles at all,' objected David.

'My powers do not permit me to intervene to prevent a building from falling down. They do, however, permit me to prevent it from being restored incorrectly. The tiles must be replaced and, in due course, I shall undertake an inspection.'

'We have no money for your tiles,' said Merlyn Orb.

David fell into a desperate silence, in the turmoil of which his nagging insecurities crescendoed in a – finally – concrete and vocal chorus.

No money for tiles! But no money for paint either, or for plumbers or poll tax, he realised. No money for electricity, for heating, for water. No money for the eternal eventualities of buildings, the wear and tear of climate and weather. No money to finance the war of attrition against time. Hadn't one been round a house, empty for a few months only, and smelled the smell, seen the evidence that those months had set about a process of reclamation? Hadn't one witnessed the relentless decay of a building whose inhabitants were getting old? David remembered his parents' house – fewer things repaired, more things put up with; soon it would no longer be their problem, so why muster the energy to get someone in to replace the panes, fix the dripping overflow? New people would take over – young marrieds with bright ideas and abundant strength – renovate, renew, restore; time would sit back and watch. A short respite and then it would return. That was the nature of things. The sole variation was the speed with which it happened. The squat was the fast-forward version: the comings and goings, the disintegration. Poverty was the fastest of consumers: it used up buildings, it used up life. Without money to maintain it, the squat would rapidly revert; unless it was in good condition, neat, clean and acceptable, the council would be considered justified in condemning it.

It was one thing to renovate a building; quite another for the inhabitants to be able to afford to live in it: *that* was what they had failed to take into account. That was what they had failed to take into account *again*. The situation was horribly familiar. A house that could not be lived in. An existence that couldn't be properly used. David should have known. He should have thought. The squatters' problem was the same as his own.

'They'll just have to get jobs, that's all.'

Henry and the others were sipping chilled wine in Henry's kitchen; a long, beautiful room, festooned with great copper basins, dried herbs, ladles, enormous whisks, white porcelain dishes, jugs. The impression was of a place in which jam was made, butter churned, bread baked, cream skimmed off new milk. The truth, however, was that Henry and Colin mainly ate in the restaurant, except on the occasions that Henry fried up a couple of magrets and steamed some mange-touts. If Henry was away on business, Colin sent out for pizza. Right now, he was eating chips with ketchup.

'If jobs existed for the squatters, Henry,' said David, 'then there wouldn't be a problem.'

'Gary's got a job,' said Colin. 'Only thing is, Hen isn't paying him anything for doing it.'

'I am loaning *you* to the project,' said Henry. 'Isn't that payment enough?'

'Well, matter of fact,' said Colin, 'I've 'ad enough of the cooking caper.'

'The cooking caper?'

'Yeah. I'm going back to brickwork. So you'll 'av to take Gary on, or advertise. Though, since you're raking it in 'and over fist, I'd hang on to him.'

'And call it "Henry's Caff", I suppose? And cultivate a beer belly and a stinking apron? Resign myself to the eternal presence of giant cans of baked beans and economy tubs of lard?'

'You could do worse. And another thing,' Colin winked at David, 'if we've got to find jobs for 'em, why not get that girl, Becs, doing her trompe l'oeils for your London crowd? They'd love nuffing better than cats on window sills that they wouldn't have to have earth boxes for, and flowers they wouldn't have to water.'

'Don't anybody worry: Henry Pearl will provide! Let us deposit the onus upon him.' Henry poured himself another glass of wine, looking, nevertheless, decidedly taken with the suggestion.

'I think it's a wonderful idea, Henry,' said Fay. 'And Becs could be on a sort of percentage of any commissions. There'll be masses of them, I'm sure. And, anyway, you needn't bear the whole brunt.' Now Fay looked, rather furtively, at Rick Farr, who was lighting a cigarette in a candle. 'Couldn't Al do something for you, Rick? I mean, he said he was in computers. Maybe he could . . . mind the shop, and let people see the things they wanted to see, while you were . . . doing other Internet things.'

Rick leant back in his chair, took a quick puff on his fag, then knotted his hands together on the top of his head. Henry pointedly pulled the cord of the extractor fan.

'Would if I could, Fay, but I haven't got any surplus requirements.'

There was a pause. David's enthusiasm and relief mounted. He was not alone; he should have realised. It was the sole recompense for this ghastly situation. Express doubts, fears for the future, to ones who were in roughly the same boat – a greater number than he had ever taken account of, a vast, human ark of them – and those swelling, private anxieties got whittled away by discussion, by a simple movement from mouth to mouth. Their sharp edges were smoothed by bickering and interchange, diminished by the conversation's tendency to veer off at a tangent.

'Supposing, Rick,' he said, 'Al looked after Just The Business while you travelled around the area, trying to sell your services? He could be on a percentage of any increase you made as a result.'

'Travelled round selling?'

David realised that he had touched a nerve.

'Rick,' said Fay, 'the problem is, I think, that people don't realise how useful you can be to them. They just see the jellyfish and they don't understand.'

'Jellyfish?' cried Henry. 'What is Rick doing with jellyfish? If you've got one of those glorious executive tanks, Rick, with little castles and koi and lucent anemones, I feel we might have been invited to admire. I supervised an aquarium feature for an office in the City and the director told me his clients talk of nothing else.'

'And Dave cn'av Merlyn Orb,' said Colin, finishing his last chip.

'I can *what*?' David's relief was instantly replaced by an intense yearning for the open road, a stick made of cherry wood, a dog, a rucksack, a sleeping-bag. He thought of tramps, wandering minstrels, gypsies, nomads, sailors, Jehovah's Witnesses.

'Though I know I shall, doubtless, be jumped on for expressing so crass and right-wing a view,' he said quickly, 'Merlyn Orb is completely unemployable.'

'He didn't make a half bad job of that roofing,' said Colin.

'In the process attracting the attention of Brian Baffle and all those in Pitsbury who weren't dealing with their own structural problems. But, in that case, let him work on the building.'

''S nearly done. Besides, it was a one-off.'

'Well can't someone else have him?'

'He *is* a poet, David,' said Fay.

'That, I suspect, is highly debatable. And, anyway, the man has expressly stated that he doesn't "believe in books".'

'He was probably exaggerating.'

'I am sorry, Fay, but that doesn't strike me as the kind of statement that is open to a variety of interpretations.'

'He probably doesn't mean *books* books,' said Rick. 'He probably means the kind your average bloke would pick up, not the sort you're pushing.'

'You make it sound as if I hang around outside the gates of primary schools with illicit copies of Provençal verse.'

'It's only fair,' said Henry. 'And don't say you aren't getting a few sales from the students I am drawing into the area.'

'I scarcely think, Henry, that you are in a position to take the credit.'

'I'll give Al a whirl if you try Merlyn Orb,' suggested Rick. 'Can't say fairer than that. How's about it?'

'At least Al appears to have some vestiges of normality. At least his presence isn't like that of some deranged Druid.'

The others looked at him. There was a pause.

Then, 'Watch my lips,' said David: 'I am smiling ruefully. I am smiling pretty bloody ruefully.'

Henry Pearl made kissy sounds into the air. Nobody spoke. David threw up his hands in a gesture of defeat.

'All right. I give in. I shall take on the wretched individual, even though I am at a complete loss to imagine what he can possibly do that could be anything other than a hindrance, and I can only pay him a small fraction of any of the week's takings.'

'He could post off your mail orders,' said Fay.

David sighed. 'Yes, I suppose he could. At least that will give me an excuse to install him in some distant cupboard, where he won't be able to engage me in what passes for conversation. Even Merlyn Orb should be capable of packing up books and sending them to people.'

A rare expression of optimism, which was not wholly misplaced. Merlyn Orb was, indeed, capable of packing up books and sending them to people. Which books, however, and which people?

The consequences of employing Merlyn Orb were to affect the rest of David Marsh's life.

14 ∫

Happy Hour

Fay's suggestion that Al might mind Just The Business for Rick Farr was to have far-reaching consequences, also.

Nor was it entirely disinterested. Friday morning, Rick carefully hung his jacket on a coathanger above the back seat, popped some mint gum and zoomed casually off for a day's punting. Leaving his enterprise in the care of one who passionately believed in communication.

Snew?, Al's duplicated news sheet, was free and angry and it wanted to get everywhere. It spat and swore, talked of deaths in cells, arms broken by bailiffs, demos, protests. And then it erupted into desperate evocations of beauty and justice, mainly in the form of truly awful or mind-blowingly obscure poetry. In the High Street, Al waved it beneath averted noses.

Barely had Rick Farr hit the road, barely had Fay waved him good-bye – an excuse to check that he really had gone – before Al was in front of all the screens, banishing the low-key jellyfish and summoning up gaudy, blinking visuals. As Fay watched, there was a Beethovenish explosion of chat and gossip, exchange of ideas, cries of commerce, discussion. Al reminded Fay of those people who make a living by spinning dozens of saucers on poles simultaneously. Having switched on the planet, he lit joss-sticks, did a bit of fiddling with Rick's personal stereo and rigged up some speakers in the shop. Suddenly, there was music, dreamy and repetitive; it made Fay think of washing machines.

But the screens! She couldn't take her eyes off them.

Puerto-Rican whores. American high-school kids. Academics. Sci-Fi freaks. People who were into collecting Tintin comics. Faces, quickly forming in a rush of coloured lines. A hub-bub of wisdom and stupidity, half-baked notions and profound insights. Rogues, villains, saints and dingbats. You could have a box of oysters on your doorstep by morning, or spices, or a bunch of balloons, or six dozen carnations. If you wanted to talk about herbology with people who really were interested in it, you could.

Fay was astonished. She was even a little cross that Rick Farr had managed to turn these Aladdin's lamps into dull, grey boxes. In her entrancement she forgot that she had mainly suggested that Rick should employ Al because she was pretty sure that he wouldn't object to giving her access to David's E-mail; forgot that she was only there in order to follow the advice that Ruth Carpini had given her: to ascertain that David was faithful and then to stop worrying about it. Instead, she stood, her head whirling, surveying the lively, garrulous world. Somewhere amongst it, it occurred to her, was Jez from the Cybercaff in Romford, probably still trying to get his five pounds out of Phil: not a wandering, ghostly mistake as he had seemed when she had been in the company of Rick and Sam Bullock, but an intrinsic part of things.

'Can you communicate with Romford?' she asked.

Al looked at her and smiled, revealing his chipped tooth.

'didyou get your 5er, Jez?'

'didI shit.'

'oh. shame.'

'life.'

'A toothpaste-type stripe, but rainbow-coloured,' said Al, 'Becs could do it. Painted secondhand chairs and tables. Perhaps picking up the rainbow theme. Cheap Net-surfing sessions. Free for UB40's. Leaflets about them – along with *Snew*? – at Gary's Café.'

'Net surfing?'

'Touching down in various bits of the culture. Much, much faster than paper.' Al looked wistful.

'Less enduring, perhaps?' Fay ventured. 'But do you think Rick will mind? I mean, I don't think any of his businessmen surf.' She imagined them in pinstripes, with briefcases, trousers rolled up, on wooden boards, cresting aquamarine waves. But if Rick did mind, in the long run, did it really matter? The jellyfish could always be put back, the rainbow greyed over. Since Just The Business hadn't worked, why shouldn't he try other things?

'Good day to yer. But what have we here?'

Fay's heart sank. It was Sam Bullock, red-faced and smelling of early-morning whiskey, exuding the solid well-being that comes from the ownership of land. Now there would be an endless, silly conversation about things that didn't exist. Fay remembered watching a sad programme on television showing how, not far into the future, one would be able to wander around places such as the BARG-MART GINORMOUS DIME-O-STORE, just by sitting on one's sofa, wearing a sort of virtual hat. You chose your virtual shopping and paid by credit card and then waited for your purchases to arrive. The idea was presented as largely positive (except that you wouldn't be able to squeeze the fruit) but it had dismayed Fay, just as Rick and Sam Bullock had dismayed her with their invisible assets and virtual cows. She hadn't realised that another possibility was a crazy, talkative, cosmic bazaar with people discussing, arguing, putting the world to rights on every corner: the verbal equivalent of that market in Arles they had been round on their honeymoon – irregular tomatoes, the scent of thyme, wine-drinking peasants, slamming fists down on tables and gesticulating to heaven; poor, bloody, rabbits and fluttering hens.

Now that Fay considered it, wasn't it rather odd, in the light of the farming crisis, that Bullock looked so cheerful?

'Sam Bullock. Cattle farmer. Boss around?' asked Bullock, his eyes scanning the shop, as if he thought Rick might be under one of the tables.

'Rick's away,' said Al. To Fay's relief, he didn't look greatly inclined to chat with Bullock.

Bullock sniffed. 'Explains the rumpus.'

'I think the music's nice,' said Fay.

'Inform him I'll be getting E-mail shortly and he's to call me when it arrives. Tell him I'll be wanting my conference – South America and Holland.'

'These must be bad times for you,' observed Al, coolly.

'How so?' There was danger in Sam Bullock's expression.

'Mad cow.'

'Mad cow?' Bullock gave a disparaging snort. 'There's only one group is mad, laddie, and it's not the cows.'

'Nevertheless.'

'Nevertheless nothing. When's the boss due back? Tell him I'm lunching at the Royal Hotel with my brother . . .'

'Oh dear,' said Fay. She had been to the Royal once, for a wedding reception. It smelled of gravy and dust. Lukewarm plates of dried-out game were produced from under domes of silver. And yet, a certain portion of Pitsbury society patronised it when in the mood to celebrate.

'He can join us for brandy and After Eights, if he's a mind.'

'Rick's gone all day,' said Al. He looked weak and milky in comparison with the ruddy Bullock.

'Tell him to contact me on his return, then.'

Bullock left.

'Nasty piece of work,' said Al, when the door had closed behind him. 'Do you want to surf?'

'Yes,' said Fay, her mind still half on the cattle farmer. 'I mean . . . um . . . no. Not today, anyway, but perhaps sometime.' Then, forgetting Bullock, 'I came to look at David's E-mail box, since he's my husband. I suppose that'd be all right, wouldn't it?'

'Sure,' said Al. 'Need help?'

Fay nodded. Suddenly, with Al's back to her, her eyes flooded with anticipatory tears. Ruth could be wrong. Maybe there would be a whole correspondence there between David and Clementine Dee. Secrets, shared jokes, mutually understood references, revived discussions, intellectual arguments: all the things that made up a relationship. Well, most relationships – *good* relationships.

Fay had never considered you might get junk in an E-mail box. She felt as if she were leafing through floating paper. There were also some questions about books, she noted, inquiries that could have led to orders; but they, like most of the junk-mail were out of date now. Having taken the box, David couldn't have bothered to check it. Ever.

Fay leant back in her chair and watched Al tracing parallel

lines, in pencil, along the wall, using a ruler. She waited for the sense of relief: Ruth Carpini had been absolutely right. There really was no reason to worry, nothing to be unhappy about. The marriage was still as intact as it had ever been.

'Yellow. Indigo. Violet,' said Al.

'Lovely,' said Fay, distractedly. Still she waited. But the relief didn't come. Instead, she felt . . . disappointed.

'"Oh? Henry's!" "Café Henry". "Henry's Café".'

It was Happy Hour. Colin Rutt was up his ladder, painting out the sign which said Marauding Hordes. Within, the discussion about a new name for the restaurant was becoming progressively more animated, due to the copious downing of Tiswin Surprise. (Gary's invention. Basically, a mixture of semi-frozen tiswin and Ribena: Ribena and chilling to take away the taste of the tiswin; tiswin to burn off unwanted brain-cells – two for the price of one between four and seven, or a special value pitcher for groups.)

Henry Pearl and his old friends, Sven and Barney – finding Henry's latest foray delightfully louche, and eating chips and Hellman's with plates of (white!) bread and marge (marge!) – were holding court to a group of young homosexuals from the university's Gay Lib Society. Sven and Barney were there to discuss *trompe l'oeils* with Henry's newest find, Becs, who was a bit surly but, apparently, highly gifted. Macaws had been toyed with. Orchids. Bottomy peaches. Or perhaps something more restrained, like a dragonfly. Then the students had arrived and thrown the conversation into charming disarray by suggesting a life-sized puma with jewelled collar. Then Sven and Barney had stood everyone another pitcher of Tiswin Surprise and the conversation had moved on to a name for Henry's enterprise.

Almost all the tables were full. A mix of people. Beefy lorry drivers. Students. Women with toddlers. Firemen. Even the odd middle-class artsy. The waiters and waitresses were quaint and not impeccably clean, but, in the light of the quantity of the food, the value for money and the all-round lusciousness of it, no one was objecting. Every minute or so, loaded plates were deposited on tables and dowsed with ketchup, Mongolian chutney, mustard, vinegar. There was a tangy quality to the boiling air.

'How about "Henry's Tummies"?' said Sven.

'"Henry's" I like, "Tummies" I don't,' said Henry Pearl.

'We must get back to our *trompe*,' said Barney, looking at his watch. 'We're due in Hammersmith *now*.'

He picked up a Sunday supplement and, licking a finger, started leafing through it in search of inspiration.

'Oh look, oh look.' Barney pointed to a long, lavishly illustrated article entitled THE CANNINGS IN PROVENCE. A full-page picture, captioned 'Roo discusses a scene in Mowbray's *A Right Wonderful Error* with wife Immie', portrayed Immie Canning in off-the-shoulder bodice against a backdrop of glacier-blue sky and frigid castle, looking at a script with Roo who was wearing a full-length coat, scarf, gloves, boots and ski-socks.

'They say he goes both ways,' remarked Sven. 'Goodness! Hasn't our Im put it on round the hips?'

'Could you do that?' Barney asked Becs.

'Do what?'

'This very vista. Sky. Chateau. Tudory figures. Lose the coat and jeans, substitute jerkin and codpiece.'

Becs sniffed and coughed a minute, swallowed a noisy slurp of coffee, wiped her nose with the back of a hand. 'It's fucking big,' she said. 'It'd take up a lot of wall.'

'Big?' Henry looked over Barney's shoulder. 'Yes, but so *you*, Barney. So *Sven*. Any time, any cost would be more than justified.'

'Where's all your dosh come from, then?' Becs asked Sven and Barney, with a belligerent look which took in Henry.

'Home baking,' Sven replied. 'In our other incarnation, we are Mrs Gibson.'

'Cakes!' said Becs, her barbed wire voice softened a fraction, her eyes suddenly thick with memory.

'Cakes!' cried Henry. 'Cakes! I am to be paid in cakes. The wretched girl negotiated it before I could so much as utter. *And* I only get ten percent of them. This month it's a Mrs Gibson's Traditional Dundee for me, but five for the squat, as well as three Mrs Gibson's Jamaican Gingerbreads and two Tyrol Cakes. Sven also said they'd throw in a six-pack of Eccles, though it remains to be seen whether I get my three-fifths of a one. Next month it's five Morello Cherry and five Coffee and Walnut for them and a Madeira for me.'

'But Henry,' said David, reflecting that a Mrs Gibson's Traditional Dundee would be infinitely preferable to the company of Merlyn Orb, 'That strikes me as in many ways ideal. It means that some of the money the squatters might have spent on food can be put aside for other things. It also means, incidentally, that you have to find no cash yourself.'

'Do you know what I could have charged? Do you know? "So sorry, Mr Bullock, I can't pay the bank what I owe it this month, but perhaps you'd accept a Mrs Gibson's Lemon Sponge?" I believe there's been a run on the Battenburg but the Chocolate Brownie is remaining stable against a basket of Butterfly Buns. And Sven and Barney are such gossips! It'll be the talk of London. Soon nobody will be bothering with cheques for Henry Pearl. My travails will be recompensed in Gorgonzolas, lhasa apso puppies, home depilation vouchers. Don't bother to pay back what you owe me, David, I'll take a complete set of *Malory Towers*.'

'The future is barter,' said Merlyn Orb, who had appeared halfway through Henry's speech. David had installed him in the priest's hole but, although he seemed rather taken with it, he emerged depressingly regularly, not to ask questions, but to make comments.

'I fear, Henry,' said David, 'that a complete set of *Malory Towers* is likely to be all that I will be able to offer you.'

Horatio Bullock had phoned that morning. Since Fay was out, David had had to answer.

How far away was the bank? Ten minutes on foot: it crouched in Pitsbury High Street, emitting letters. And yet, it had seemed as if Bullock was speaking at a great distance from normal life.

Bullock's favourite word was 'surprise'; he seemed to pass his existence in a permanent state of astonishment at the errant behaviour of his customers – a wonder that led him not to expect them to act as sensible mortals might, in similar situations. He had professed his usual amazement about David's failure to reply to his letters – though what could he have imagined there was to say? (Sorry? Have a Mrs Gibson's Shortbread?)

David had pointed out that business was improving slightly.

'Big ocean, Mr Marsh,' observed Horatio Bullock. 'Small drop.'

Had David taken Mr Bullock's advice and considered that, if the supposed development project went forward, it was more than likely that the diminished value of his property would not be on a par with his borrowing? (A roundabout way of indicating that the bank viewed David as pretty much fucked.)

Had he *considered* it? Had he considered it?

For hours, days, weeks, David had done nothing else. Who would not have? And yet, so perverse did Bullock find his customers that he appeared quite capable of believing that – out of silliness or naughtiness – David could be going about his life as carefree as a young sailor scrubbing the decks of the Titanic.

Did any of Bullock's customers behave in that way?

Throughout the conversation, David had been aware of a whistling coming from above. Colin Rutt was replacing David's lost tiles – as he had replaced Merlyn's efforts on the squat, as he had dealt with the holes on Rick Farr's. Colin's efficiency was phenomenal. It was largely due to him that the renovation of the squat was now, to all intents and purposes, finished.

It was a beautiful autumn day with bouffants of pale clouds and the scent of smouldering grasses. Pitsbury was a mass of scaffolding and ladders – repairing itself, as it had done since it was first a habitation. Briefly, David had imagined the resourceful Friedaswida, busy with a hammer; the laughing Hermia Mowbray, mopping up a flood of well-water; those stone Archbishops, whose only companions now were pigeons and swallows, discussing with masons the cathedral they were one day to become a part of.

Yes, David supposed that in a way Bullock's customers did appear oblivious to their plight, though it wasn't in the least surprising that they should. Placed as they were in the quotidian foreground, even though the backdrop was debt and decay, people simply got on with things. It was that, or collapse onto the floor of Marauding Hordes in a shower of coley.

It would be reckless to maintain that Horatio Bullock didn't matter, but he didn't matter quite as much as David had hitherto supposed. Now, in the light of Henry and Becs' jolly cakes, he struck David as drab and old-fashioned. Barter had not been a rip-roaring success much after something or other B.C., but surely the species that could remain unbowed by rain, porosity, wind, banks, BARG-MARTS, journalists, charities, conservation officers could come up with something better than it had tolerated for quite long enough. Let the future be buns and sponge cakes rather than grey men in suits.

'I'll do a free performance of my verse,' said Orb, 'one evening, in the shop, by candlelight.'

'Mr Pearl?' said Al, popping his pale face round the door of David's shop, 'They told me I would find you here. Mongolian chants? Inner Light Recordings? Can I borrow?'

'If you play an audio tape backwards,' said Merlyn Orb, 'you hear messages from spirits.'

'Which, if they are so stupid as to send them in such a convoluted fashion, can hardly be worth listening to,' said David. 'And, while I appreciate the offer, Merlyn, I don't have live performances.'

'Be my guest,' said Henry to Al. '"Henry's" resonates to the inanities of Des Grate, "Radio Pitsbury's zaniest DJ".'

'Thank-you, Mr Pearl,' said Al. 'What time is tonight's reading, Mr Marsh?'

The Friday freebie rag plopped onto the mat. The newsboy's luminous jacket briefly caught the beam of a passing car. It was a cold evening. Just The Business's screens blared into the dusk and reflected, in disco colours, on the faces of the clusters of excited young people sitting in front of them. The roofs of Pitsbury were black silhouettes against a lemon sky. The illuminated cathedral was a honeycomb of light.

'A missive,' said Merlyn Orb.

Grim-faced, David was putting more candles onto saucers. Some were lit already, Fay's therapeutic ambergris ones which she had donated to the occasion. Henry Pearl had contributed two bottles of tiswin at cost price and loaned the glasses.

'Oh,' said Fay, who had picked up the paper and was looking at the letters page.

David glanced over her shoulder, his brief touch was rather heavy on it.

'Dog owners should be banned?'

'No.' Fay pointed to a letter from a Mrs Sugg.

David read it, and then went on to look at several others.

There was a satisfied pause.

'Now,' he said, at last, 'we could be getting somewhere.'

Mrs Sugg started by drawing readers' attention to the fact that she had lived in Pitsbury all her life, and was secretary of the Pitsbury Historical Association. In view of rumours about a supermarket development on the wasteland next to Weaver Street, Mrs Sugg was most alarmed at the thought that Pitsbury Council might also be planning to demolish the last remnant of that area, namely a rather lovely Tudor building which was of considerable historical interest.

A Mr Growbag was similarly concerned, and a Lady Cobble claimed that what was now the squat had been requisitioned for the treatment of the wounded during the First World War.

The door of the bookshop opened. A figure in an anorak entered. David looked up. It was the young journalist he had met at the first night of Marauding Hordes and, again, at the instatement of Archbishop Struther on his niche.

'If you're here for the poetry reading, it doesn't start for another half hour.'

Though this didn't seem to make any difference to a group of students, who now came in behind the journalist, poured themselves large tiswins and started wandering around the shop, pulling out and looking at volumes. How, in God's name, had Orb managed to conceive the idea of performing his verse at David Marsh Antiquarian Books, and then publicise it, unknown to David, but with sufficient success to be going to have – the door opened on another group of people – what looked like a more than reasonable turn-out? Could Merlyn Orb, possibly, have a literary following?

Now Fay lit all the candles and switched off the lights.

It was strange how you buried memory, thought David, startled. Maybe it was because, deep down, you felt that each stage of your life was not so much over as left behind. Or perhaps you kept your younger self hidden away somewhere, due to a sense that you had betrayed it. Standing amidst the dipping shadows and murmured conversations, David remembered that this had once been the goal of his endeavours. He had discussed such events across coffee-stained formica with a plump-faced Fay. Of course, then, they hadn't imagined it like this – not a disparate gaggle of students and squatters and other unknown and, in some cases, unlikely individuals; not him and Fay middle-aged – it had been meant to happen much sooner than that. But then, somehow, somewhere along the line, David had forgotten that it had been meant to happen at all. Today, though, it had. And today David remembered, for the first time in ages, that his younger self had planned that it should.

'Not my scene, literary readings,' said the journalist. 'Got wind of some squatter thing you've got going here. Checking it out.'

'Well I hope you will report it more accurately than you did the accident to the Canadian academic.' David's tone was brisk.

The journalist looked blank.

'She didn't break her arm really,' Fay explained. 'I met her.'

'She did. Right arm. Several places. Wouldn't get it wrong, my colleague; one of the best in the business for in-depth accuracy.'

'Yes, the local paper is famed for its profound insight and searing attention to fact.'

'Honest! Anyway, what's the story here then?'

The phone rang.

Rick Farr burst through the door, leaving it wide open. David noticed that the rooftops of Weaver Street were sparkling with ice crystals. The first frost of the year.

'They are painting rainbow stripes along my walls!' Rick said.

'As you can see, we're very tied up here,' said David to the journalist. 'Perhaps tomorrow?'

'Why not go to the cafe opposite now?' suggested Fay. 'If you ask for Gary?'

'Try his chutney and chips,' somebody said, overhearing.

'And that killer drink he does,' said another.

The telephone continued ringing, ever more crossly.

'Could someone grab that?' shouted David.

'Booze? Chips?' The journalist hot-footed it into the night.

'Listen, Rick,' said David.

Rick's cheeks were flushed. He smelled of cold.

'Listen,' David repeated. From over the other side of the shop there was a gale of laughter. 'I think,' David said, 'that the problem, all along, has been that we never took into account what people really wanted. Perhaps we never took account of what we really wanted ourselves.'

'They aren't even all paying,' said Rick.

'No,' said Fay, 'but there's an awful lot of them. So, perhaps, better some not paying anything than basing it on rich people who prefer to be virtual.'

'I owe the bank 70K.'

Rick looked dog-tired, the sheen of businessman rubbed off by the day's efforts. How old was he? David asked himself, suddenly realising that Rick could be less than thirty.

Silently, Fay placed a glass of tiswin in Rick's hand. He took a sip automatically, choked slightly.

'I've driven the length and breadth of the county today, speaking mainly to bastards,' he said. He took another sip. 'No, not bastards,' he corrected himself, putting the glass down. 'Weary blokes, too wrapped up in their own problems to be able to spare a thought for mine. But I couldn't make out I had problems. I had to be upbeat. Then I come along Pitsbury High Street. No one about, except round Quik-Potato and Burger-Fish and the like. I think of getting a takeaway but, quite frankly, I can't face the thought of queuing. Come into Weaver Street. Your place is a mass of candles. There's a dozen down-and-outs sitting in Gary's. There's juggling with flaming torches on the wasteland and firelight from the squat. And there's my place, like Piccadilly Circus, stuffed with students and oddballs eating Eccles cakes and gingerbread and talking rubbish, nine to the dozen.'

Rick's eyes filled with tears. Maybe as young as twenty-seven, twenty-eight, David thought.

'And there's stripes along the walls,' Rick went on. 'Someone's painting a broken chair purple. And I think, Jesus, this is my *home*, even though the building belongs to the bank, and it's the first time I've ever come back to it when it's been anything but empty.'

'I'm phoning long-distance, from Provence. I've been waiting an eternity for someone to answer. Is that David?'

'No, it's Merlyn Orb.'

There was an irritable silence.

'Who are you?' asked Tony Gilbert. 'Where's David?'

'He's in the shop. I'm on the extension because it's noisy in there. I'm a poet.'

'Do you work for David?'

'In a way.'

'In what way?'

'I pack up books and post them to people.'

'Good. Listen. I'll tell you what's happened. You'll be aware that Roo and Immie Canning are filming Hermia Mowbray's *A Right Wonderful Error* down here?'

'No,' said Orb.

There was a pause.

'Well they are,' said Gilbert, crossly. 'And Mark Casey, the acoustic guitarist, he's been creating a score for the song and he was supposed to do a jester cameo. Rupert Canning is, invariably, the easiest of people to collaborate with – and so is Immie. They are both very giving. So it's probably Mark's bout of bronchitis that's made him feel that he can't produce the level of performance, the level of musicality, that the project obviously deserves. And maybe he doesn't feel that Zucchini is quite the person to appreciate what he's – as have we all – put into this of himself. You understand what I am saying?'

'Yes,' said Orb.

'The result being, Mark's left for the Seychelles and we're doing an out-and-out re-think. Which means I would, after all, like that edition of Provençal poetry that David had earmarked for me. We'll probably be underscoring the song in *A Right Wonderful Error* with an earlier burden, as originally planned. So could you whizz it off to Provence A.S.A.P.? I'll give you the Comte's postal address, though really – he's so eminent – just the name of the Comte and France would probably do. What time is it with you?'

'I don't know.'

'Well, could you get it packed up now, so that, at the latest, it can go by morning?'

'Yes,' said Merlyn Orb.

David stood in the bathroom drinking water from a pint glass. He swallowed down a couple of aspirins. His mouth was dry and his head was pounding but, all in all, he didn't feel too bad. It wasn't the debilitating hangover of middle age; it was the hangover of student days that you could sleep off. And he would. Merlyn was looking after the shop. David needn't rise until noon, if he wanted. Then, maybe, he and Fay should go to Gary's and have a fry-up. It would be like when he was a student; those non-existent Saturday mornings after Friday nights spent celebrating the end of Fay's working week at Langley The Chemist. Sometimes they'd fetched up at an all-night place at the bus station that was used by the drivers and by cabbies, and nurses from the hospital going off duty. David wondered whether it was still there.

Then, as now, the night before had seemed to divide into sections which the booze whittled into fragments, which you attempted, in vain, to assemble into a coherent whole, Saturday lunchtime – having remembered, just in time, that while saying good-night you'd arranged to meet up again at The Bell.

Then, as now.

David ran the cold tap for more water. He stood drinking it, looking at his somewhat worn reflection.

Without doubt, the reading had been a success – though whether this was due to the tiswin and the candlelight or to the actual content David was at a loss to say. In truth, he hadn't really had a chance to concentrate on Orb's contribution to the event; the verse had, mainly, reached him in bursts while he was pouring drinks and admitting latecomers. One poem had struck him, though, for strangely it had appeared to be a sonnet; not a form David would have expected Merlyn Orb to be conversant with or, if he were, to approve of.

Was that long before Merlyn had, dismayingly, produced a guitar and looked very much as if he was planning on playing it? At which point Henry Pearl had, rather splendidly, seized the instrument and thrust it into the hands of a friend of his called . . . Len? Ken? Sven! . . . thrust it into the hands of a friend of his called Sven who, David remembered, was there with someone called Barney. They were meant to be in Harrogate but they hadn't been able to resist the pull of evensong and then the Cock and Hen, after which they'd realised there was no way Barney could drive, so they'd turned up at the reading in search of Henry to ask him to put them up for the night. Henry had demanded that Sven who . . . had been a treble? Had studied at the Royal College of Music? . . . should play a galliard. Which he had done. And they'd spilled out onto the street but, by then, it had become a hokey-cokey. And into Rick's. And Henry Pearl had re-opened Gary's and then explained to the police that it was a private party, though David did seem to recall having parted with a fiver at some stage.

Shrieks and laughter, clear and unmuffled in the thin, cold air. It was a wonder they hadn't all been put in a cell.

The cathedral clock struck coldly. David raised the bathroom's sash-window. The cathedral was out – a chalky blue slab of stone against the fragile light of a silent autumn dawn. The ivy on the grey walls was sugared with frost, the Ebb was a fuzz of mist. Patches of lawn were asbestos mats.

Now a face flickered through David's brain; one which he could not place. Nor could he be sure exactly when, during the evening, he had seen it. A cool, woman's face that had seemed to be making notes.

As, indeed, it was.

15

The Paper City

The annual visit to the Royal Society for the Help of the Homeless.

The worst thing about which – other than the boringness of it – was the sandwiches. It was one of those working-type events at which handshakes were swift; no waves at the press or crowd; instead, zoom inside, looking businesslike and ready for bundles of administration. And, in keeping with that thorough mood, lunch would only be tiny little flat sandwiches, filled with slivers of smoked salmon, and mineral water and coffee. No pudding, of course.

It was funny how, as soon as the weather changed and the children went back to school, everything seemed to go brown and grey and woollen. Duchess Harriet looked out at a group of slim, intense young girls in the thick, dark uniform of the Queen's School, waiting to cross the road with bags of crisps in their hands. Probably one of the princesses would have to go to the Queen's School. Well, there were worse places.

Thank God for London, though. Thank God for her sexy, rich, Latin Giorgio, who kissed Harriet's fingers and bought her bracelets and said she was so-oo clever. As the days huddled in on themselves, Duchess Harriet had observed that you needed more of that sort of thing to combat the drabness. They were a necessity: nights glittering with flash-bulbs; operas; clubs, left late late late, when the sweat of the disco meeting a brief blast of cold, just prior to the warmth of the car, gave you a tingly, champagney sensation.

In the cathedral precinct there were more Queen's School pupils, purple-legged and red-cheeked, in lacrosse kit. Duchess Harriet looked at them with utter pity. Those endless, draughty, almost pitch-dark afternoons in goal.

'Ms Court is the Society's Director,' said her lady-in-waiting as they drew up outside the charity's headquarters. 'You have met her before, on all your previous visits to the R.S.H.H.'

'*Tennis* Court?' asked the Duchess, who was considered witty by her friends.

Ms Court it was whom David had seen but been unable to identify. And it was not a love of verse – though she was fond of the Lake Poets – that had brought her to Weaver Street. Because of what she had noted that evening Ms Court had, since, visited Weaver Street at various times of day in order to check up on the details of what was happening there.

Ms Court was a woman imbued with that upper-class desire to feel that she was doing good – the icing on the cake of an already richly-mixed life. She lacked, however, the energy, imagination or genuine altruism to achieve anything but the most cursory of benefits to her fellow kind. Enough for her own satisfaction, but not really enough to justify her copious salary or, this year, to look sufficiently impressive in her report to the Duchess of Pitsbury. Who, like Ms Court, was a caring individual but, unlike Ms Court, a hyperbolic one who might be unable to appreciate that slow and subtle improvements are as good, in their way, as the large, flashy variety.

Ms Court had toyed with the idea of putting something more ordinary in this year's sandwiches – Brie, perhaps, or avocado – as an indication of the charity's sense of solidarity with the less fortunate, but came to the conclusion that this, alone, would not suffice. True, the Duchess was usually completely happy with her charity's endeavours but, at present, the pressure on her to look good was at its most intense. Divorce negotiations were the news of the day and, in the poor Duchess's position, Ms Court knew that she would be making a play for public sympathy, approval, admiration: in short, whatever was likely to result in the best deal.

It was, also, more than possible that Ms Court herself might be questioned by the press, and the year's star initiative, unfortunately, did not bear much examination, having been scuppered by the very people who had profited so greatly from it.

This star initiative had been the formerly homeless family that Ms Court had dangled in front of David as evidence of the charity's success. Not terribly long after their conversation, however, the mother had quit her cleaning job at Bus Station House, apparently when someone (not employed by the Bus Company, so goodness knows what they were doing there) had pointed out to her that she was being paid a pittance – less than the dole, this person had worked out. (Yes, but surely work brought its own rewards, not all of which were financial?) Then the husband had objected to being transferred to another branch of Burger-Fish – which would only have meant an hour or two's travelling a day – and had subsequently been given the sack. The family's rented house, on what used to be the Elizium Forest Council Estate, flooded (just an inch or so) in the storm, and a social worker managed to get it deemed unfit for human habitation. Currently, the family was in a bed-and-breakfast.

Ms Court knew better than to expect the poor to be grateful. She did, nevertheless, feel that they might make more of an effort. Ms Court could scarcely hold up as a moral trump for the Duchess a family which had been in rented accommodation for barely six months before slipping back into homelessness and unemployment.

Though there was precious little else.

Except for Weaver Street.

Now Weaver Street's imaginative decision to do up a squat and then, it appeared, establish a sort of cooperative system of employment was not, strictly speaking, anything whatsoever to do with the Royal Society for the Help of the Homeless. But it might have been; if the Society had had the idea, it would have – subject to the agreement of various committees. So to say to the Duchess that a wonderfully original experiment in the grim battle against homelessness was presently taking place in Weaver Street – without going into details as to who instigated it – would not be unreasonable.

David Marsh's motives in getting the Weaver Street squat done up were now clear to Ms Court, in the light of the certain truth of the planned supermarket development and David's alarmed, and unlikely, visit to her around the time that the development had first been mooted. In which case, if it were to come to David's attention that the Royal Society for the Help of the Homeless was claiming credit that was not its due, he would, surely, quickly reflect that the Society's endorsement of the renovated building could only strengthen his position.

Ms Court wore an elegant charcoal suit with slim-cut skirt, blunt-ended black suede shoes, a heavy gold chain. The Duchess was in pillar-box red. She was, as was customary on the occasion, seated at Ms Court's desk, beneath her own picture. Most of the meeting she had spent looking out of the lovely, delicate Georgian window, now framed with flaming Virginia creeper. Perhaps to admire the half glassy-blue frost, half sodden emerald grass of the Queen's School Quad. Perhaps to help her to concentrate.

'. . . coffee morning, attended by the wife of the archbishop, bringing together various distinguished professional women in order to discuss what, if anything, the private sector can contribute to a consideration of the problem,' said Ms Court.

The Duchess remained silent. Her lady-in-waiting gave a small smile. Those members of the charity eminent enough to be allowed to attend cleared their throats. Lady Cobble, an elderly woman whose soft skin was the colour of mother-of-pearl and whose father had bequeathed this building to the charity, stroked one many-ringed hand against the other.

'But, in time-honoured fashion, I have saved the best for last,' said Ms Court. 'What one should call, perhaps, the *Renaissance* of Weaver Street.' (There was an appreciative ripple of cultured amusement from the eminent, in order to show that they were fully aware of Pitsbury's Tudor connections.) 'In particular, the renovation of a dilapidated but historic building in the Pitsbury Without part of Weaver Street by the squatters who are living there – a situation which had, previously, been causing considerable concern.'

Yes, she had struck a chord. Duchess Harriet's attention was snatched away from the window and her eyes glued themselves to Lady Cobble who now, serendipitously, had begun to voice her own pleasure at the renovation.

'During the First World War,' Lady Cobble continued in a clear, old-fashioned voice, whose slow enunciation resisted the cracking of age, 'the building was used for the treatment of wounded. Those well enough to do so would sit in the grounds. They were very lovely, then, you see. There was a kitchen garden, with herbs – rosemary, lavender, thyme. There was a knot-garden, and a well. Roses, of course. And a sun-dial. But *all* that area was rather nice. Small houses, mostly, though not entirely, with bath-tubs hanging on hooks outside and their own little gardens.'

'Gardens?' exclaimed Duchess Harriet.

'Yes, my dear,' said Lady Cobble. 'During the Second World War they were full of potatoes. I remember their purple flowers.'

'But isn't the squat condemned?' asked the Duchess. 'What's the point of doing something up just to pull it down again? Isn't there going to be a big new complex that'll need the access?'

Say what people might about the Royal Family, thought Ms Court, they certainly did their homework; which those who agitated for their abolition ought to take into account.

'There are rumours of a complex. A supermarket, in fact, Ma'am,' she said. 'But, fortunately, enthusiasm for the Weaver Street initiative is running high.'

'We are delighted,' said Lady Cobble, 'to see a building such as this get back on its feet. I myself have written to that effect to the local newspaper. As have others.'

'You need not worry, Ma'am.' Ms Court noted the Duchess's expression of dismayed concern. 'Pitsbury opinion about the renovation is such that you can be sure that any attempt, now, to demolish the building in order to allow for a new development would meet with intense opposition.'

Late afternoon. That desperate period between lunch and dinner. The lights were on in some of the shops already and the shoppers scurried, heads down, with bags of groceries. The bridge which led to Weaver Street was illuminated. As the Jag bobbed over it, Duchess Harriet caught a glimpse of luminous, lime reeds and thumping moths.

Considering its attractiveness, it was odd that she hadn't noticed Weaver Street before. The pavements were full of people talking. There was a bookshop, in its window wine-and-gold-coloured volumes and soft, grey-lined paperbacks. There was an aromatherapy and herb shop, with a display of baskets of mushrooms and sacks of nice-smelling looking things. There was something a bit like a disco, giving off hypnotic music. A café.

'Stop the car,' said the Duchess. 'Two jam doughnuts, if they have them. If not, a sausage roll.'

The driver got out. The Duchess and her lady-in-waiting watched a tattered girl juggle firebrands, tip her thin face backwards – a mass of orange light and purple hollows – and swallow the flames.

'They don't have doughnuts after elevenses time, Ma'am. And they've run out of sausage rolls. They can, however, do you a hot-dog with chilli sauce.'

The wasteland hadn't changed, thank goodness. What with this unpredicted obstacle in the shape of the renovated building, in front of which the car now stopped, and the thought of Giorgio's fiery Latin temper, Duchess Harriet had almost expected to see people digging up potatoes, hanging washing, heaving their bath-tubs inside for soaks in front of the stove. She had almost expected to see gardeners trimming low box-hedges and shell-shocked young soldiers in striped pyjamas smoking pipes among the roses.

Instead, the wasteland was still the same jig-saw of broken things. There were pools of flood-water reflecting icy pieces of young, autumn moon.

Duchess Harriet swallowed the last bite of her hot-dog and wiped her chin with the paper napkin. The restored squat was quite a different matter, however. That had undergone a metamorphosis, and no mistake. The Duchess still preferred the convenience of split-level living, but even she could see that here was a Cinderella of a building, blossomed into loveliness, all the more compelling for its merry touches.

There was a slim, sturdy, red-bricked chimney, crazily high and puffing silver smoke. A funny little attic window reflected a small portion of moon. The building's brickwork was in herringbone patterns, held, corseted, between strong, dark, curving beams. Through a downstairs window, Duchess Harriet could see part of an enormous, mausoleum-like fireplace. The brightly-painted ceiling of an upstairs room was lit by candles: ivory ruffs, ruby caps. There was a dense oak front door, loam-coloured and covered in bolts and hinges, studs, deep locks – the kind made for heavy, trefoil-ended keys. Stone sills terminated in carved wiggles.

'You can drive on,' said the Duchess, thinking, as the car pulled off and the squat dwindled to a reflection on its shiny boot, that well done-up as it was, there were lots of houses, every bit as nice as that one, all over the place. Heaps of Harriet's friends lived in them. So why did people get so steamed up about heritage and what-not? It was evidently absolutely imperative to get the building pulled down – p.d.q., pronto – as agreed, and before any silly old biddies got too organised and up in arms about it.

A job that was down to Horatio Bullock, whom Duchess Harriet now got onto her portable blower to and asked what the hell he thought was going on.

A city is a large place and one cannot have eyes everywhere. Nor can one be expected regularly to pore through the local paper on the off-chance that it may contain something of relevance to one's own activities. Duchess Harriet's point, that she found time to do just that – and not merely the local, but almost every single national – took no account of the fact that bank managers who are also mayors are, perhaps, a trifle busier than members of the Royal Family.

It was a rum do, though: that much the Duchess was correct about. And Horatio Bullock knew, better than he let on to her during their conversation, that if there was one thing that Pitsbury got worked up over, it was architecture. She could partially thank her brother-in-law for that, though Bullock did not voice this observation.

He was in the bank when he received the Duchess's call.

Autumn was a demanding season, in both his capacities –
a time of loans and civic duties, in particular the Pitsbury
Hallowe'en celebrations, which brought people in from all the
surrounding towns and villages. Horatio Bullock did not see
himself as doing anything so undignified as *juggling* his time.
Instead, he pared it into neat pieces: now Mayor, attending
meetings with Mummers, Fire Officers, Morris Dancers, Brown
and Tawny Owls; now bank manager, negotiating mortgages
and interest rates.

It was very rare, though not totally unknown, for him to blur
the two categories.

Horatio Bullock knew that people mainly saw the bank as
something that spat out money in return for a hit of plastic.
Or as a malevolent presence, formalising their mistakes. Both
views were simplistic. Truly, the bank was the repository of
the city. All Pitsbury's facets resided there, in paper form.
Horatio Bullock could – and sometimes did, when school
parties arrived at his bit of their tour – summon from the
vaults thin deeds in browned, illegible handwriting, sealed
with a squelch of wax. (Though he also, invariably, had a
computer-generated sheaf of correspondence about the same
properties; to him, just as interesting.) In the bank, Bullock
held sway over a paper city, more relevant in many ways than
the material one over which he strutted his Mayoral office in
Neo-Gothic school halls, cuboid council rooms, presbyteries and
palaces, disinfectanty gymnasiums, chlorine-smelling lidos and,
of course, in the cathedral, where Pitsbury's Medieval burghers
grouped around the Holy Family in deliberate, stained-glass
anachronism.

When Bullock did things with paper, the results manifested
themselves in concrete, brick and stone. There must be no breath
of corruption. This was why he was scrupulous about keeping
his roles separate, except when it was absolutely necessary to
do otherwise.

Such as now.

As a result of the Duchess's phone call, David Marsh lay before
Horatio Bullock on his rectangular slab of desk, compressed
between green cardboard.

So, for good measure, did the rest of Weaver Street.

The chairs and tables, crockery, cutlery and mutating invoices of Henry Pearl's restaurants. The commerce between David and Fay Marsh and Henry Pearl Interiors. Corpulent cheques from Henry Pearl to Colin Rutt; smaller ones to 'The Three Mongols Dancing Trio', 'Inner Light Recordings', 'The Terrence Higgins Trust' and 'Save The Dolphins'. The wills of David Marsh's parents. The sum David Marsh paid for his initial investment in stock for his bookshop. Fay Marsh's standing orders and a plethora of little payments to her from the Shaman Of Mysterious Hope, Aldershot. On David Marsh's credit card, two tickets to *Loving Wisely Well* during this year's Pitsbury Arts Festival. On Rick Farr's credit card, his Rolex – and everything else now, including supermarket bills.

Then, the letters Bullock had sent to them. Form ones, mainly. Colin Rutt exceeding his overdraft limit by several hundred pounds, (a cheque from Henry Pearl in response). Reminders to Rick Farr about his seventy thousand. Reminders to Henry Pearl that, though Henry Pearl Interiors was in the black, Grandmother's Footsteps, Marauding Hordes was showing a worrying deficit. The early, polite concern, letters to David Marsh (a few covering cheques from his wife); the sterner, more worried, phase; extreme misgivings; intense surprise; alarm; threats.

Quite enough.

Mr Marsh would not be able to claim that he hadn't been warned.

But this was only one avenue of assault. There were others.

The Mayor issued commands to a very reluctant Ms Court at the Royal Society for the Help of the Homeless before making his way to the Conservation Department.

Brian Baffle's office was the campaign headquarters, from which he mounted his offensive against those who sought to muddle time.

It was mostly fairly clear what had been done, and when. Baffle had maps from all periods of Pitsbury's existence, right through from the city's scrawny, Roman stage to the jostling present.

Horatio Bullock did not know what he was looking for, but he trusted that some era would have left something lying around which he would be able to put to his purpose.

'Eighteenth,' said Baffle. His hand scuttled across Pitsbury Without, sparse and separate; a little village, huddling up to the city wall.

Bullock, as Mayor, as banker, had never – when he thought on the topic – viewed history as having much to say for itself before the nineteenth century. Nevertheless, he forced himself to pause over the map.

'What's this?' he asked, pointing at a small circle in the grounds of the confident squares and oblongs which would one day be the squat in Pitsbury Without.

'A well,' said Baffle. He sniffed and stuffed an inhaler up each nostril. Pitsbury's wells had mainly sunk beneath the surface now and, though Baffle's subconscious would have liked to worm its way underground to check that each era was behaving itself, his conscious admitted that, for the most part, wells had got away.

'It's here also.' Baffle replaced the eighteenth century with the seventeenth. The squat had fewer outbuildings then. 'And here.' He swept the seventeenth century to the floor and put the sixteenth on the table, then the fifteenth, flipping maps as if to animate a cartoon, until the building had vanished and only the well remained.

'Accuracy becomes less absolute the further back we go,' said Baffle, his voice rich with condemnation for the slip-shod past.

'Continue,' said Horatio Bullock; an ambiguous command. Baffle, however, produced the nineteenth century and both men bent over it, breathing heavily.

'Ah,' said Bullock with approval.

The railway. Solid, middle-class houses, elbowing their way into the spaces in the city centre. Pitsbury Without, a mass of spruce tenements and terraces, crowded around the earlier buildings; little shops and businesses: tailors? cobblers? dress-makers? bakers? blacksmiths? Horace Bullock did not bother to speculate. Instead, he shoved a blunt finger at a tiny square next to the well.

'What's that?' he asked.

'W.C.,' said Brian Baffle. 'There are those,' he added, 'who look upon the nineteenth century as the age of the toilet.'

Which might have been something of a disappointment to the many lavishly breeding patriarchs who now slumbered complacently in the white spaces which were Pitsbury's Victorian cemeteries.

'Might I inquire, Your Worship, what exactly we are seeking?' asked Brian Baffle, in the silence that followed.

There was no reply. Bullock was stroking his chin thoughtfully.

'Pipes,' he said suddenly. 'Nineteenth-century pipes. Have you got any maps of them?'

He was not to know that the subterranean strata were a sore point, nor that the nineteenth century was not a favourite, the resourceful empire-builders all too often lacking a proper sense of what should be where – partly forgivable, due to diminishing space, but cavalier, nonetheless.

'Many Victorian sewers were built onto Roman ones,' Baffle ventured; a fact that would have clinched them as beyond the pale for him, but which did not trouble Horatio Bullock.

'Maybe I could take a look at them?'

'It would mean going down the corridor to Environmental Health,' said Baffle.

This was no obstacle either.

'This evening's a curry and kebab swoop,' said the secretary, 'that's why there's no health officers here.'

'We could return at a later date,' tried Baffle.

'We wish to look at nineteenth-century pipes and sewers,' said Horatio Bullock. 'And get out the present water-system, too.'

'Just a moment, Your Worship.' The secretary picked, pulled, looked, put back. 'Yes.'

Two neat, flat facsimiles.

'I'd hate to encroach on another's territory,' said Baffle.

'I don't see any other,' said Bullock, smiling, 'and your presence can save me time.'

Pitsbury's Victorian plumbing system. Straight lines and right angles, laid out like a computer circuit.

'My colleagues in Environmental give me to understand that many of those early pipes still in use are caving in now,' said Baffle, privately reflecting that that was what you got for jumbling epochs. 'Though the Victorians built thoroughly.'

'But not forever?' said Bullock, seeming pleased at the thought.

'They expected us to concretise their achievements,' said Baffle.

'Many of them, we have,' said Bullock. 'Where on this map would Pitsbury Without be?'

'Here,' said Baffle, after a moment.

'And the Weaver Street squat?'

'Here.'

'And this,' pointing, 'is the well?'

Baffle nodded.

'And that is the sewer for the squat's W.C.?'

'Possibly *was*,' said Baffle. It now dimly occurred to him that his desires, as Conservation Officer, and Horatio Bullock's, as Mayor, were not necessarily identical.

'Why *was*?'

'Demolition. War.' Said Baffle.

'Which could have affected beneath the surface,' said Bullock. 'New networks might have replaced the old.'

'Possibly,' Baffle agreed.

'In which case, I'd now like to look at the contemporary piping,' said Bullock.

Baffle unfolded the second diagram.

'The war did a lot of structural damage to the system,' observed Bullock after a moment, evidently discouraged. 'Much of it was apparently made defunct.' However, after further investigation he added, excitedly, 'But the well is still there. And so is the old sewer. Very close to one another, don't you think? The well's still the squat's only water supply. And they're using the nineteenth-century sewer.'

Baffle considered the squat's current plumbing.

'The well shouldn't be marked,' he said quickly, displeased by the inaccuracy and becoming increasingly nervous about the possible outcome of the Mayor's discovery.

'How so?' Bullock looked perplexed.

'The subterranean structure is certainly there still.' Baffle's expression indicated that, when things sank beneath his juris-diction, he would just as soon they ceased to exist completely.

'But the above-the-ground portion of the well is no longer visible. Though there could' – gaining hope that accuracy might be salvaged – 'be some remains that I didn't perceive because they were covered by the flood-water.'

'The flood-water!' exclaimed Bullock.

'When I was checking on it, I noted that much of the land adjoining the Weaver Street squat was submerged,' said Baffle.

Then, noting the triumph on the Mayor's face, he wondered if it might have been better if he hadn't.

16

Repossession

The day began peacefully enough.

The room was full of cold, white, morning sunshine. Fay lit a match.

'Why is it *rosemary* for remembrance?' she said, reaching into the grate. 'Why isn't it . . .'

'Daffodils,' said David.

'Formaldehyde,' said Merlyn Orb.

It was the first fire Fay had had in the shop this year. She'd also lit one in the sitting-room. David watched last February's newspaper, the kindling and the pine-cones, dried crisp and pale by the summer, begin to flame. Merlyn was going to look after the shop for her while Fay went to Just The Business. She had been going there, daily, for the best part of a week.

Fay wore a big chestnut knitted sweater and a long cord skirt. She had written an itemised list of things that Merlyn should (and should not) do, including on it Rick's telephone number in case Merlyn needed to get in touch with her. She had also made a list for herself of what she wanted to achieve that day.

As far as David could gather, she was establishing a planetary web of aromatherapists and herbologists.

Until recently, David had assumed that it was a coincidence that Marsh Meadows had always run at a smaller loss than the bookshop. Now, he was not so sure. Fay's shelves, the drawers, the filing cabinet were arranged ever more methodically. When a letter came asking questions which she could not answer, Fay consulted the esoteric volumes in her bookcase – Chi'en Nung, Pliny, Rhazes, Linnaeus – with practised ease. She had, apparently, already mastered the Internet sufficiently well to be able to discuss herbs and aromas with other experts on the subject. Papers covered with notes and correspondence were the result of each day's visit to Rick's. They were carefully gone through and carefully filed. The queries and observations which resulted from them were written down for Fay's next session.

The fire was crackling.

David had seen only ferns and fronds, diluted soups; a slim girl holding a can of lager in a pale hand at the end of a burgundy, drawstring sleeve. This girl still existed – emerged, from time to time, in tears and sugared violets and terrible words like 'icky' – but a sturdy, at home woman had come to inhabit the space also.

How long had she been there?

It was the kind of day – so fraily bright, so pale and drifting – that felt as if it could, at any moment, crumple into dusk. David thought that he would put on his sheepskin jacket and walk by the river. It was the kind of day you looked at the yellow leaves and the motionless water and pretended to yourself that you did not mind walking alone. David could have asked Henry to come – Rick and Colin didn't understand walks – but Henry made such a song and dance of what ought only to be a peaceful occasion: all scarves and keys and speculations about umbrellas. David would have liked to ask Fay but (he did not think to wonder which had happened first) just as he had begun to want to know her again, she had begun to move away.

Contact between them used to be fraught with meaning – heavy, portentous, liable to lead to all kinds of emotional debris spontaneously crashing down out of nowhere. Now their marriage seemed to carry less weight.

'Wouldn't you think that Sam Bullock should be worried?' said Fay, interrupting David's reflections. 'I saw him the other day but, with everything else, I'd forgotten about it. I mean, wouldn't you be in a bit of a panic if you were a cattle farmer?'

She was looking at the fire, thoughtfully.

David's eyes followed her gaze to Sam Bullock's grainy face on a white, as yet unburnt, triangle of newspaper.

'I would,' he agreed, 'though mad cows are fairly low down on my personal hierarchy of worries. Had I the leisure, however, I would doubtless be making a mental assessment of the likelihood of having eaten contaminated beef at some stage in my life.'

'Everything is contaminated,' said Merlyn Orb.

'Some things more than others, Merlyn,' said Fay.

'It seems to me that these "everything" and "nothing" tags can, with a spurious semblance of profundity, be applied to everything,' said David, irritated.

'Like you are now,' said Merlyn.

'Don't be nasty, David,' said Fay. The flames were gaining on Sam Bullock, though his satisfied expression remained, oblivious. 'He's part of the Net, Sam Bullock,' she added.

'I wouldn't have thought a farmer would have much use for the Internet,' said David, surprised.

'I could see what it is that he's doing,' said Fay, softly.

'See?'

'Look.'

David raised his eyes to meet those of his wife but, at that point, conversation ceased for, 'It has been vouchsafed to me!' exclaimed Merlyn Orb, suddenly, pointing in the direction of the window.

David looked out.

Marching past, unmistakably towards the squat: greys, duns, dead blues. A rush of determined, thorough, conscientious faces.

'It has been vouchsafed to me also,' David observed grimly, reaching for his jacket with an awful sense of foreboding, 'and lest, Merlyn, you be tempted to imagine that you and I are receptacles of spirit wisdom, I suspect it has been vouchsafed to Fay as well.'

'It was vouchsafed to you first, Merlyn,' said Fay, grabbing her poncho.

David flung the front door open. Everyone in the street seemed to be heading in the same direction.

The phone gave an agitated squeal. Fay scuttled back to answer it.

'Yes, we've seen, Henry.' She cupped her hand over the mouthpiece. 'He's upset because Colin wants to bring a kosh.'

Brian Baffle, looking unaccustomedly sheepish. Ms Court. A couple of policemen. The journalist from the local rag. Firemen, nurses, students, business people, mothers, children, adolescents who'd been eating in Gary's or surfing the Net. A big group of tall, wide, solid, chewing men with folded arms and crew-cuts, lined up in front of the squat. Accompanied by an entourage of council officials, Horatio Bullock holding a tannoy.

When Clementine had gone, nothing had felt desirable to David, except a stifling weight of duvets and pillows to bury himself under. In the face of the bank's inexorable letters, just to have blanked out the windows, sealed up the doors, done clever things with ropes like the squatters did.

Now, once again, rock bottom looked like a very solid place indeed compared with Weaver Street's late, airy strivings. The squat was naked and exposed. Its thin glass. Its easily fractured woodwork. Its vulnerable rooms. No longer a place where people could go to be left alone and forgotten, it had staked a claim which forces had come to persuade it to relinquish.

Amongst the crowd of spectators David spotted Gary's round face. Merlyn Orb was dark and incongruous in the sunlight. So were all those squatters marooned outside: a grubby debris, used to darting between shadowy places. David experienced a terrible stab of guilt. They had taken away the squatters' only insulation. Had the Council, unopposed, pulled down their shelter on the edge of the wasteland they would have been able just to seep into other unwanted places; where, as long as they remained undemanding, they would have been undisturbed – at least until those places, in their turn, were otherwise required. Exist in a corner and the squatters were permitted that corner to exist in. Indicate that they were planning to live in it and, suddenly, they had overstepped the boundary; they had become inconvenient.

Very inconvenient from the look on the face of Ms Court.

'What is going on? What is going on? Who are those brutish boys in those nasty colours?'

'Bailiffs, Henry,' said David.

There was a horrified pause.

'And Becs and Gary considered I looked like *them*? Even Rick, even Rick in the heyday of his hair oil, looked marginally more soigné. I must apologise to him this instant.'

'Where's Colin, Henry?' asked Fay.

'I locked him in the coal shed. I pretended I was sending him in there for a shovel for me. He's never admitted it, but I suspect, in his reckless youth, Colin may have been,' (whispered) '*inside*. He's prone to taking the law into his own hands.'

'Does anyone know what's about to happen?' asked Rick Farr, appearing.

'Rick! Rick! Let me abase myself.'

'Henry, could you shut up a minute?' said David.

Horatio Bullock had lifted the tannoy and words were crackling out of its metal lips.

'Firstly, let me extend my sincere congratulations to the citizens of Weaver Street for a truly exceptional, and timely, highlighting of the plight of the needy among us.'

The speech bounced off the walls of the Weaver Street squat in a shrapnel of static. Its colours exaggerated by the paleness of the day, the building seemed a wavering backdrop, painted on the sky. In the absence of any physical barriers, those inside had reverted to the only means of protection they had left: silence.

There was a ripple of applause from the council officials.

'As a direct result of which, Ms Court, of the Royal Society for the Help of the Homeless,' Bullock continued, 'has been inspired to guarantee, to all those *willingly* vacating the Weaver Street premises, bed-and-breakfast accommodation until more suitable measures present themselves.'

Ms Court forced a smile.

David's voice quickly inserted itself into the pause which followed.

'Since the building has been renovated, and is clearly in good condition, might I ask why the squatters cannot simply stay there?'

Heads swung round.

The tannoy gave a pip of surprise.

'Research undertaken by Mr Baffle of the Conservation Department,' said Bullock with a soft gesture towards the unhappy looking Baffle, 'has revealed that the Weaver Street squat is unfit for human habitation.'

Henry Pearl gasped and threw a hand across his heart. 'That building is a triumph! A triumph! My own sweat is mingled with the plaster.'

'No!' cried Fay.

'It's our *home*!' shouted someone.

Rick Farr lit his first cigarette in a fortnight.

'What, in God's name, is that supposed to mean?' exploded David. 'When it was collapsing, when it was leaking, when the roof was caving in and damp was exuding from its every pore: then the squat was considered perfectly fit for any wretch who cared to doss down in it.'

There was a new, rather louder, round of applause which frothed through the crowd without definite location. Then a frozen moment of silence. Martins dipped over the wasteland. The day, the light, the timelessness of the sky, swallowed David's words up.

'A map of Pitsbury's plumbing system,' Bullock continued, metallically, 'reveals that the water supply to the squat comes from a well. This well is next to the Victorian sewer. In gross danger of contamination. The flooding of the area by the recent rain may, quite possibly, have occasioned fractures in the structures of both well and sewer. Though disappointing to every one of us, I would be failing in my civic duty if I did not require the building to be boarded up pending further investigation.'

The bailiffs swayed on their stiff, slightly-apart, legs. They were evidently used to this preliminary blather, the flutter of legalities before the nitty-gritty. From inside the building, in another, uncertain silence, David thought he heard Becs coughing. He imagined Al's damp hand poised, still, on the duplicator. He wondered how Al's tooth had got chipped.

For once it seemed that there was a row of simple, neat, clear-cut decisions to be implemented.

Bullock, for whatever reason – oiled palm? because that was the sort of thing mayors liked?—was, apparently, doggedly in favour of the BARG-MART, and had brought his heavies in to make sure it happened. There was nothing for the squatters to do but to take Ms Court up on her offer of temporary accommodation. They had to. The alternative was violence, siege conditions, twisted limbs, broken teeth.

Probably it was a lie about the sewer and the well; or if it wasn't, their juxtaposition was no truer of the squat than of numerous other buildings in Pitsbury. Beneath the shallow skin of earth, any amount of structural betrayals doubtless awaited. The Weaver Street squat, however, was the one that would be boarded up. Then Bullock need only stand back and winter would do the rest. By spring, the building would have died. To inter it with the other remains scattered across the wasteland would seem like a logical conclusion. This, David and Fay and Rick and Henry and Colin must try somehow to combat, before it was too late – if it wasn't too late already: nowhere seemed to be able to persist unless it was properly inhabited.

They must also, each consider what of their own livings there was left to salvage.

Resigned, calm reflections which were immediately interrupted by the sight of Colin Rutt, smudged with coal dust, his arms covered with splinters of wood, making his way along the ridge tiles of the squat's roof carrying a kosh and a shovel. Colin disappeared behind a chimney. David glanced around quickly. So absorbed were the rest of the crowd in terrestrial developments that no one else appeared to have noticed Colin's presence.

'That is the end of that, therefore,' concluded Bullock, 'and let us hope it is a temporary one.'

'There are no temporary endings, my friend,' declaimed Merlyn Orb in a ringing tone. 'We are not departing. We live in Weaver Street. Our work is here.'

It was news to David that Orb felt anything but the most tangential of relationships to his mail-order activities.

'Merlyn . . .'

A chicken, upside down, in a market in Arles, flapping its gaudy colours. A pearly bone being chopped on a butcher's block.

'You are afraid for us.'

How David wished Merlyn wouldn't talk like that. How he longed to know what the hell Colin Rutt thought he was doing skipping about the roof like a black bloody Santa.

'Quite frankly, yes.'

'I'm not leaving "Gary's Caff",' yelled Gary.

There was a rough round of applause from a group of burly firemen.

'Gary's? So it's Gary's now, is it? Bailiff Pearl merely provides the crockery.'

'You believe the charity lady?' asked Orb.

David sighed.

'Quite frankly, no. But, Merlyn, this is no time for heroics. It doesn't matter to you where you are. You might just as well be in one place as another. It's only us it makes a difference to.'

The bailiffs had terrible cheekbones, they were shaven close as rubber. The squatters couldn't run that risk, they couldn't afford to demand a corner of Pitsbury.

'When is the time for heroics, David?' asked Merlyn Orb.

Colin Rutt emerged from behind the chimney. In a desperate bid for a chance to consider the situation, and without thinking, David lunged at Bullock's tannoy, grabbed it from his hand and aimed its funnel shape at the rooftop.

'Don't do it, Colin!'

'Colin? Colin? Colin's in the coal shed.'

'Don't do *what*?' mouthed Colin from the rooftop. As David had guessed, he had evidently planned to sit it out up there for a while – a Turkish Delight bar gleamed in his back pocket – a little head banging, maybe, but nothing so grand as a suicide threat.

'Don't *jump*,' said David.

Fortunately, Colin cottoned on. He gave David a rather obvious thumbs-up and did a truly spectacular edge along the ridge tile plus pretence to nearly slip.

'I am going to faint. I am going to faint.'

David lowered the tannoy. 'You know Colin's as happy up there as a mountain goat, Henry,' he said softly.

'They'll shoot him down.'

'Nah,' said Rick, treading on his fag end.

'Clumsy though our police force is, Henry, I don't believe that is their favoured means for dealing with potential suicides.'

There was no doubt, however, that those who could be expected to deal with the matter were looking distinctly discomfited. The bailiffs were shifting from foot to foot, their expressions suggesting that suicide rather went and spoilt things. Bullock was in discussion with the police. His entourage's gaze was fixed on Colin, who executed a beautiful loss and gain of balance.

'He should have had a ballet training,' said Henry.

The journalist from the local rag was scribbling in his notebook. David wondered at what point in the proceedings Colin would become newsworthy.

It was the stalemate which David had wanted and which he had suddenly, fortunately, remembered was a part of such events. For whales and for nuclear disarmament – though, principally, for Fay – David had traipsed, with splintery placard, up to London on the train, down to Brighton for a madly located international whaling conference. A bit of shouting. Tremors of rumour and causeless excitement. But mainly, great blank spaces of empty time when the protesters looked at the police and the police looked at the protesters, and everyone wondered what to do next.

'Mr Marsh, a word,' said Horatio Bullock, breaking away from his group.

Surprised, David passed the tannoy to Henry, who spontaneously entered into the swing of things.

'Colin! Colin! Think of all you have to live for! Cuddles, Lake Geneva, Maltesers, bacon sandwiches.'

The latter seemed to strike a chord with the crowd. As David and Bullock made their way up a deserted Weaver Street, a chorus of comments broke out:

'. . . close the "Caff"?'

'They'd have to.'

'. . . someone else?'

'Like Gary does them? No way!'

Then, extrapolating:

'. . . well Farr's got the know-how but not the . . .'

'He's not tuned-in.'

'He is, currently, but how long for? Net's tumbling over itself . . .'

A gleaming car pulled up outside Henry Pearl Interiors. Henry's friends, Sven and Barney, leapt out in a waft of musk and entered the building discussing Becs' *trompe*.

'Mr Marsh,' said Horatio Bullock. 'I sense that we have here a tense situation.'

They stood on the bridge at the end of the High Street, Bullock's back against the stone wall, David leaning over it, looking down into the water.

A quivering city.

'Forgive me for not complimenting you on your astuteness.'

'Perhaps, in the past, Mr Marsh, I have underestimated your intelligence.'

'The thought has crossed my mind.'

'You believe I'm a fool.'

David shrugged.

'I must balance needs.'

'Starting at the top?'

'Mainly the middle. But anyway, Mr Marsh, this is not the time, nor the place. You are ringleader?'

'How can a ring have a leader, if we must use a playground term?'

Below, the floating buildings.

'You are in charge,' Bullock persisted.

'I suppose in as much as anyone is.' Though the term struck David as inexact and coarse. 'My influence is limited.'

There was a silence.

'I've reviewed your case,' said Bullock.

'My case?'

'Notwithstanding the fact that there are worrying deficits – which it surprises me that you haven't addressed with greater urgency – or that a supermarket development might precipitate a downturn in Weaver Street, it is possible that a deal might be done.'

'If . . . ?'

'If, Mr Marsh, you are sensible about change.'

'Otherwise?'

'Repossession is a distinct possibility. In fact, I have a Statutory Demand in my pocket.'

'I've no idea what that means.' Though David could guess.

'What it means is that, unless the money owed to the bank is repaid within the next three weeks, bankruptcy proceedings can then be put into motion.'

The flat, flawless sky. Shrouded willows. Roofs and chimneys.

Slowly, 'I see. Though if I am "sensible", as you put it, I would still be living in a house without any real value.'

'You wouldn't be unique. And anyway, what is "real value", as you put it?'

A stone 'O'. One half in water. The other in air. David's self and his reflection, two, human hands on the clock that was the bridge that led to Weaver Street. Not, as when one was young, those two vast peaks, *either* and *or* – diver or astronaut; pilot, biologist – but paths so close that, at times, they barely diverged; two human hands, interconnected, turning together. A David who made one decision. A David who made the other. What, in the end, was the difference? The ultimate repossession lurked anyway: be brave and decent since, for oneself, the outcome would be, either way, the same.

But for the great, rolling 'O'?

David suddenly realised Horatio Bullock believed that he owned Pitsbury. He thought that its controlling mechanisms were the bank and the council offices. He thought it was *these* that lent Pitsbury's buildings to their occupants.

David's reflection smiled back at him.

'Real value, I would suggest,' he said, 'is what something is worth now.'

'Which, Mr Marsh, is exactly what hangs in the balance. I can make you worth nothing.'

'No, Mr Bullock, you cannot do that.'

17

Colin's Leap

'It must be something he learnt at Knobworth.'

'Knebworth, Henry.' David smiled into the fog.

Henry Pearl strode along the glistening pavement wearing a cashmere scarf, in off-beige, a full-length camel coat, and a hat that Sven and Barney had given him as a souvenir of Bergen. The pubs were turning out. Dark, trudging forms appeared and disappeared. The cathedral had vanished. The acrid smell of fog, mixed with rotten leaves, tingled in David's nostrils; his cheeks were coated with moisture. The Ebb, which they crossed now, was heavy and panting.

'He had fun with the blanket,' said Henry.

'Yes, he did.'

Racing to one end of the roof, shouting ''Ere I come'. Watching the burly firemen rush their suicide blanket after him, adjust and position for a neat catch, then racing to the other end.

'It makes you wonder about the Fire Service's success rate in such cases,' Henry remarked.

'Most people are probably more willing to be caught.'

'Even so, they were none too nimble.'

'The crowd and the bailiffs made the job difficult.'

'I cannot believe that there isn't usually a crowd of onlookers. If Colin had been in earnest, we'd be spreading him on our toast by now.'

The thought of Colin Rutt spread on toast was oddly appealing.

'Do you know where we are, Henry?'

'I haven't the slightest notion.'

'Is that St Oswig's?'

Skewed stone tongues above drenched grass. A slimy path. A perspiring tower.

'It has the look of it.'

'We can't be far from the ring-road. Those are the Queen's School playing fields: that's the Hallowe'en bonfire.'

'We shall be found in the morning. Little birds will have covered our bodies with leaves.'

Spongy turf. Mud dotted with boot-marks. The empty white rectangle of a netless goal. The first damp layers of the Hallowe'en bonfire.

'The drama,' Henry exclaimed, 'of his eventual leap!'

Sliding down the roof and then, with amazing confidence, arms spread – not a leap actually, more a collapse, onto a well-chosen section of those gathered below who, probably also having been to Knebworth, knew crowd-surfing when they saw it. Though the bailiffs and council officials apparently did not. Their plan appeared to have been either to arrest Colin Rutt for something or other (more police had been summoned), or to take him away to hospital (an ambulance was on stand-by): whichever seemed most appropriate. It was, quite obviously, a shock when Colin, splayed out, borne up by shoulders and palms, roller-coastered his way over waves of individuals to the edge of the assembled group and hot-footed it off. In the resultant commotion, the bailiffs let their cool slip; temporarily, but long enough for a swarm of people, led by Merlyn and Gary, to hurtle between them into the squat and jam pack themselves inside it.

'If the Weaver Street squat were a giant jelly-mould,' said Henry, 'one could have lifted it up, given it a little shake, and, behold: a perfectly-shaped house made entirely of people.'

'If the Weaver Street squat were a giant jelly-mould, Henry, do you think the little shake would be necessary?'

'You can briefly dip them in water.'

David and Henry stared, silently, at the dark criss-crosses of the Pitsbury Hallowe'en Bonfire, the annual lighting of which – by the incumbent Duchess of Pitsbury – traditionally marked the climax of a strange and anarchic day which, in spite of intense official pressure for them to do otherwise, most people – especially those who did not actually live in Pitsbury – greatly enjoyed. Every year there were calls for the event to be banned. Every year someone was rumoured to have been stabbed. Every year there were letters to the local newspaper. The bonfire, twenty feet across, was built by Queen's School first years, supervised by a master in a tracksuit. It was lit with a brand made from wood salvaged from the previous year's fire. Now, in this dense dome of fog, it was impossible to believe that those gleaming leaves and clammy branches could ever catch light.

'Why do you think the people went inside the squat, Henry?' asked David.

Had they, like him, experienced the desecration of something important and beautiful that to neglect it would be? Were human beings sometimes inspired, *en-masse*, towards goodness, just as they were, more often, inspired *en-masse* towards evil?

'The ant syndrome,' said Henry.

'The ant syndrome,' David repeated. 'You're going to have to enlighten me.'

'You've never studied ants?'

'Not everyone has, Henry.'

'Oh, you should. You'd be amazed. There are farming ants, harvester ants, hunters, herders, even slave-owners. They are capable of making nests constructed of nothing but themselves suspended from one another.'

'The relevance of this temporarily escapes me.'

'Are they one thing or many?' Henry turned to face David, eyebrows raised. 'Nest-wise, they act as one. For other purposes, they act as many.'

'They could be both.'

'Your guess is as good as mine. But people and ants behave with remarkable similarity.' Then, 'Watch my lips, David,' Henry said, 'Watch my lips. They are blue with cold. Everything I am is shivering and shrivelling.'

The bus station was a candyfloss of orange light. A solitary vehicle chugged. People sat inside it, dozing and yawning, waiting for the driver. All the other buses were switched off, dark and numberless.

The café was still there – getting on for twenty years later – still fulfilling the same function. There was the same old fug, the same smell of frying, the familiar gurgle of the cappuccino machine. Two young nurses were smoking cigarettes and drinking black coffees. There were cabbies. A uniformed driver, reading the *Sun*. A table of scarfed students, drunk and loud and showing off a little.

'What can I get you gentlemen?' wiping the formica with a j-cloth and swopping ashtrays, running a hand through grey hair, smiling through thickened features. 'Well stone me! It's Dave, isn't it?'

'It is.'

'What are you doing back in Pitsbury then? It must be, I don't like to think how long. You used to come in weekends, with the pretty blonde girl . . . what was her name?'

'Fay,' said David.

'So what can I get you?'

The nurses looked at their watches and got up from their table. The students lolled and laughed and tried to keep the night going.

'Or it could just be that people were loath to lose Gary's cooking,' said Henry, as a chip-filled net was plunged into sizzling oil. 'Since his seems to be the only cuisine which speaks to them.' He took a sip of cappuccino. 'A new door for the coal shed! I could weep. I nearly did. And, of course, it will be Bailiff Henry who picks up the splinters.'

Architecture. Food. The impulse to group together. Solid structures: creators of cities. Along with these, though, probably a whole host of spurious reasons, thought David: curiosity; the desire to impress, follow, piss off, be in on what happened next – an indefinite number of feelings and emotions could fit into one building. Anyway, too much attention as far as the officials were concerned. Horatio Bullock, Brian Baffle, Ms Court, the other council people, the police, had gone into a nodding, consultative cluster, occasionally looking over at the bailiffs – who had regained their Action Man stances – seeming suddenly aware that they might strike the watchers of the local news as not awfully benign-looking; and the team from Aspect South, now arriving, typically, after everything of interest was over, would have nothing much but them to show shots of.

David sighed. 'They'll be back.'

'Who will? David, do you think we dare a consolatory doughnut?'

'Bullock. The bailiffs.'

'Ah yes, but the drawbridge is up.'

Wooden eyelids in the windows again. Heavy objects against the doors. Ropes.

'And for me, too. I'm a squatter now, Henry.' With a shaky scaffolding of accountants and solicitors, who could prolong the process but not prevent it.

'At least you have your health.'

'Yes, at least I have that.'

'How about if we ask for one between us, and a knife to cut it in half with?'

When David and Henry had gone off on their walk, Colin came out of the priest's hole and Fay made them both scrambled eggs on toast.

It had been silly for Colin to be up there in the first place: if they'd wanted to arrest him or put him under psychiatric observation, it wouldn't have been hard for the authorities to ascertain his whereabouts. Probably, Fay thought, the reason they hadn't was because they didn't want to do anything that would draw media focus back to Weaver Street. Probably, Henry had realised this too and the thing he'd made about concealing Colin was really to do with Henry being upset about the door to the coal shed. Over the eggs, Colin told Fay that he hadn't minded it in the hole, anyway, so it didn't matter. He'd been very comfortable, actually; Merlyn Orb had made quite a nest up there: newspapers, orders and receipts, copies of *Snew?*, a battered old kettle, a chipped mug, cushions, a blanket, bits of chocolate, books, a flannel and a bowl and an old piece of soap to wash with.

When Colin left, Fay pulled the sitting-room curtains against the dark, floating night. She bent to put another log on the fire, which was a mass of orange embers.

Poor David, wanting air. Though Henry's presence would prevent excessive melancholy, in spite of the fact that he'd said he was only accompanying David because he couldn't stand to be in the same building as Colin Rutt a moment longer.

Fay collapsed into a kneeling position on the woven rug in front of the hearth. This is not my home, she thought, looking at the flames. Horatio Bullock is going to take it from me.

But that felt stark and incorrect and Horatio Bullock struck her as a red herring. Fay wished she could discuss what had happened with Ruth Carpini, but Ruth had said she wouldn't be around, and Fay had sort of got the feeling that she didn't want to meet up again. Talking to Ruth, though, Fay had felt like a capable adult. Partly, perhaps, because with new people you got to be whatever age you walked into their lives at: to Ruth Carpini, Fay wasn't twenty years old and David's wife. Possibly not to others, either.

Now, suddenly, it seemed to Fay that she had read herself through David's eyes for so long that she had overlooked another, equally valid, version of her story. Had the recent changes in David's attitude towards her, she wondered, been the result of David also coming to this realisation? Of seeing that Fay's career moves, which had led, as logically as if it had been planned, to Marsh Meadows and now the Internet, could be interpreted as not random, but intentional, albeit subconsciously so? Of eventually noticing that he didn't live with a wispy young girl any more, but a purposeful woman with clear ambitions and a life mapped out as much for herself as for David? It wasn't a different plot, but a different slant on it: another reading. And who, looking at the facts, looking at the emotions even, could say which was the more accurate, which Fay Marsh was the more authentic?

Maybe, it occurred to her, she shouldn't have felt intimidated by the thought of the courageous Friedaswida. Maybe it was wrong always to place herself at the window of history, watching events unfold, shaped by others. Mightn't an early Fay have been at the doorway with the rest of the women, helping hold back what they didn't want to enter, protecting whatever sheltered within? Might she have been the one who the perceptive Friedaswida had had her eye on, ever since she was a novice, to take up the mantel of Abbess?

The telephone rang into a silence broken only by the crackling of the fire and the ticking of the clock.

'Could you tell me what is going on?'

'I'm sorry?' said Fay.

'This is Tony Gilbert.'

'Oh. I should have recognised your voice, Tony. This is Fay. David isn't here at the moment.'

'Isn't he?' Tony Gilbert sounded as if he wasn't sure he believed her. 'I'm phoning from the café. There are problems with the line to the chateau. Immie Canning is tearing her hair out and Roo's taken it upon himself to drive to Nice, in the Ferrari, to give France Telecom a bollocking in the morning.'

'Oh dear,' said Fay.

'So we didn't need to be confronted with anyone else's inefficiency. For aeons I'd been waiting for that volume of Provençal poetry David's employee swore he'd send to us. I say *I*, but actually we'd all been on tenterhooks: since Roo had had to take over the direction of *A Right Wonderful Error*, after the horrible let-down by Zucchini, he'd felt he just couldn't call the re-think terminated before we'd dealt with a variable as crucial as the score is. It was agony convincing him otherwise. Then, what arrives this morning, much too late to be of any use, addressed just to the Comte, France, no post code (which explains the inordinate delay): a copy of *A Right Wonderful Error* which, since we're filming it, you will not be surprised to know we have scripts in abundance of; tucked into it, a grubby, smudgy, aggressive sheet, entitled *Snew?*; and a book about the sardine industry. Well, Immie just burst into tears.'

There was a silence.

'I'm not really responsible for David's business,' said Fay, in a faltering voice. Perhaps it was the stresses of the day that were causing terrible coils of threatening laughter to form in the pit of her stomach. 'You didn't speak to David about the Provençal poetry? You spoke to Merlyn?'

'I didn't speak to David. I don't recall the name of the person I did talk to.'

'It must have been Merlyn, Tony. He's rather . . . um . . . lateral. Did you mention Rupert and Immie Canning to him?'

'I forget. Possibly.'

'Well that might have been what confused him and made him think of sardines.'

There was a pause.

'I fail to see how the two great luminaries of the British theatre could make anybody think of sardines,' said Tony Gilbert. Fay clapped her hand over the mouthpiece. 'Hello? Hello? Are you still there?'

'Yes, I'm still here, Tony. I've got a cold and it makes me sneeze sometimes.'

'We've all got colds, too. Particularly nasty ones. Immie's face is a mass of blotches.'

'Tony, if you give me your address again, I'll make sure David sends the book out tomorrow.'

'Oh, as I say, it's too late for that. We're running over budget, which is how Immie managed to persuade Roo to opt for the usual Tudor – it's rare for Roo to make artistic concessions. Though he wasn't happy about it. Not at all happy. It took a lot of soul-searching for him to come to terms with it. At least, that's what we assume he was doing; he was gone for twenty-four hours. Then, that got over, the sardine book arrives and it feels like the last straw.'

'Tony,' said Fay, in a desperate attempt to change the subject, 'I met Ruth Carpini.'

There was a pause.

'Ruth Carpini? Whatever is she doing back here?' Tony sounded astonished.

'Back?'

'She broke her arm, in several places, and was forced to return home. Pitsbury College, Canada . . .'

'Pitsbury College, Canada . . . ?'

A smirk appeared in Tony Gilbert's voice.

'Pitsbury College, Canada, sent over her colleague, Clementine Dee, as replacement.'

Slowly, Fay put down the receiver.

18

Trouble In Provence

A week spent doing London, as if London was a verb and not a noun, with a girlfriend from Languages, *en route* for a semester's guest lectureship at the Sorbonne. It had made Clementine feel like a person again with a bright and lively context; not just a silent academic haunting a dusty office in Bus Station House, trying to get enough of a hold of a bit of Mowbray before it was auctioned off and buried among the rest of some rich guy's stash.

She'd stock-piled Top-Value Tibbles – New Rabbit Flavour In a Rich Jelly. ('Hey look, Ol,' she'd said to Oliver, showing him the can, 'you get to eat *new* rabbit, not old, clapped-out rabbit like I'll bet some cats do.') She'd arranged, at a stupid price, for one of Tony's neighbours' kids to come and feed Oliver once a day, and check the spider plants hadn't dried out too much. She'd left keys, phoned up, phoned in, set papers, faxed Ruth, called a taxi.

London glittered and vibrated. By day it was pearly, at night it was accordions of neon. Clementine played the game of academic-about-town – both her and her friend all thin heels, lots of plum and chocolate and white wine in cafés in Covent Garden, while music student chamber orchestras ground away like crazy.

It didn't work, of course. Her heart was broken and, along with it, those notions of self she'd boasted of to David back in

April. *Where to place your love is in part a decision like any other.* And Clementine Dee made cool, rational decisions, didn't she? Right! Like falling in love with a married man. (Dippy.) Like coming back to Pitsbury. Like entwining herself so much in the place that, as the filthy train shed wiser mortals at more accessible locations, even as she waited for her connection, on a draughty platform, sipping brown liquid from a plastic cup, Clementine's spirits mounted. Pitsbury was some sort of home, simply because it was where she'd best loved someone. That love had settled all over Pitsbury, like this wretched British rain – minute droplets that turned the cathedral, now coming into view, into a mass of seething atoms just beginning to be singed by a pale sun.

The buildings looked spattered. The trees were losing their auburn tints. Then the train entered the Victorian palace of a station – metal filigree and rose windows. Doors opened. Clementine looped her light, woman-who-knows-how-to-pack-to-travel bag over her shoulder and got out.

She felt the excitement immediately. Pitsbury was small enough to be filled up with it; in London, you met excitement in pockets, each with its own discrete cause, its fading boundaries. Here, when something was in the air it had one cause only. Which was what, Clementine guessed, was meant by provincialism.

Being Canadian, not British, she collared a railway worker.

'What's happening?'

'Leaves on the line.'

Clementine could never get over the enchantment the British had with their climate, each season treated like the first of its kind. Had leaves not fallen on the rails every autumn since there had been rails for them to fall on?

'No, I mean, is something happening?'

'All Souls.'

Then he started waving an arm and blowing his whistle.

As an explanation, this wasn't up to much. As a phrase, however, it had a doleful resonance. And anyway, by the time Clementine had walked to the centre of town, to have lunch and wander around some before getting a taxi back to the Ebb Valley, the posters all over had explained it.

Evening service in the cathedral, attended by Harriet, Duchess of Pitsbury. Official Hallowe'en Bonfire Lighting at midnight, at the Queen's School Playing Fields, by Harriet, Duchess of Pitsbury. Official Fireworks. Numerous side events in the streets of Pitsbury – most of which, Clementine discovered, had been cordoned off to traffic – and in the cathedral precinct.

A Pork Roast, organised by the Pitsbury Round Table, was being set up, the rain now having stopped, just inside the cathedral gate. Fresh-faced young fathers were applying matches to wood-chips; one of them was trying to get an apple to stay in the mouth of the pig carcass. The Guides' stand, due to sell buttered sowans, Thor cakes and champ, was also in place; the cold sowans and champ in giant saucepans, ready to be hotted up on a primus. The posters also advertised Bobbing For Apples for the Mentally Handicapped; W.I. hand-knits, in aid of the Homeless; a Children's Procession Of Turnip And Pumpkin Lanterns; Trick-Or-Treat Fancy Dress, With Prizes; Souling Songs, Performed By The Pitsbury Players; and a Pie And Mushy Pea Stall, laid on by the Cock and Hen. In passing, the posters mentioned that most pubs would have extensions and that there would be A Parade Of Brotherhoods.

The interior of the cathedral was full of blond light and echoes, and mouse-women, sorting sheets and hymnals and arranging chrysanthemums with curled, pink fingers. A thunder of voluntary started and stopped.

'I think you are fond of our cathedral?' said a voice beside her.

It was the tall Canon in the long black cloak, who had nodded at Clementine that night in April when she was taking one of her secret walks in the locked precinct.

'Today, I'll have to admit, I'm here out of plain curiosity. About All Souls.'

'An event with many aspects.' The Canon smiled. 'It sounds so wholesome. And, of course, they publicise it as such. In vain. That is, perhaps, a consequence of appropriating someone else's festival: it's imbued with a vestigial paganism.'

'Celtic, aren't they, the bonfire festivals?'

'I believe so. Though at the cathedral we claim today, All Souls Eve, for those saints – unlike our Oswig and Friedaswida – who have no day allocated to be their own. Then tomorrow, All Souls Day, for everyone who has died, remembered or forgotten: a kind of all-encompassing spiritual tabulation, like the general blessing.'

'And the paganism?'

'Yes, that is where, with respect, popular interest mostly lies. Pub extensions. Drunkenness. Fights between the Brotherhoods and between others. Conflagrations.'

'Misrule.'

'Doubtless it has its function. Probably it will continue long after Christianity has vanished.' Again, the Canon smiled. He sauntered away in a shush of garments.

Curious, thought Clementine, this British capacity for double-think. She could only suppose that the race that had painted the planet with empire, littered it with colonies, had taken as its motto 'The Show Must Go On'. Which required the adaptability and compromise that, in their turn, resulted in the world-weary cynicism which seemed to Clementine the best characteristic of the British. North American optimism was so brittle, so unyielding.

She walked past fluttering Catholic candles, beneath the arched window where Pitsbury's Medieval bakers were preparing the Last Supper.

It was late afternoon. The clouds had dissolved. The sky cleared. The temperature tobogganed down.

'Be all right for the fireworks tonight,' said the taxi-driver.

Before she'd even got out of the car, Clementine knew that someone had arrived at Tony Gilbert's. The lights were on inside.

She scrambled out. There was lots of slamming of doors and getting of luggage, counting of change, thanking for tip. The taxi pulled away. A flinty arrow of geese honked above, flying south. There was the sound of a distant dog barking.

It could be the cat-feeding kid. But she bicycled down in her jodhpurs after pony club, and Clementine couldn't see any bicycle. The garden gate was just a little open. It could be Fay Marsh, let in to wait for her by the cat-feeding kid, who knew that Clementine was coming back today. Or someone from the university, though it was doubtful they'd have stuck around in her absence.

Or it could be David.

You played out scenarios in your brain, time after time, almost without being aware you were doing so. *Clementine opened the front door. She put her things down. The house was warm, not cold and unlived-in. The curled form of Oliver glistened in panes of sunlight. A kettle was coming to the boil. There, standing by the kitchen table, just for this moment unaware of her presence, the worn, handsome form of David Marsh.*

The sleek, cross figure of Tony Gilbert. On the table, a letter-opener. In one hand, a sheaf of letters. In the other, a tin of New Rabbit Flavoured Top-Value Tibbles.

Gilbert swung round.

'What is this? Where are Oliver's "Yum-Yums"?'

The *ancien régime* was back. Oliver opened his eyes and gave a look of such pathos that, had he been a child-star, it would have won him an Oscar. It even seemed to Clementine that he sucked in his bulbous stomach in a vain attempt to reveal some ribs.

'He does okay on "Tibbles".'

'He's lost weight.'

'He needed to.'

'And you've altered the temperature of the freezer, and both the temperature *and* the timing of the heating system.'

'Tony, did you honestly expect me to live here a whole year without changing anything?'

'Yes, yes, yes.'

'Well I couldn't, couldn't, couldn't.'

Gilbert started grinding coffee beans with an exactitude that set Clementine's teeth on edge.

'So, where have you been, Clementine?' He'd evidently decided to go off on another tack.

'London, for a week.'

'Leaving Oliver to starve!' Gilbert was unable to prevent himself from bursting out again.

'Leaving Oliver to be fed, daily, by the kid of one of your neighbours.'

'You've changed, too, Clementine. And it's not just the hair-cut.' Gilbert was a man who thought women liked it when he made personal observations about them. 'You've become cooler, less easy-going.' He percolated in silence, leaving Clementine to ponder this insight.

A – predictably – completely wrong one. No less easy-going, just less willing, at this precise moment, to put herself out any for Tony Gilbert. Cooler? Well only a hundred and eighty degrees off there, Tone.

He'd scattered stuff everywhere, marking his territory, letting it be clear whose cottage this was. There were three unopened bags in a corner of the kitchen, an open one on the table, half-unpacked. Books and scripts from out of it mingled with Clementine's own books and Mowbray notes, left neatly on the table and the dresser, now knocked askew. A chic carrier was also half-emptied; floured saucisson, oozy cheese, brioches, baguettes, a pink, beribboned, patissier's box – all well and good in their place – seeped, leaked and crumbled among Clementine's things. A gaping grip on the floor revealed puffy white shirts. There was a case of wine bottles. Another, full of some other kind of liquor. The open washing machine was choked with dirty laundry. Chestnut leather boots leaned sideways. There were cufflinks every which way.

'Skimmed or semi-skimmed?' asked Gilbert.

'Neither, I just had some.'

Gilbert seated himself at the table with his coffee.

'So: London,' he said.

'Yeah.'

'Let me guess: Oxford Street, the Tower, Hyde Park Corner, the Changing of the Guard, Harrods.'

'Actually, not. Covent Garden, the new wing of the National, the Museum of the Garden, Neal Street, Soho, the South Bank and the new Globe. You've seen the new Globe, I guess?'

'Well, no, I haven't. I've been tied up with other projects.'

Now it occurred to Clementine to ask what Tony was doing back in England.

'You mean you haven't seen? You haven't heard? From what I've gathered, it's been headlines in the English press – and the American, and on their network television news – ever since three days ago, when the ghastly story broke.'

'I haven't read a paper or watched TV for a week. Maybe I

noticed something about the Cannings on a news-stand, but I didn't pay it any special attention.'

'Well it's been bloody. Absolutely bloody. And it doesn't help to come home and discover my heating system has been fiddled with.'

'What's been bloody, Tony?'

Gilbert took a sip of coffee and stood up. He got two wine glasses and two small tumblers out of a cupboard, inspected them for smears, and pulled a bottle out of each of the cases on the floor.

'I can't even begin to talk about it without some plonk.' He took the bottle opener down from its little hook and removed a cork. 'I say plonk, but actually this is a wine Roo discovered at a small co-operative miles from anywhere, and if the London restaurants ever got wind of it, they could sell it at silly prices. It's young but full of character. This,' pulling the stopper out of the other bottle, 'is another of Roo's finds. It's made of walnuts steeped in *eau-de-vie*.'

'None for me, Tony, I'm driving later.'

Gilbert poured himself a large glass of each, took a swig of the wine and did strange, hamster things with his cheeks and lips for a few moments.

'It was blown up out of all proportion,' he said, eventually.

As the tale unfolded, this proved to be one of Tony's few observations with which Clementine was inclined to agree, though for a different reason: in choosing a focus for its attention, the world's media might have occupied itself somewhat better than with the marital upheavals of Roo and Immie Canning.

Along with her many other talents, Gilbert informed Clementine, Immie was a quite superb cook. (In fact, she was toying with the idea of a cookery programme, with accompanying book.) Cassoulet. Confit. Gratins. And she was not tall. Though internal fuel was needed against the bitter cold, and most people thought a little *rondeur* became Immie rather. But if you were a man with the looks and stature of Roo, well, women threw themselves at you. Not that this was a question of a woman as such, though the French girls did mature earlier than their British and American counterparts. Zucchini's protegée,

Veronique Poubelle, had been around for some time. Ever since, in fact, she had starred at the age of fourteen (opposite Gamin) in *Les Enfants qui Pleurent*, an opalescent evocation of lost innocence which was showered with praise by the critics. Now, at nearly seventeen, Veronique was no more inhibited or aware than a wild kitten. So it was crass to dub what had happened as a tawdry *affaire* between her and Roo; it had more been a mutual, totally unselfconscious, physical exploration. If you'd forced Tony to give you an adjective – Clementine did not, but he furnished one anyway – he would have characterised the whole business as 'holy'.

This was not how Immie Canning had viewed it, however, when the photographs of Roo and Veronique, very much together in Nice, appeared in *Paris Match*. Though, as far as Gilbert was concerned, if there had to be recriminations, it was probably Immie's paranoia about her hips and the – rather good, but insensitively conceived – solo adaptation she'd just completed of *Vanity Fair* that had driven Roo to perform holy acts upon *la jolie Veronique* in his Ferrari.

Zucchini was gone. Roo was distraught about his potential knighthood. (Tony poured himself another large glass of wine and of walnut stuff.) Immie flew into Gatwick, in a flurry of solicitors. Veronique Poubelle was rumoured to be negotiating a nude spread in British and American *Playboy*. The whole Mowbray project was put on ice and the entire crew – which had been so *close*, so *integrated* – mooched home with their bags of duty-frees and their *pains au chocolat*.

At this bitter thought Tony speedily drained his wine glass in a careless fashion, which Clementine fancied he thought looked French, and filled it up again. She watched him in silence, wondering what implications Gilbert's return would have for the Quik-Potato Visiting Fellowship. The Fellowship stipulated that the visiting academic should reside in the property of an absent British colleague. Did it have a clause which addressed the eventuality of the British colleague's unexpected return? And even if it could be squared with Quik-Potato, sharing a house with Tony Gilbert for an entire academic year could not be contemplated.

'So what are you planning on doing next, Tony?'

'Next?' Gilbert had got himself a plate, and a knife with two erect triangular spikes. He now proceeded to tear off peasanty hunks of bread in a lava of crumbs. 'Clementine, this is a famous French cheese, it's been made for centuries in an identical way.'

'I just ate, Tony.'

'You must be unafraid of trying new things.'

'What are you planning on doing next, Tony?'

Gilbert was now rough-hewing the saucisson. It occurred to Clementine that people such as him should never travel.

'I'll tell you what I thought,' he said. 'What say I grab a couple of hours of shut-eye while you prepare some vegetables and defrost us a couple of steaks? Then I'll Béarnaise it up for us and we'll open a bottle of Beauje.'

The idea of Gilbert fiddling around with egg-yolks was awful.

'Actually, Tony, I thought I'd spend the evening in Pitsbury. It's the Hallowe'en celebrations tonight.'

There was a pause.

Then, 'Oh, all right,' said Gilbert.

'"Oh, all right" what?'

'Oh, all right, we'll go and see your fireworks.'

There was another pause.

'No, Tony, I couldn't ask you to do that after your travelling. Anyway, I was kind of planning on going alone.'

A silence.

'I see,' said Gilbert, in a nettled voice.

He took a gulp of coffee, then a gulp of walnut stuff. Clementine suddenly realised that somewhere in Gilbert's luggage lurked a blue peasant beret that he'd have purchased at some market and, as soon as he'd got properly unpacked – Jesus, perhaps tonight even – he'd be wandering around in it, telling people how functional they were.

'Can I give you a piece of advice, Clementine?'

'No, Tony.'

Gilbert reached across the table and grabbed her hand.

'We both know what's standing in the way.'

'In the way?'

'Of us.'

He let her hand drop and pulled off some more baguette, keeping his eyes upon her face.

'Us?'

She might have guessed Tony would favour the lunge. Clark Gable. John Wayne. She was expected to hammer at his big chest with her little fists, and then succumb.

'If you do not get your two hairy mits, and everything else, over the other side of this table in no minutes flat, I am going to ensure that you never have grandchildren.' Though Mother Nature looked like she was doing a pretty switched-on job of ensuring that anyway. Gilbert had evidently been kneed in the groin enough times in his life to be inclined to give Clementine the benefit of the doubt.

'I see you're still besotted with him.'

Reproachfully, Gilbert snipped the pink ribbon of the patissier's box with a pair of grape scissors, revealing a three-storey caramelised construction.

'I am "besotted" with no one.'

'Oh you are. But it's no good, you know.' Gilbert poured a fourth glass of wine, or was it a fifth? He bit into the caramel thing. Confectioner's cream adhered to his upper lip. 'You will find in life, Clementine, that the moral act is, most usually, also the expedient one. It was only right to nip it in the bud.'

A chill ran across Clementine's whole body. A cold calm. Was it possible that David had confided in Tony Gilbert?

'What do you mean?'

'You haven't met Henry Pearl, have you? Gay.' There was a pause for her to appreciate his liberalism. 'Gossip, like they are. All I had to do was to mention something to him about you and Marsh to be sure that it would get back to Fay – that's Marsh's wife. Though I gave the impression that Fay had met you, on the off-chance that Pearl might feel he should cover for David, or spare Fay's feelings.'

'And why did you do this, Tony?'

'For you. For us. Ultimately, for David and Fay. No good can come of deception and marriage-breaking. Forewarned was forearmed in Fay's case. There must have been discussion and negotiation. I'm sure the relationship was stronger as a result. Built on much solider, less assailable, foundations.'

'And you feel yourself qualified to interfere in such matters?'

'I've been around a bit, which makes it incumbent upon me to intervene where I feel my guidance is necessitated. Have you heard from David?'

Automatically, Clementine shook her head.

'In that case then I'm totally vindicated. He's known for at least a week that you're in the area. Perhaps longer. Unless of course Fay hasn't mentioned it, and that's unlikely. If he was going to make a move he'd have done so by now.'

'Fay knows it's me?'

'And not Ruth Carpini? Yes. I can be sure of that. You see, I was the one who told her. What are you doing? Good God, woman! I'll have you know, that cost sixteen francs.'

'Well how's about we take it off what you owe me for Ol's "Tibbles"?'

'They're baked fresh daily by a woman who's nearing ninety. Clementine. Clementine. If you do anything to that saucisson, I'm afraid it may threaten our continuing to live together.'

'See this saucisson, Tone? Let's imagine – we're not talking size now, you understand – let's imagine it's part of your anatomy. Let's imagine this cheese knife is even blunter than it is.'

'Are you expecting your period, Clementine?'

The knife went hurtling into a corner.

'How could you do it, Tony? How could you do that to Fay and David, just on the off-chance it might facilitate you getting your leg over? Can't you imagine what they'll both have gone through?'

A phone call for a taxi. The strange lightness of empty suitcases, pulled off the top of the wardrobe, out from under the bed. The flu-day outfits, handfuls of underwear, spring layers, summer cottons. Letters, essential oils, nail-clippers, hose, earrings. Then, from the dresser, from the kitchen table, covered in grease and crumbs, cream, pastry, caramel: Mowbray notes, hardbacks, paperbacks; pored over, unread, pencilled in the margins, pages marked with bits of torn newspaper.

Gilbert watched; sipped self-righteously. The door-bell rang. Clementine counted her bags, checked her credit cards and cash.

'Your keys, Tony. Bye Ol.' A quick towzle of his fat head.

The taxi took her back up the lane, along the floor of the Ebb Valley. The sky was dark. Clementine opened her window a crack. The air smelled of gunpowder. Far off, a white firework effervesced, low on the horizon. She caught the sound of its desperate wail.

He had not come. David had known she was here and he had not come. Until now, Clementine hadn't been aware what a powerful comfort her invisibility had been to her. If David didn't know she was in Pitsbury, then there was a reason – an excuse – for him not to act. But if he did know, and still did nothing . . .

Clementine thought of Hermia Mowbray. A saucy face. An arched eyebrow. Plays, poems and fragments.

I must gather myself up again. I must amass the pieces and re-construct in a way that makes sense. I must figure out why what fetched-up where it did. A kind of spiritual tabulation.

It did not seem too bad that some saints had to do without their own days – they still got to be saints, for chrissake. But those anonymous departed souls, stuffed into twenty-four hours; that was so sad, if she didn't watch out she'd start bawling about it.

So she looked through the window at the vanished landscape, the cold sky, beginning to be littered with dead stars. So intently that she did not notice that the taxi passed a Volvo driven by David Marsh, travelling in the opposite direction.

19 $\int$

The Going Away Pattern

There was a theory about the human foetus that David always used to find implausible: that, while in the womb, it passed through all the evolutionary stages that the species had stopped off at *en route* to becoming *homo sapiens*. Now, however, re-enactment struck him as a tiresomely integral part of human development; he remembered, from some distant lesson, that the French word for *rehearsal* was *répétition*. Over and over until, one day, you got it right, or at least a few more bits of it right than you had before.

David had returned from the bus station café, intending to tell Fay about the pretty girl she was remembered as there, to a scene that could have been summoned up by the memory. Bitterly sipping wine. Blotchy. Worst of all, unforthcoming and silent. Something was wrong but, as of old, no words were spoken: it was all soggy atmosphere. And this had seemed a bit much on the day that had transformed penury from hazy threat to house guest. There was some tired bickering. Loaded sighs. In bed, they lay awake, back to back. David fell asleep well after a wretched, damp dawn had fuzzed away the darkness.

Day two, they wallowed in the swamp. Day three, they both went out. David to the Cock and Hen, which appeared to be stock-piling mushy peas, presumably against some imminent Armageddon. Fay to God knows where, but she came back with a basketful of terrible roots which, sadly, proved edible.

Day four, David rediscovered satire which Fay smothered in reproach, but at least she had stopped crying. Day five, there was a Weaver Street meeting about future strategy in relation to the squat. Fay rediscovered language. Day six, she went to Rick's to use the Net. David consulted a solicitor about their financial situation. They discussed it that evening.

Today, day seven, All Hallows Eve, dawned icky but cleared into a great, glassy chill. They went walking together in the afternoon, Fay's hand light in the crook of David's arm; her idea.

The streets were filling rapidly with a mixture of people, some belonging to the impending occasion, some not.

Office men and women in raincoats and suits queued in Cagmag's for things to grill. Yobs stood in pub doorways with pints, or grouped in the pedestrianised areas, gulping from cans, swearing, throwing sparklers. Burly choristers strode towards the cathedral. Vicars and their behatted wives, in puces, mauves and emeralds, early for the service in case of traffic jams and parking problems, wandered the precinct making polite comments to Guides who were selling flapjacks and slight portions of lukewarm mashed potato. A man carved a mahogany pig, watched by a Danté-esque line of people. There was a large police presence. Wardens in luminous jackets checked the passes of the few cars admitted. In the back of one there was a purple flash of Archbishop.

By the corner of a curving side street, on a brazier of glowing coals, a chestnut-seller turned nuts with a narrow shovel, emptied scoops into brown paper bags. They tasted burnt and bitter and sweet and musty.

Scattered along the path by the Ebb were the large yellow leaves, teardrop-shaped, that children make herring-bones out of.

At the precise moment that the bells started ringing, the cathedral was switched on, the bridges, churches, Roman ruins flooded with illumination, Fay said, 'You don't love me any longer, David. Not like you love Clementine.'

'You can't go down there, I'm afraid, sir. It's cordoned off for the Duchess.'

'Then how do you suggest I get to the taxi-rank?'

A group of pirates, one falling-down drunk – intense early drinking, a tradition among the Brotherhoods – surged forward at that moment. A burning torch catherine-wheeled through the air. People screamed. A bottle was broken. The upsurge was caused by the parade of a rival Brotherhood – Spaniards. Police pushed into the hubbub. From what David had heard, the Pitsbury Brotherhoods with their boozing and fights and stealing of each other's bonfires, spent the rest of the year working in insurance offices and making their exotic costumes. People said the tradition went back to an ancient, atavistic fear of the foreign which bravado dictated should be trounced by emulation of it. People said the tradition went back to a group of shipwrecked, persecuted, Catalonians who, for some reason, had settled in Pitsbury in the fourteenth century bringing the remnants of an earlier festival. People said the tradition went back to 1930 when it had been thought up by a bored naturalist.

'How do you suggest I get to the taxi-rank?' David repeated to the policeman, who was trying to pull a bleeding pirate to his feet.

'No point, sir,' over his shoulder. 'Town's closed to all traffic for at least another hour.'

Flanked by a grim guard of parents and Brown Owls, a hundred or so bobbing heads went by, their hollow, orange and white interiors lit by candles. Grinning, gaping, skeleton features. Single, skewed teeth. Globules of floating shadow.

In the interior of an ageing Rolls was Horatio Bullock, plus Gloria, the Lady Mayoress.

'Would you like to give a contribution to The Mission to Seamen?' asked a tweed-haired woman at David's elbow, trying to press a sticker onto his sheepskin coat.

He had to get to Clementine. Now. This minute. David had the sense that the two of them were standing in the brief, honey spotlight of life while, from all sides, twitching arms of darkness pulled and pawed and tugged. Even now, Clementine could be being walked backwards, away from him – waist encircled, breast clamped, limbs pinioned – by the hideous, triumphant, secret police, army, undercover agents of chance, randomness, disease, etc.

Etc.

Bo-peep. Humpty-Dumpty. A plethora of lazy-mothered ghosts in sheets with eye-holes. Quite a few more (miniature) pirates. Gypsies, tramps and beggars. Lumbering through the waves of the procession, a slow iceberg of ambulance. Crowds of people, choc-a-bloc down to Weaver Street and beyond.

Burping police radios.

'Someone's been stabbed,' said a woman.

A child was crying.

David thought of Alice in Wonderland, when all the cards fly at her. He wanted to be Colin Rutt, swimming his way along the streets of Pitsbury, leaping from rooftop to rooftop among empty martins' nests and stairs of smoke. He wanted to be the sound of bells, hurtling through the cold air.

Two large brigands upended the Mentally Handicappeds' Apple Bobbing barrel, soaked ghosts and nursery-rhyme characters. Gleaming apples bounced on the cobbles, tripped up a Pitsbury Player dressed as a Souler, who dropped his horse's head, interrupting the other Players in the midst of a Souling Song ('*Fu canny is the steering mon/Wa kens his gless o' strither*').

Excited cries. The crowd leaned and tipped and David found his head pressed against the window of a monstrous, sleek, black vehicle, contained within which was Harriet, Duchess of Pitsbury in a hat the shape of a flowerpot. Beside her, holding hands, a white-suited man, who could have been appropriated from an aftershave advertisement.

A plain-clothes person pulled David away, evidently fearing that his obvious adoration of the Duchess might inspire him to perform undesirable acts.

'Is there no means of getting out of Pitsbury?'

'Well I don't reckon she'll give you a lift, sir.' Guffaws.

David got boxed in by a tortuous construction of metal scaffolding, awnings, trestle-tables, vats and burners.

'We've got meat and carrot, meat and potato or meat and curry spice. You can have red or brown sauce on your peas.'

'I don't want a pie.'

'Single or double peas?'

'I don't want peas either.'

'Then what are you queuing for, mate?'

There were a couple of drunks – a mariner and a pirate –

fighting, in slow motion, in the Ebb. They were attempting fisticuffs but gave the impression of some Japanese martial art where you fell your opponent without ever actually touching them. Of course, the bridge was blocked solid with gormless watchers.

Henry Pearl was seated in his kitchen, drinking a cup of lapsang souchong and reading Proust.

'Colin's off guzzling toffee apples but I cannot stand the bangs and the throng.'

'Lend me the Volvo, Henry.'

'You know she isn't happy in third, and she is rather low to the ground, so don't bottom her. Though I have no idea how on earth you're going to get out of Pitsbury.'

'Neither have I at present.'

Henry jangled keys. 'I am thinking scratches. I am thinking finger-marks. Could this not, perchance, wait until Pitsbury is one giant hangover and the streets are deserted?'

'Henry, I'm in love ... I'm in love.' David said it twice, because it felt like a shouting avalanche.

'Does Fay know?'

'Yes. She's all right about it.'

'Then tell. *Do* tell! But what am I saying, when all you want is to hasten?' Henry placed the keys in David's palm and gave it a little pat. 'But at least let me know the name of the lady. It *is* a lady?'

'It is, Henry. Her name is Clementine Dee.'

'She lurks in my consciousness, for some reason.'

'She's bloody invaded mine.'

'The tank's full but, remember, she's not happy in third.'

'Wot's up?' Colin Rutt was holding a beehive of candyfloss in one hand and a hot-dog in the other.

'Curtains!' Henry exclaimed. 'For Sven and Barney. Candy-floss chiffon.'

'I'm borrowing the Volvo, Colin. I've got to get to the Ebb Valley.'

'You'll never make it out of Weaver Street, Dave. There's two Brotherhoods giving each other knuckle sandwiches city wall end. Tun'v rozzers. Coupla vans they're putting the ones they've arrested in.'

'But surely someone's getting through?' cried Henry. 'Surely, our Emergency Services . . . ?'

''Mergency, yeah, probly.'

'And is not *Love* an emergency?'

'Henry, I cannot believe that the Pitsbury Constabulary would view it as such.'

'Baby. 'Pendix.' Colin took a bite of his hot-dog.

'Well we can't, with any credibility, do baby, so it will have to be appendix. But bags I be patient. David, driver. Colin, succour.'

'Sucker?'

'Help. Comfort in time of trouble. He has *no* education.'

Valuable moments were wasted while Henry rubbed flour into his face, for a look of pallor, and put on an exquisite pair of white silk pyjamas (hand-made in India) and an embroidered, Chinese dressing-gown.

'You only need a cigarette holder, Henry, and you could pass for Noël Coward.'

'Oh, thank-you! Thank-you!'

'Yes, but this is not the impression we are attempting to give. You must try to look frightened and distraught.'

'I shall think of the coal shed door. Not that blanket, Colin: it's so army.'

'There's a long hold-up, sir. We're advising motorists to delay their trips.'

'This isn't a trip, officer.'

'Nah,' said Colin Rutt, aggressively from the back, nearly spoiling everything. 'It's a 'mergency.'

'We suspect our friend has a ruptured appendix,' said David.

The policeman peered in through the window at where Henry Pearl, half propped against Colin, wilted, iridescent beneath a woven throw.

'Coal shed,' muttered Colin. Henry gave a pathetic wail, more suggestive of inner angst than pain.

'Excuse me, sir?'

'Ruptured,' said Colin. 'Right through, more likely than not.'

Now Henry gave a shriek of real pain. 'If you do that again, Colin, I swear . . .'

'He's delirious,' said David.

The policeman made a decision, spoke rapidly into his radio.

'It's like the parting of the Red Sea. And then all the Egyptians, or was it the Israelites . . . ?'

'Do shut up, Henry.'

'That's right: shower me with thanks. *Grace à* Colin here, I doubt I shall be able to wear anything tighter than a yashmak for over a month.'

David dropped them off by a narrow bridge, the other side of St Friedaswida's. Pitsbury was a bonfire of lights.

'You'll be all right getting back?'

'We'll stroll along the river. Who knows? It might even be romantic.'

'Here's your coat, Henry. I hope you don't get any problems over the pyjama trousers.'

'People will think we are our own little Brotherhood. We shall skirt through back alleys in utter secret, then we shall gather up a Chablis and visit Fay.'

'I'd appreciate that. I appreciate everything.'

'Be off, you're supposed to be ardent.'

The receding city sent flares, screams and low shouts into the darkness. Soon, these subsided. David drove through a domed landscape with only the lights of a few thinly scattered cottages and barn-conversions to interrupt it.

He thought of Clementine. He thought of Fay. He thought of how these two women had woven the fabric of his life and had therefore been able to perceive in it patterns which he, himself, had not been able to perceive.

'The going away pattern,' Fay had called it. A dance with mirrored footsteps. She loves him. He is indifferent to her. She is indifferent to him. He loves her.

Though this was a simplification of the real situation. Fay had not loved, she had obsessed. David had not been indifferent, merely minimally affectionate. So, gradually, Fay had got interested in other things, which had filled the space that her obsession had once occupied. Freed from the claustrophobia of the relationship, David had begun to respect and admire his wife again. He had been willing to call this rediscovered emotion, 'love'. And, had there been no one else, Fay said, that might have been wise – it was comfortable, kind, would have stood the course.

Almost, for a while, in the awful tangle of feelings, walking with his wife by the river, David had thought that maybe he loved her and Clementine both the same, or Fay more, perhaps, because of what had existed between them.

'I know what you mean, David. I've experienced it myself. All this week I've been trying to be the person I used to be. I tried and tried to be upset and jealous . . .'

'The performance was impeccable. I must admit to having been convinced.'

'But I couldn't keep it up – and you wouldn't be able to keep up thinking you were still in love with me. There were roots . . .'

'Please, Fay, I beg you, since we appear to be standing amidst the debris of our marriage, if roots are your major consolation for the situation, refrain from listing the others, I fear it might depress me.'

An orange rocket sped up the sky and shredded. David rubbed the corners of his eyes.

'But they're not consolations, Davey, they're replacements – the Net, the Web, Marsh Meadows . . .'

'Will they be enough, though?'

The thin hand stiffened. A brand new annoyance brought a sharpness to Fay's voice.

'You aren't my only available future, David. There's nothing that says only one of us gets to be happy.'

Available future.

But was Clementine available still? David thought of tight-jeaned undergraduates, academics, ski-tanned Canadians, viscounts, rock singers, poets, farm-hands, rugby-players.

The road along the bottom of the Ebb Valley was deserted. The only other vehicle David passed was a taxi. The lights were on in Tony Gilbert's cottage, however. On in almost every room, in fact. A beacon, drawing him in, illuminating a future which had seemed impossible. David knocked on the door, heard footsteps, took a deep breath.

'So you've come crawling back, have you? I thought you probably would. I've even started . . .'

'Tony?'

'David?'

There was a pause.

'You'd better come in,' said Tony Gilbert, turning and leaving David to follow through a house that looked as if it had just been searched by a particularly assiduous drug-squad. On the kitchen table, amongst strewn books, papers and breadcrumbs were two slabs of frozen steak, apparently put there to defrost, in the process of being licked by a large cat. Steam was rising from a saucepan. There was a pungent stench of tarragon vinegar. Tony went back to what he had evidently been doing before David had interrupted him – separating egg yolks and whites, rather unsuccessfully, with an Errol Flynn sort of movement and much dangling albumen.

'Pour yourself some of that,' said Gilbert.

'Is it tiswin?'

'It's French. Walnuts.'

David picked up the bottle and give it a sniff. It smelled like the stuff Henry used for lighting his barbecues.

'I suppose you've come to apologise about the sardine industry,' said Gilbert. 'Well it's too late for that, much too late, as you must have read in the papers.'

By now, David was becoming accustomed to discovering all kinds of things for which he turned out to have some degree of, hitherto unimagined, responsibility. He had not envisaged, however, that his area of accountability could be expected to span the plight of an ailing fishing industry. Had Tony Gilbert, he briefly wondered, some kind of link with The Mission to Seamen?

'I don't really think you can hold me to blame, Tony,' he ventured cautiously.

'Well if not you, I don't know who.' Gilbert started doing things with the hot water, egg-yolks and a whisk.

'The Ministry of Agriculture and Fisheries, perhaps. The Common Market. Pollution. Oil spills. But, please, not me, Tony. Not sardines too.'

'In that case, why are you here?' asked Gilbert. Then, after a little pause during which he bitterly clipped tarragon, 'No, I can guess. But it's too late for that also: Clementine's gone.

And anyway, David, I think that perhaps I should warn you, the woman has a nasty streak to her, a violent tendency that appears to erupt from nowhere. I would guess latent schizophrenia, manifesting itself as phallus-envy.'

'She kneed you in the groin, did she, Tony?'

'Luckily I was too quick for her, but it was close. Bloody close. David, I'm going to have to defrost these steaks in the microwave, since the Béarnaise is nearly ready. I like mine rare but I expect you eat yours incinerated to a crisp. I'll open a Beauje, as we seem to have demolished this bottle.'

'Actually, I like mine rare also. But I can't stay to eat, Tony. Tell me when this happened.'

'After the departure of Zucchini, but before Veronique. Well I say before, but . . .'

'Zucchini is here?'

'Is he?' Gilbert sloshed wine, unsteadily, into two glasses and puffed, rinsed and gargled a gulp round his mouth.

'Tony, when do you expect Clementine back?'

There was a maddening silence, during which Gilbert whisked, microwaved and tasted again.

'I don't,' he said eventually. 'She's gathered up her things. Though you can never tell with the unstable.'

Plunging, breathless, flailing feelings assembled in David's chest.

'Where is she now, then?'

'Now? *En route* for Canada? Heading back to London? Your guess is as good as mine. Though, if you want my opinion, you're better off with Fay.'

There was a stillness the size of a cathedral inside Fay Marsh. She felt, not empty, but hushed.

David had turned on the path for a moment and walked a few paces backwards. She'd shooed him on his way with gestures, and watched the sheepskin jacket vanish into the darkness at a bend obscured by willows. He might have been nobody. If she had been someone else, taking a shortcut along the river to avoid the crowds for All Souls, he would have been. If she had been Friedaswida's novice, he might have been walking above her bones. If he had been born as little as forty years earlier, she might only have encountered him as a mound of flowers or a name on a memorial.

So it was silly to . . . Anyway, it was a big consolation to make your own decisions, even if they . . .

She'd retraced David's footsteps, though more slowly; it was herself she was going home to.

After Tony Gilbert's revelation, Fay had spent a horrible night and a terrible day piecing together lies.

One thing, however, in spite of all her efforts, had doggedly refused to fit: the fact that Clementine had encouraged her to look in David's E-mail box, knowing that there was no correspondence between herself and David in it.

Probably only to throw her off the scent, though, she'd initially argued. Probably only to throw her off.

But she hadn't really been *on* a scent, had she? All she'd been experiencing were the same, usual, vague suspicions and insecurities. Clementine had had little, if anything, to gain by what she'd said.

Nevertheless, she *did* lead Fay to think she was still in Canada (perhaps the better to facilitate an affair), Fay had reminded herself as she'd gathered wild carrot and horseradish beneath a leaden sky. Immediately considering, though, that as Clementine had pointed out, there was nothing Fay could ever have done to make David stay if he'd decided not to. Even coal sheds proved unreliable. A cool sun had seeped out in white capillaries. Its unyielding light made everything perfectly clear. If David were to decide not to stay, in terms of what Fay Marsh was and what she wanted to be, would it desperately matter? It would matter, yes, but would it matter desperately? And suddenly, Fay had felt that it wouldn't, and impatient with despair.

The telephone rang and rang. Once, a young girl answered and said that Dr Gilbert was in Provence and Dr Dee was in London for a few days.

Pushed towards trust, Fay's rational self told her, in Clementine-type tones, not to be ri-di-cu-lous but to take things at face value: could someone be eating bacon and peanut-butter sandwiches with you one minute and plotting against you the next? Yes, her other side maintained. Well, yes, the Clementine voice conceded, but, realistically, didn't the sandwiches make it a whole lot less likely?

You couldn't study the ways of plants and herbs and aromas, you couldn't think of nature spirits and ancient wisdom without believing that certain things were meant to be. Once back at the empty house, with David gone in search of Clementine, Fay had cogitated on the frying-pan and the butter-pat. Or carob bars and *Fantasy Island*. But the solemn, cathedral feeling had led her instead into the street, along the crammed pavement to Just The Business.

She journeyed in darkness through the Web, the Net, the Enchanted Forest that Clementine Dee had led her to.

Outside, a flare went up. The street was dyed crimson. A thin wafer of ruby spread across the carpet.

Fay thought how far away and dead the universe seemed unless you named the constellations. Then, there scarcely seemed room for all of them. How silent satellites and airwaves, until you watched, until you heard, the trillion, crystal, criss-crossing, intersecting, weaving voices that bounced on them; helter-skeltered down their spirals; made them springboards for leaping across space into other people's places, across time, into other people's mornings.

Fay drifted without purpose through shoals of ephemera, into weather and traffic, movement and commerce, eventually finding herself in Sam Bullock's E-mail.

Virtual, was her first thought – great herds of nothing, driven westwards by bobbing cowboys riding air. But then she noticed how securely these virtual herds were hitched to the earth. There were ships and trains, schedules, names which recurred, references, confirmations.

Another flare, more sanguine light, seeping into everything.

Sodden fields. Bony flanks. Oval, innocent eyes. Splayed, teardrop ears. Cows. Real cows. Thousands of them.

20 ∫

No Room at the Inn

The rented room smelled stale. The light from the wan bedside lamp accentuated stains and cigarette burns and where the candlewick bedspread had worn thin. A dingy end to a nightmare journey, lugging impossible bags from the very outskirts of town where the taxi'd dumped her, through crowds that had pinballed her all over the shop.

Clementine switched the light out and opened the window that gave onto the fire-escape. Still, icy air and the blended scents of applewood, gunpowder and chestnuts; an underlying, burny, caramel tang.

The cathedral was a swarm of saints. The mortal plane, a mass of faces. Bigwigs. A Mayor-type. Clerics. Worthies. Jerks hurling bangers. Families. Kids. A plump woman in a disastrous hat, obviously chief V.I.P., surrounded with security, was handing out prizes to costumes.

The bells were still at it. Clementine imagined them flinging themselves about up the top of some cold tower. She thought of moonlight, the Roman ruins, the smell of daffodils. April seemed a long distance off; dead and buried. She should never have come back to the Cathedral Inn. Having once been in this room, David would be here always.

The telephone was covered in a thin layer of grease. When Clementine eventually got reception there was the sound of a radio playing in the background. It took several goes to get her an outside line. Fortunately, Ruth Carpini wasn't one to be phased by suddenly being confronted with several thousand miles worth of boo-hooing (at a cost of Christ knows what per minute). Yes, the arm was soon to come out of plaster. Yes, she would replace Clementine if the Fellowship's stipulations could still be met. No, it was not stupid to have your whole existence turned upside down by love; it was nothing new and nothing unusual – hadn't Renaissance comedy taught Clementine anything?

This was a comfort. When she'd put the phone down, Clementine thought of those Tudor dances – usually horrendously executed; a way of getting everyone cheerfully offstage. You worked your way up to the top of the line, palm to palm, doing the same as the couples before, the couples after. You cast off. Nothing new. Nothing unusual. The same boat. Ruth had unerringly homed in on the one consolation. That great recording of the eternal similarity of experience.

Now the room was freezing, but Clementine couldn't bear to close the window. She called the airport, then opened a bag and pulled out a comforting old, misshapen, unravelled, droopy sweater. And a beret, not hers. It must be the one she'd suspected Tony would have purchased, somehow scooped up along with her clobber. She opened another bag into which she'd stuffed everything to do with Mowbray. Her hand closed round a volume of *A Right Wonderful Error*. Clementine started reading by the light of the cathedral. Then stopped, puzzled: this wasn't her copy; it must be Tony's also. The bells abruptly ceased. The sound of the crowd was a low, close hum. Clementine felt it reverberating in her ears and fingers. A folded piece of paper fell out of the book. She picked it up and opened it. It was entitled, *Snew?*, grubby and badly-printed, with idiosyncratic spelling, but Clementine was used to manuscripts: angry voices; angry events; poignant evocations of Justice. And . . . a sonnet. One that Clementine had believed, up to this moment, was known to nobody other than her and Ruth Carpini. One of which, Clementine had believed, up to this moment, there was only a single extant copy – at Bus Station House. But here, word for word, signed 'Merlyn Orb'. Clementine picked up the book again and gave it a shake. Another piece of paper fell out: an invoice for *A Right Wonderful Error* and for *A Potted History of the Sardine Industry* from David Marsh Antiquarian Books.

'All right! All right! My goodness, what impatience!'

The door was opened, not by David or Fay, but by a tall man wearing silk pyjamas and an embroidered dressing-gown.

'Is this David Marsh's house?'

'That is a matter of considerable controversy, but he does presently reside here, yes. You'd better come in,' with a beckoning motion, 'the streets are so savage we're in imminent danger of an invasion of Brotherhoods if we don't shut the door pretty hastily. I *love* your beret.'

'They're very functional.'

'Are they? Well you mustn't say so. It spoils it somehow.'

In April, they hadn't closed the curtains. The room had filled with floaty sunshine. The fireplace had had dried flowers in it.

'You must try some of this luscious Chablis,' the tall man continued. 'And join in our conversation about cows and see if you can throw any light upon something of a conundrum.'

There was a beautiful black man in skin-tight jeans, eating mushy peas, seated on the rug in front of the fire. There was a fidgety guy wearing a thick gold watch in one of the armchairs. No David. But, on the sofa . . .

'Hello Clementine,' said Fay.

'Hello Fay,' said Clementine.

'Yes, well that is who you would be,' said the man in pyjamas, looking at her with interest. 'I assume, I *hope*, that something intelligent is being done with the Volvo. Tell me, Clementine – I may call you Clementine, mayn't I? I am Henry Pearl. This gorging person is Colin, and that is Rick. Tell me, Clementine, why does one say "fishy" and not "cowy"? Why are fish so much more dubious than cows? Is it something to do with the sea, do you think?'

'I guess I hadn't . . .'

'One assumes, of course, that there *is* an answer. Just as one feels, in one's heart of hearts, that there is a key that opens every door.'

'Hen, she don't know what you're rabbiting about.'

Hen? Rabbit? Fish? Cow? The distance between the two Englishes had never seemed so great.

'It's to do with the movement of cattle, Clementine,' said Fay. 'There may be nothing in it, but it does seem a bit strange.'

'Did you ever empty your mother's sewing-basket onto the carpet?'

'My muvver din't sow. Run off with a bookie.'

'Well mine *did*. Her stitching was exquisite. Anyway, what we have here are metaphorical odds and ends.' Henry passed Clementine a drink. She took a sip, feeling like she'd walked into topsy-turvydom. 'Let us empty them onto the rug of our consciousness. Many many unfortunate bovines appear to be leaving Sam Bullock, the Mayor's brother's, establishment, travelling to Venezuela and, one suspects, no happy outcome. Thence they are transported to Holland and afterwards, in less animate form, they are imported into the U.K.'

'By a Giorgio Fernandez,' said Rick.

'Who's porking the Duchess of Pitsbury.'

Fog on the freeway. A car cutting in on her. Distracted by the whopping cowboy, the colossal letters, the surprise that BARG MART were still allowed to trade in Britain. For a moment, Clementine forgot about the Mowbray sonnet.

'The Giorgio Fernandez who owns the BARG MART GINORMOUS DIME-O-STORE?'

Actually, David Marsh's guess as to Clementine's whereabouts was considerably better than Tony Gilbert's.

He could have been wrong, though. She could have taken the taxi straight to the airport; in which case, he would have had to regret, for all eternity, not having driven there, overtaking every taxi he spotted on the way, in order to look and see who was in the back of it. And do what if he saw her? As David had sped back in the direction of Pitsbury he'd imagined ramming the taxi sideways on to make it pull over, like they did in films set in Arizona. Or maybe he'd have opened the door of Henry's Volvo and yelled out of it, in order to attract Clementine's attention. What if she'd ignored him, though? Then he could have leapt onto the taxi's roof, he supposed, leaving the Volvo to float off into a gulch, like they did.

There was also the London possibility. He could have hared up the treble clef of motorways that linked Pitsbury with the Capital, acting similarly, praying he'd see Clementine before she was gulped up by the Metropolis and lost forever.

It was a risk, opting for the Cathedral Inn.

At the thought, and entering Pitsbury's gloomy suburbs, David had hammered his foot down on the accelerator.

A sleeping policeman, wide as a water jump.

There was a terrible scraping, jamming sound. The Volvo limped to the side of the road where it collapsed in a petulant heap and something rolled off it.

David ran. Past bungalows and double-glazing shops. Chippies and Kebabs. A small version Quik-Potato. Characterless pubs.

He thought of cranes; bulldozers; tanks; those little tractor-things with enormous, fat tyres that could cross anything; land-to-water craft able to float down the Ebb into the town centre.

Instead, however, as the roofs became more complex, the pavements narrower and the vistas older and more scenic, he was confronted yet again, *yet again*, with ever-growing, ever-drunker mobs of people; ever-more-numerous, ever-less-patient troops of security. The Duchess of Pitsbury seemed to be being moved to another location; had she come to Pitsbury with the express intention of making life difficult for David Marsh, she could not have succeeded more gloriously.

The dank, shortbread-coloured exterior of the Cathedral Inn looked, to David, like the portals of Heaven. The mother, sister, aunt, daughter of the woman who'd been presiding over Reception in April seemed to him the Recording Angel as she confirmed that a Dr Dee had, indeed, checked into the hotel, though when she would not say, nor whether she was still in her room.

'What number is it?'

The woman's lips formed a little line of cross-stitch.

'The Management has a policy which prevents it from allowing *men* in the rooms.'

'It didn't in April.'

'It does now.'

'So you rent only to women?'

'Of course not.'

'But any male who decides to stay in this establishment is obliged to sleep in the corridor?'

'We do not allow men, *who are not guests*, in the rooms.'

'The goal of this being to achieve what?'

'It is the Management's policy.'

'That you have already told me. What is it designed to achieve?'

'I imagine,' said the woman, looking at David as if she suspected him of being a rent-boy, gold-digger, gigolo, wandering rapist, 'I imagine it is so that ladies are in no danger of being harassed.'

'And nobody capable of harassing a lady would be able to afford the price of one of your rooms, so that they could go up the stairs, unhindered, and knock on the doors of as many females as they cared to?'

'If you do not leave I shall phone the police.'

'At least, please tell me whether Dr Dee is up there.'

'Up where?'

'Where, in God's name, do you think? On the topmost spire of Pitsbury Cathedral? In the bell-tower? Floating westwards in the basket of an air-balloon?'

'She did put in a phone call to Canada. And then she phoned the airport.' The woman's voice reeked of triumph.

'And then?' David's dismayed heart felt as if it might explode.

'I have already compromised my position.'

Light tumbled out of the cathedral onto the congregation of Worthies departing into the darkness. A stained-glass jumble of shapes and colours. Horatio Bullock and the brassy Gloria in their glad-rags. The Archbishop, pink-nosed, sneezing into a snowy handkerchief. The Lay clerks and boys, shivering in their red and white, the Lay clerks looking at their watches and assessing how long it would be before they were leaning on the bar of the Cock and Hen, discussing which of the trebles was the prettiest. Harriet, Duchess of Pitsbury, in her flowerpot, still hand in hand with white-suited Aftershave Ad.

There was no light on in any of the rooms at the back of the Cathedral Inn. For a desperate moment it occurred to David that this might only be because the majority of those broken enough to stay there lacked the energy, gumption, initiative to flick a light switch. But then it seemed to him that most of the rooms did have an unoccupied air, in which case Clementine, given a choice, would have taken the one she had had before.

Like Peter sodding Pan, David climbed the fire escape, wondering whether the building supported it or it supported the building. He cupped his hands round his eyes to blank out reflections and peered through the window of the room that had been Clementine's. There was the merest fraction of residual illumination from the corridor, in the form of a smear of forty-watt which only accentuated the imprecision of square and oblong shadows; they could be suitcases and travel bags but might, just as easily, be pieces of disparate furniture and dysfunctional electronic amenities. Or gravestones. Or megaliths. Safes. Henges.

'You are to come down immediately with your hands above your head.'

It took David a moment to realise that this remark was addressed to him. He turned and breathed in a sharp lungful of cold air, startled by a blast of beauty. The weathered face of the cathedral. Saints with worn noses. Angels with worn wings. Ridged, icing-bag rosettes and traceries. All bathed in golden light. Above, a hailstorm of stars. An indigo sky.

'I repeat. Raise your hands above your head.'

Now David noticed that the bottom of the fire-escape was ringed with policemen, several of whom were holding machine-guns pointed in his direction.

'Why?'

'You could be a sniper.' The officer addressing David seemed rather thrown by the question.

'I could be, except I don't have a gun.'

'I'm afraid we can't trust you on that.'

'Anyway, who would I be planning on shooting?'

'The Mayor. The Duchess. The Archbishop.'

'In ascending alphabetical order, or in order of preference? I repeat, the only people carrying guns in this precinct are yourselves.'

'Perhaps, sir, you could keep your hands above your head while we discuss this.'

'I most certainly could not.'

'Oh do, David, *do*. Think how silly all these stalwart men are going to feel pointing their contraptions at you if you don't look impressed by them.'

'Henry?'

'Look, this man is named David Marsh. I can vouch for him. And I am speaking as a local businessman.'

'Rick?'

'I don't see why they should be especially impressed by that.'

'I know you, don't I?' Colin Rutt stared, meaningfully, at one of the policemen.

'David, aren't those steps terribly rickety?'

'Fay?'

'Officer, if you are willing to view this simply as a merry Hallowe'en escapade, I will personally make sure that a Mrs Gibson's Vanilla Sponge is delivered to the Station, with my compliments, along with a bottle of tiswin and a thank-you card.'

'He doesn't look very merry.'

'He never does,' said Fay.

'Could he just raise his hands for a moment or two, since people are watching? Then we'll let him go home.'

'Oh, he isn't going home. He's going to a sort of party.'

'Henry, the last thing I am in the mood for is a party, of any kind whatever.'

Clementine almost certainly on her way back to Canada. The evacuation of the squat only a matter of time. Ditto his own eviction. The wasteland imminently to be desecrated by the construction of a soulless BARG-MART GINORMOUS DIME-O-STORE. In the process of being stared at by an enormous crowd, made up of the residue of the cathedral congregation, a multitude of insurance agents, dressed as pirates, sailors and Spaniards, half of them too drunk to stand, and a whole pile of infants holding pumpkins. David also noted the presence of the journalist from the local rag. Ms Court. Mr and Mrs Brian Baffle.

'You'll be in the mood for this party, David. I promise. Just raise your hands once. For the sake of our Emergency Services. Imagine you're being crucified.'

21

All Souls

Weaver Street had emptied now. Clementine walked through the keyhole gap in the city wall and entered Pitsbury Without.

There was a candle burning in an attic window. The others were boarded up. There were people at home, though. The building contained life. Clementine felt its pulse as she lifted her hand to the front door and, prior to knocking, ran her fingers gently down it, touching the lovely, warm tree limbs, the joints and crevices.

It was a little, polite, friendly knock, with nothing of official-dom to it. The kind that must have sounded on this wood many thousands of times over the centuries. Perhaps that was why, in spite of everyone's warnings, the door was opened immediately as if she had been expected.

There was a rug on the floor. Wall paintings. People. Light came from the flames of an enormous, throbbing fire over which hung a cauldron. A pierced, shaved, coughing, tattooed woman was juggling oranges – glistening dawns; black, dead spheres; flaming sunsets. A very pale-faced man was turning a duplicator wheel. There was a smell of burning meadow grasses. Bunches of herbs and dried flowers were suspended from hooks in the beams. There were a couple of bottles of clear liquid on a long table, glasses, a large earthenware bowl of hot chestnuts.

'I'm looking for Merlyn Orb.'

'You've found him.'

He was leaning against a wall. Tall, dark and thin with a large nose. She hadn't noticed him among the beams. The dancing firelight on his face made it, though serious, appear suddenly to flash with laughter. His eyebrows arched and dropped.

'I know this sounds crazy but I guess . . . I mean . . . is it possible that we've met some place before?'

Or was it that just for an instant his expression had made her think of Hermia Mowbray?

'Anything is possible.'

A round man entered, chewing on an Eccles cake, carrying a slopping metal bucket. He poured water from it into the cauldron, which gasped and exhaled a great breath of steam. Some droplets splashed onto the flames, which lit up sulphur and showed Clementine that some of what she had thought were shadows were people and some of what she had thought were people were shadows.

'That water. Does it come from . . . ?'

'Well well well,' cried Merlyn Orb, making Clementine jump.

'You're a poet?' she asked.

'I am.'

'And you work for David Marsh. You put *Snew?* in the Mowbray play and sent it to Provence.'

Merlyn Orb merely smiled and suddenly, startlingly, Clementine was overtaken by a violent desire to hurl herself at him, to shake his bony form, to yell at it 'Tell me! Tell me! Tell me!' To dive her hands inside him and rifle through heart, lungs, kidneys, liver, in search of the secret. In the middle there, surely, someplace, must be the hidden nugget of explanation. She wished he wouldn't look at her like he knew her thoughts – like she was a thin pane of glass, a mirror. Then, just as suddenly, the sensation flew off. Merlyn Orb was only a street person – one of millions – who had, by some means or another, got hold of a Mowbray sonnet. This building was only a done-up squat at the end of the twentieth-century.

The firelight was orange again. It reared. Orb's face laughed. Clementine heard a giggle. A snort. Clear as a bell. It was a child in an upper bedroom. It was a couple making love. It was Hermia Mowbray, guffawing down the corridor of time. And now, with a neat little tap, a vital but simple component of what Clementine was at found its place in her brain. A reason for those afternoons in Bus Station House. A reason for spluttered calls across the Atlantic. A reason for grabbing books and holding them above your head while the quicksand sucked you under.

Laughter.

She'd always loved the comedies best.

Farts and yokels. Pratfalls. Somersaults. Mirth. The possibility of rib-tickling, leg-crossing laughter. No one's possession. Everyone's right. It seemed to her now that this must be the true purpose even of tragedy: to show how things should not be, that they might be swept away to make room for laughter.

Take laughter seriously, said Hermia Mowbray. *Take it very seriously indeed.*

Well well well *that suckled me from birth to pryme.*

'Tell me where you found it,' said Clementine to Merlyn. 'I'm an academic. I have to be curious.'

'Where I found what?'

'The sonnet.'

'What is a sonnet?'

'A poem. A kind of poem. You know the one. I don't care that you say you wrote it. Hell, maybe you did, maybe it's a group of sounds that wanders about looking for someone's mind to set up in. But tell me where you found it. I'm an academic – only a guinea-pig in reverse, I guess, unshredding as opposed to shredding – but it's what I do.'

Clomping footsteps on a broad wooden staircase which lurched and concertinaed in the unreliable light of Merlyn Orb's dripping torch.

The room was an ice-box. And yet, people slept in it, or maybe they were dead: motionless, frozen dunes upon the floor. Upon the floor of a painted cave. While others watched them from the ceiling – warmer, jollier people who could afford to be amused by the perplexities of life, being so very far away from them.

The pierced, shaved, tattooed, coughing woman raised her face, shivered with a blackcurrant yawn. 'Henry said it's Victorian Gothic.'

A draught. The torchlight streaked across another area of

ceiling revealing ivory Tudor ruffs; ruby Tudor caps; round, worthy, provincial faces; *timbers carved, like faces* . . .

'Henry was wrong,' said Clementine.

'I painted it.'

Gold. Crimson. White. Yellow.

'You got the colours spot on.'

''Sobvious.'

. . . *like faces*, comma, *with my rhyme*: Sobvious indeed, thought Clementine; and she'd extracted and inserted more commas into student papers than the average dentist had pulled molars and put in crowns.

Here were the carved Tudor faces.

There, along the length of the *oaken beames*, carved into the wood, the Mowbray sonnet.

If Clementine had been standing in a hot room she'd probably have gone icy cold. In this icy chamber, she came to the boil.

Not Mowbray's handwriting, but that wasn't surprising – she was a playwright, not a wood-carver; it would have taken *skil* to make wood loop and curl and flow like that, *skil* that would have existed in abundance in Tudor Pitsbury.

A proud father.

'Thy sonnets are so greatly to my pleasure, daughter, that I shall cause that one be carven on those beames which saw thy lyfes first day.'

Clementine plunged into a glacial lake. Her body was steaming. She was numb with cold. Then, again, she was an electric ring. She felt dizzy. She felt like she'd got flu. It was too much. Great, subterranean sobs gushed to the surface. Her stupid eyes were a couple of hot taps. It was too much. She wanted to turn her back on it and think, instead, about sheep dog trials and stencils.

She was standing in the birthplace. In the very room where those saucy, inquisitive eyes had first opened; that witty mouth first taken breath; the reeling focus of a newborn struggled to make out its mother's lips and these homely, wooden, Tudor burghers that would fascinate Hermia her entire life. So that, one day, she would incorporate them into a sonnet which her father would cause to be carved upon these very beams, and which would wind up, in manuscript form, as a saleable investment at Bus Station House.

Clementine said nothing. Waved her hand weakly at the Tudors as if to say 'You tell them'. Eventually managed to croak, 'I need a drink. I need a drink now.'

From below came a gay cry:

'The players are come.'

On top of it all, if Fay and the others had found him, if her guess that he would go to the Cathedral Inn in search of her was correct, Clementine was about to see David Marsh again. The person she loved best in the world. The man she ached for as much as she ached for knowledge. And here she was, looking somewhat akin to a floor-cloth.

The mounded people were rising. Feet pattered down the staircase.

With an extremely irritating beckoning gesture, Merlyn Orb stretched a long arm out to her and said 'Come', which was irritating also.

Now the kitchen table was covered in bottles. Henry Pearl was setting out paper cups. Colin was peeling chestnuts. Rick was talking with the pale-faced duplicator man. Fay was unloading hefty baps and earthenware bowls from a rush basket. And David Marsh was standing, looking down into the fire, a hand resting on the stone mantelpiece.

Clementine imagined David's eyes witnessing a life's first day. Even the best of carvings were only faint approximations of the crammed, real, human face. He looked tired, a bit battered, though even more handsome than she remembered him. Did he know she was here? No, he had the air of someone dragged along.

Clementine's spirit rushed over to him, touched the hunched shoulder, watched the head raise, the expression grow incredulous, placed her lips on his lips in a hearty, furious kiss.

'Oh David, look! Look! I am thinking happy ending.'

'We said you'd enjoy it once you were here,' said Fay.

'Toldja,' said Colin.

Rick twiddled a gold cigarette lighter.

Almost, Clementine dissolved. But wait. Did David think, did he really think, that he could just swan in, in October, and reclaim what he'd discarded in April? And who, now she considered it, had asked Clementine her opinion on the matter? It had been assumed, merely because she'd told them where David would probably be, that she was still in love with him, still available – and, in the daze of things, she'd gone along with it – but, consigned to the realm of martini and peanut butter, might not her fancy have led her into dalliances that David Marsh and his friends knew nothing of?

'Clementine,' said David, his expression growing incredulous. 'What are you doing here?'

'It seems pretty obvious: I'm in the middle of a set-up, laid on for you by your companions.' They were not the words she meant to say, but she couldn't stop them. Now the plaster was ripped off, she knew how terribly badly she'd been hurting. Worse than it might be possible to forgive him for.

'I think I'm going to weep tears of joy.'

'Do shut up, Henry,' said David.

'Don't be nasty, David,' said Fay.

'I am not "being nasty". It's just that, in the light of what Clementine has just said, tears of happiness appear somewhat premature.'

'Oh, I'm sure they're not,' said Fay, smiling at Clementine.

'Nah,' said Colin, winking at her.

Rick clicked his lighter on and off.

'I don't really know any of you . . .' As she spoke, Clementine's rage mounted.

'But you will! You will! Watch my lips: friends for life.'

'And, what is more to the point, none of you really knows me. I'm sorry to cheat you of your love scene, but I am afraid that I have a life too, and I am not simply going to drop everything and rush into the arms of a man who has had the gall to say that a relationship with me would be a risk.'

The pierced, shaved, tattooed woman clapped.

'Oh David!' said Fay.

'*All* relationships are a risk, David. All *life* is a risk. Love is an emergency.'

'Yes, I know that now, Henry. It just so happens that I didn't in April and I have to say that I feel it is scarcely fair for Fay to upbraid me for my loyalty and Clementine for my honesty.'

'I was taking a risk, too, you bastard. Don't you think I felt a complete ass when I got rejected?'

'It seems to me . . .' said Merlyn Orb.

'Do not go on, Merlyn. If you wish me to remain civil, do not go on.'

'Wot else you know now you didn't back then?' said Colin through a mouthful of chestnuts.

'Why, for God's sake, should my soul be the only one to be anatomised? Could we not, perhaps, ask Dr Dee why, since it transpires she was requesting me to end my marriage, she did not hear me out rather than exiting into the fog?'

'I thought I was acting wisely. I thought I'd be able to call it a day and it'd be over. So I was wrong. Burn me at the stake, why don't you?'

''Ang on harfa mo. If you woz wrong . . .'

'Oh Colin. Yes! Yes! I knew there was a reason why I tolerate you.'

'If Clementine was wrong, that does not necessarily imply that, in the meantime, she hasn't got over . . . whatever there was to be got over.' David looked broken. Clementine's wicked heart whooped, even as it was wrenched apart with pity.

'This isn't how it was supposed to be, Davey.'

'No, Fay, I daresay it isn't. And once I would have said that I have grown accustomed to things not being how they are supposed to be, but the truth is I haven't, and I don't think I will now. I don't think I even want to.'

Clementine's wicked heart danced a mazurka, even as it was wrenched apart with pity.

Now there was a knock on the door. Merlyn Orb opened it.

'I am Merlyn Orb. Enter.'

'Oh, so it's you who think that Roo and Immie Canning are sardines. Well you couldn't be more wrong, though even sardines would have been better than Top-Value Tibbles.' Slightly unsteady on his feet but radiating good health and dressed like something out of a menswear catalogue aimed at County types, Tony Gilbert.

'What are you doing here, Tony?' exclaimed Clementine and David in chorus.

'Dr Dee and I have a date to see the fireworks.'

'And you didn't reckon that that arrangement – such as it was – was negated by your attempt at a pass causing me to smash your pastry and take a knife to your sausage?'

'A knife to his sausage!' gasped Henry.

'Fuck me!' said Colin.

'His saucisson, for Chrissake. It would not be worth going to gaol over Tony Gilbert's worthless member.'

'Clementine, I realise that, in your unsophisticated Canadian way you view this kind of horseplay, this kind of repartee, as flirtatious . . .'

'Flirtatious?'

'How did you get here, Tony?' asked David.

'Have to admit, finding you again was bloody, after you'd ditched the Volvo.'

'You were following the Volvo?'

'Ditched? Define "ditched" for me, Fay, in a way that will cause the minimum of distress.'

'I'm sure Tony means "parked", Henry.'

Gilbert gave a little barking laugh. 'But I was sure that, wherever you were, Dr Dee would not be far behind. Got to the precinct, found everyone talking about a nutter who tried to scale the side of the Cathedral Inn . . .'

So Clementine had been right. The Cathedral Inn was where they'd found David. And he had tried to scale it! To get to her!

'. . . figured that could only be one person, bearing in mind Clementine stayed there in April. Heard you'd been carried off by friends. Arrived at Marauding Hordes, of which, quite frankly, I could not believe the transformation – I suppose it does make some sense to chase the lower end of the market but . . . Anyway, it was closed, but two young gentlemen outside Henry Pearl Interiors told me I would probably find you all here. The rest is history. Clementine, I know there's oodles of time yet, but if you want a proper view of the Duchess, we really . . .'

'Horseplay?' said the tattooed woman, looking at Gilbert as if a prison sentence held no fears.

'Repartee?' cried Fay.

'"Whatever I say, wherever I go, yes means yes and no means no,"' said Henry, primly. 'And that includes pyjamas.'

'Tony,' said Clementine, suddenly realising that she could afford to be sorry for the dreadful man, though not awfully sorry. 'In April, and for the first time, I fell in love.' The simple, naked words drew an irritatingly maiden blush across her cheeks. She glanced at David, glanced away again.

'Good. Well now you've admitted it, perhaps you can put an end to this shrewish behaviour and come and watch the Duchess.'

'Not with you, Tony. With David Marsh.'

'Who is married,' said Tony.

'Who is free,' said Fay. 'Really, Tony, I don't think you should have been driving.'

'Though I wasn't the one who had an accident.'

'Accident? Accident?'

'Fussbout nuffink probly.'

A gold cigarette lighter, tossed into the air and caught, tossed and caught.

But the sound had been turned down on them. They were background noise only. The room was glowing, golden and beautiful. Clementine waded, floated, danced towards David, her legs, arms, bosom lapped by silken swathes of warmth, velvety swatches of intricate feeling. Then they were standing, both her hands in both of his, silent, surveying the lifetime of exchanged words stretched before them. And then, a sudden, frozen stab of terror – shared, she knew that – and then a wave of infinite regret that twenty was long gone; that there was the odd treacherous grey hair; at the hands, which were not youthful; the inescapable knowledge that the lease on all promises, all happiness, all potential, was a short one.

'"The stone that the builders rejected,"' said Henry. 'Well, my real forté is minimalism.'

'And ours,' said Merlyn.

Tony Gilbert had, mercifully, fallen asleep on the floor after a couple of tiswins. All around, people were eating and drinking.

Clementine was peeling chestnuts and stuffing them into her mouth at furious speed. David was taking big chunks of Fay's baps and dipping them into a bowl of garlicky hummus, interspersed with gulps of Henry's red wine. They had both been overtaken by an enormous hunger. David's free hand, however, still held Clementine's. He couldn't take his eyes off that intelligent face, its animation somehow heightened by the new short hair; he loved watching people listen to her.

'Gothic was an understandable mistake,' Clementine said. 'But the sonnet seals its authenticity. There is no doubt that this is the building where Hermia Mowbray was born.'

David physically experienced, in his own body, the awe-choked effort it took Clementine to say this. He didn't have to imagine, he could feel what it meant to her, even down to that selfish pang – squelched underfoot, but there an instant – that the knowledge must be shared and the world allowed to enter, clamouring for its culture. But the world being allowed to join in was the fee for the building being able to exist at all; Clem knew that also. Just as the overwhelming, tangible desire for privacy – David thought of moated castles, drawbridges, four-poster beds, curtained litters – must be subordinated for the moment to the concerns of this extraordinary group of individuals who, in a strange, circuitous way, were responsible for David and Clementine being together.

The conversation moved on to the supermarket development.

'Look,' said Rick Farr, 'this is how I reckon it works. Horatio Bullock does a deal with the Duchess of Pitsbury, which allows her BARG-MART boyfriend to buy and re-develop the wasteland.'

'Cheap. Back'ander. No prob wiv planning permission.'

'Which is why Bullock suddenly became so eager to demolish the squat,' said David, recalling the offer that the Mayor had made him on the bridge.

'The birthplace,' said Clementine.

'In addition,' Rick continued, 'it is agreed that BARG-MART will buy *Sam* Bullock's beef.'

'Made uv dodgy cows.'

'And the unfortunate creatures are shipped to and fro in order to conceal their questionable origin,' said Henry.

'Exactly.' Rick threw his lighter high into the air and caught it again.

'Poor cows,' said Fay. 'Poor cattle.'

'The trouble with knowledge, however valuable, is deciding what to do with it,' said Clementine.

'Clearly, the birthplace will never be destroyed now,' said David.

'And that, in itself, will prevent the BARG-MART,' said Rick. 'Probably, a more upmarket development will replace it.'

'A pedestrianised area,' said Henry.

There was a silence.

'Accessed from the bridges,' said Rick.

There was another silence, interrupted only by the sound of Gary's chomping, Al picking at chestnut skins.

'I have a vision of the future,' Henry said. 'Here it is. Listen. I see numerous luxury homes, inhabited by cultured, aesthetic, restaurant-going individuals. I see a French-style market. Craft shops. Institutes of higher learning, absolutely stuffed with people wanting David's volumes and Rick's . . . communications expertise. Holistic clinics desirous of Fay's beauty products and carminatives. I see a landscaped place where there are no homeless . . .'

'No, they aren't tolerated. They're sleeping in cardboard boxes somewhere else,' said Becs.

'This is banal,' exclaimed Clementine. 'It's just too frigging banal.'

Though once it would not have appeared so. Now, however, Henry's vision sounded like those diddy, metallic, juddering cities in cheap fifties sci-fi.

'It's only one possibility,' said Henry, sulkily.

'You've got to run an idea up the flagpole to see who salutes it,' said Rick, who was evidently somewhat struck with the picture Henry had painted.

'Of *course* you have.'

'No one's saluting, Henry,' said Becs.

There was another chewing silence. Beyond the windows, from across the city, came the distant, humming vibration of the All Souls crowds. The cathedral clock struck eleven. Soon, Harriet, Duchess of Pitsbury, would be transported to the Queen's School playing fields to light the midnight bonfire and to watch the fireworks.

'It's strange to think that she's here,' said Fay. 'The Duchess, I mean.'

And all the eminent Pitsbury burghers. And the Archbishop. And the Mayor. And Sam Bullock. And the journalist from the local rag. And Ms Court. And Mr and Mrs Brian Baffle. And Mr Giorgio BARG-MART. And the Canon. And the Choristers. And thousands of onlookers. And the team from Aspect South, who showed the lighting of the Hallowe'en bonfire every year, without fail, on the following day's lunchtime and evening news.

There would be an unanimated speech read by Duchess Harriet about darkness and light, or something along those lines. The cathedral, the bridges, churches, Roman ruins, all the illuminations, would be switched off. Last year's traditional brand would be fired up. In a cursory manner, Duchess Harriet would touch it to the bit of the bonfire specially designated for the purpose, one that had received a particularly heavy dowsing of paraffin. A smouldering pause, and then the dead branches would swallow the fire and the effigy placed on top of it would droop, cave in and collapse, and people would cheer. A maroon would go up, followed by a trillion screaming, reeling sparks, gasps, exclamations, quickly extinguished specks of light, popping universes, brief planetary systems.

'Basically,' said David, 'we are in charge. Not for much longer. But, at this moment, a window is open. Every possibility is within our reach. We are in a position to demand whatever we want. It's eleven o'clock. We have an hour in which to decide what that is.'

22 ∫

The Birthplace

A late June day a few years later. The trees a mosaic of gilded, youthful leaves; old walls basking in the gold light. And Pitsbury, all done up in motley.

The interior of the cathedral was a cool collision of whispers; the stained glass, jolly with sunshine, emptied a shower of jelly-babies onto the flagstones.

'I will never get used to having this around me,' said Clementine. She was staring at a mild-faced twelfth-century donkey. 'And this!' Roped off, a chequer-board of tiles depicting stylised pagan symbols.

David shifted and felt the bottle of fizz in the rucksack move slightly. His very blood could have been champagne, he thought. It was an unforgiveable cop-out to say that happiness was unattainable.

Clementine was reading the fourteen-eighteen lists now, and the thirty-nine-forty-five, looking at a bayonet-spiked carving of The Unknown Soldier. Her eyes turned to David's, very bright.

'I know,' he said. 'I know.' He put an arm around her shoulder, scooping her close.

'Dead! Unknown!' Clem exploded.

David imagined a statue of Al, The Unknown Street-Person. Pale, with a chipped tooth. Endlessly duplicating. David thought of the fraying, fading rainbow that Rick Farr simply hadn't had the heart to paint over, though it made the rest of the place look shabby. However old Al had been seemed young to be dying. Though that was the case always. Hepatitis. *Snew?* was now an archive.

Clementine strode on. Her footsteps sounded as if she was angrily kicking her way through dead leaves. Clementine rattled at the world like it was a five-bar gate. She hammered on doors and demanded things into being; refused to understand the meaning of 'impossible'. With Dame Immie and the rest of the theatrical community agog, the media screaming heritage and Tony Gilbert *somehow* having wheedled an advisory position, she'd still brawled her way to getting what she wanted for the opening of the Mowbray Theatre. No, David considered, probably more what she thought was right. Didn't they all, Clem included, somewhat yearn for the old rickety set and eminent tragedians poncing around in ermine and velvet? Dame Immie would have played Thalia for peanuts, she'd informed every television channel, daily, for what felt like the best part of a month: no, not even for that, purely for love; yes, for love alone. Tony Gilbert had pled and bled for this to come to pass. But, eventually, the Mowbray Theatre had opened with a new play, by a young, female playwright, performed by the keen young actors and the scattering of names that comprised the National Mowbray Company. Chief Artistic Advisor, Dr Clementine Dee, holder of the Mowbray Chair at the University of Pitsbury.

'We'd better get on,' said David.

'I guess,' said Clementine.

Through the cathedral doorway and into the fading light. A busker. Four jugglers. Someone performing at the centre of a crowd. A Charlie Chaplin, utterly motionless.

'It's busy now but tomorrow, when the Festival starts, it's going to be crazy,' remarked Clementine.

A man in a hard hat was being lifted up among the trees by a ladle-shaped construction. From his arms dangled a rosary of coloured bulbs.

David thought of Becs, on the wasteland, practising her fire-eating with orange brands lit from a flaming oil drum. She didn't have a cold, they'd discovered not very long before the theatre opened. She had tuberculosis. It nearly killed her.

'*Lake Geneva. Colin tells me it's Tuesday. We have found a delicious patisserie where virgins dressed like sugared almonds serve tartelettes and hot chocolate, and we do not stir until Becs has drunk at least one large cup and eaten at least one pastry. Colin, of course, is munching like there's no tomorrow. Our hotel – on the French side (much cheaper, and better food) – overlooks the Lake. Becs is a wonderful antidote to Colin and sometimes, in the evenings, over fondue and profiteroles, sometimes I actually get to indulge in cultured conversation while Colin glugs sickly liqueurs made by monks with herbs. A bientot. H.*'

David remembered driving to the airport to pick the three of them up in Henry's new car, which he had lent to David and Clementine rather than pay the airport's horrendous parking fees. They had passed what had once been the BARG-MART GINORMOUS DIME-O-STORE. A fifty-foot cowboy held a hammer above an empty building.

It had made David think of the auction at the plush auctioneers' in Bond Street; public horror having been expressed at the idea that it might leave the country (Pitsbury College, Canada's nose was twitching), money had been donated from the National Lottery to bring Hermia Mowbray's sonnet home to her birthplace. Everyone had decided that they wanted to attend. They had rendezvoused at a café in Covent Garden. Outside, a music student chamber orchestra ground away like crazy while they drank white wine and ate little bits of things from small saucers. Clementine wore plum. Fay was late. Rick, all tie and wristwatch, gnawed at an olive stone. Henry sported a brocade waistcoat and Colin, rather embarrassingly, was head to foot in black leather.

The auction viewing-room was full of the murmur of rich voices, with the odd 'New York' taking off into higher volume. Colin and Rick were, quite frankly, disappointed. Henry pretended not to be and made much of being more of a 'visual' person. But David, Clem and Fay ran their fingers along the inaudible, paper conversations, diaries, poems, notes, letters (as if to touch, as if to reach).

In-jokes. Rhyme schemes. Old pets. Shared references. Demolished houses. Common memories. First drafts. Defunct makes of car. Long ago rotted party dresses. Long ago forgotten emotions. Final copies.

It was another language; almost one's own but not quite.

David had never encountered anyone who could cuss like Clementine.

Why should a woman who, though patron of the Royal Society for the Help of the Homeless, had been instrumental in attempting to throw squatters back onto the streets; who, though a member of the little family supposedly put there by God in order to keep green and pleasant England's green and pleasant etc, had been instrumental in an attempt to pull down the birthplace of one of the world's greatest playwrights, and – as if this were not enough – to build a monstrosity which, unless Clem was very much mistaken, no one in their right mind could describe as either green *or* pleasant: why should such a woman be invited to make a speech about the newly returned Mowbray sonnet in the newly opened Mowbray birthplace?

The answer was quite simple, as David had pointed out; which Clem had found unendurably irritating. It was in order to perpetuate the pretence that the Duchess of Pitsbury, thrilled to discover the truth about the squat, had been inspired thereby to persuade her boyfriend to donate the wasteland site to the people for all eternity; and to finance the landscaping of said site by Guy Dylan (who, disappointingly, knocked nothing off); and to set up a Co-operative Trust which would provide a Centre for the Homeless, who would tend and administer the Elizabethan herb and kitchen garden and the Co-operative's shop and warehouse. This was the bargain which had been struck, so there was no choice in the matter.

In the event, however, the Duchess went down with laryngitis after a night at Mosley's and could not attend. Dame Immie Gilbert stepped in and read a bit of *Thalia* with great solemnity and bags of enunciation.

'He treats her like dirt,' remarked Henry to David as Dame Immie reverently approached the special rostrum. 'But wasn't it a lovely wedding? The bridegroom was radiant.'

They had all been present at Tony Gilbert's nuptials. David could no longer remember why, since they had, presumably, only been invited so that it would look to the media as if Tony

Gilbert had friends, too. Anyway, the outcome of Gilbert's marriage had been fortunate in that, some time before the ceremony, he had filled a plethora of suitcases with his frilly shirts and leather jackets, crammed Oliver into a cat-box, moved into Dame Immie's mansion (which boasted a rehearsal space and masses of lavender-scented guest-rooms), and put his cottage on the market.

Fay had bought it.

Now they emerged from beneath the busy carvings of the Cathedral Gate. There was the familiar, tear-gas explosion of burning fat, onions, minced meat, breaded cod, potatoes. But also, from the street-sellers: caramel, mushrooms, garlic, hot doughnuts, sweetcorn, roasting pork. There were posters for the Festival's usual bland offerings: The Pitsbury Players' production of *Oklahoma*; a performance by the Polish State Brass Ensemble in the Queen's School hall, subsidised by Quik-Potato; ('Booker nominated!') comedian, Reggie Bell, and model, Kandy Lam, reading from their new novels. But also from the street-performers; from students and hand-to-mouth theatre companies; from club-circuit stand-ups; bands. Stuffed into rooms above pubs; on the pavements; in the sagging halls of defunct religions and political philosophies; packed into disused premises out on the Elizium Forest Industrial Estate; into part of the Co-operative Trust's warehouse, cleared out and made available; into the bit of David Marsh Books which used to be Marsh Meadows: experimental drama; satire; new music; crazy kinds of performance art without classification. The paint still wet on them and smelling of sawdust.

The bridges at the bottom of the High Street had been decorated with flowers. Their pale reflections floated, mermaid-like, above the reeds.

They entered Weaver Street.

They walked past the popping lights and fading rainbow of Just the Net; the restrained gold letters which proclaimed Henry Pearl Interiors, Renovation, Restoration & Theatrical Design.

Every night, for weeks – in Henry and Colin's kitchen, eating taramasalata; over peanut-butter and bacon sandwiches and jugs of Martini, among the herbs and night-scents, listening to the last birds and the tumbling Ebb, at Fay's; once, eating poussin, at the Gilberts'; mainly, on the sitting-room rug with tiswin and a fry-up when they got hungry – Henry, Becs, David and Clementine (and anyone else who happened to be about) had discussed the interior design of the Mowbray Theatre.

'What, we must ask ourselves, does Hermia Mowbray *mean*? How can we interiorise that meaning?'

'Interiorise? Henry, must you use such appalling terminology?'

'Shut up, Dave, it's a good question.'

'I'm not disputing the merits of the question. I am merely observing that . . .'

'Clementine, shouldn't you be in a lovely squashy armchair?'

'I'm all right, Hen.'

What *did* Hermia mean?

David and Clementine discussed it beside the river, looking out across the wasteland, seeing its muddy gashes healing over with grass and borders, trees, wide vistas, shady walkways. Witnessing the birthplace's garden come back to life with vegetables and herbs – purple potato flowers, rosemary, lavender, thyme – symmetrical, knotted, miniature hedges, beds of roses, a sun-dial, the well; watching strong and lovely buildings ascend gradually, knowing that it was beneath Fay's capable hands that the Co-operative Trust was being formed.

They wove a durable fabric, Fay and Clementine.

The Centre ceased to be scaffolding and walkways along which squatters, the homeless, the formerly unemployed pushed cement-filled wheelbarrows. The resiny scent of pine gave way to emulsion. Sheets and pillowcases, toys, clothes were carried into the Centre, every alcove of which contained clean, narrow beds. In the large, airy warehouse, vegetables were stacked in crates; herbs hung to dry, ready to be bagged up and sold in the shop with the vegetables and the bought-in foreign herbs, spices and aromas, or sent to other parts of the globe.

Simultaneously, the Theatre ceased to be only labourers hammering and brushing, Henry in a tizzy and Becs up a stepladder (Becs was now Henry's permanent employee; she was also living with Henry and Colin; on their return from Lake Geneva, Henry had discovered that her company was something that he simply could not give up). The players arrived. Rehearsals began. Some were painting ceilings, some scenery; some were actors, directors, producers, others were squatters, the formerly unemployed, the homeless. They smoked together, got drunk together, seduced each other, *learnt* from each other (or so the actors told David). They lounged, gossiped, discussed and proclaimed on the Theatre's many long, external balconies, watching the cathedral go gas-fire orange at sunset, or yawning and drinking coffee as the toad-coloured St Friedaswida's turned lemon in the early light.

Had Henry's design interiorised the meaning of Hermia Mowbray? Perhaps, David thought, since the Mowbray Theatre was a building full of mirrors; square, rectangular, circular. They filled with faces and moving clouds, with river water and spires, stars and moons. Should Pitsbury subside, should the Theatre, the Centre, the gardens, the bridges, the cathedral crumble, one could imagine that these mirrors might still, unhoused, hanging from nothing, continue to gather reflections.

As they continued up Weaver Street, one of his apprentices came out of Gary's ('the thought, the very thought, that I am sleeping partner in a business which is training people to batter Mars Bars'). The apprentice handed David a carrier bag of sausage-rolls.

'Gary said to say we're up to our eyes cos the weather's got lots of people visiting the birthplace, but he's hoping to make it along later.'

They entered Pitsbury Without and took the path through the birthplace gardens, past the Centre, the shop and warehouse, the Mowbray Theatre, along the avenue of young oak trees, beneath the archway of honeysuckle, passion-flowers, beans and cucumbers. People from the Centre were weeding and gathering; the air was full of the sun-warmed scents of tomatoes, mint, new potatoes, roses, bruised stems, new-mown grass. *Thalia*, proclaimed a banner hanging from one of the Theatre balconies.

The spot where they had arranged to meet was a grassy bank beside the Ebb where wild thyme grew. A favourite place of Fay, who was spreading a white cloth and unpacking plates and bowls onto it as they approached. Colin was opening a bottle of pale-ale. Rick twisted a stalk of grass between his fingers. Becs juggled hard-boiled quails' eggs. Henry was pouring chilled champagne into saucer-shaped glasses.

'There they are!' said Fay.

'Hiya,' said Rick.

'Com'ere gorgeous,' said Colin.

'There has been a failure to syncopate tone,' said Henry.

'Meaning what, Henry?' David passed Fay the bag of sausage-rolls, which she emptied onto an oval platter.

'Meaning exactly that: sausage-rolls – from Gary, I take it. Fay has provided a most tasteful and inventive salad but Rick has brought a dozen miniature pork-pies and Colin has purchased, watch my lips, I cannot bear to pronounce it at full volume: six canisters of chilli-bean flavoured taco-chips. I have brought quails' eggs, galantine of maize-fed fowl, and four varieties of Moroccan olive, which I have marinated myself in oil with cracked coriander and bay-leaves.'

'Sounds good,' said Clementine. 'We brought more champagne, and smoked salmon sandwiches.'

'Well that restores some equilibrium to the celebration.'

'Did you take her to the cathedral and round the town?' asked Fay.

David nodded.

'Then consider yourself thoroughly welcomed into your new surroundings,' said Henry, expertly opening a champagne bottle. 'And now let us drink to your future.'

The first thing Hermia ever saw was a smiling face looking down at her. Then, her mother's lips.

Soon, other faces.

The world was a mass of shapes and colours, sprayed lights, movement.

Hermia learned to differentiate some things from others. Her mother's voice from her father's and theirs from other people's. Though sometimes her mother and father's voices would twist together, spiral into sounds that she would one day know as conversation, argument, discussion, and (the one she loved best) laughter; in tones that she would one day identify as merriment, sarcasm, disagreement, assent, satire.

Sometimes Hermia was bounced past grey stripes and balanced above the ground on slim fingers. Then, her eyes reeled as they sought perspective. What was close, what far away? What was small, what was large?

Sometimes, from a lap, she looked into infinite darkness, dotted with lights.

Sometimes Hermia saw two cities, one against blue, one against green: upside down, downside up; a small girl with a little 'O' mouth looking at her from the green city, alone in having no counterpart in the blue one.

She saw a donkey. Heard music. Things flew through the air and got hooked on branches. She smelled food and flowers. The green city was full of quivering blossoms and snakey grey arcs. Then Hermia was moving beneath golden, ivory, purple, scarlet, emerald arches and the green city had lost its glassy sheen and become coarse and rough and springy. Now, her head was in the crook of a black, salt-and-citrus-smelling, triangle. There was a pop. A tiny bit of bitter, wet tingliness was run along her lips.

Hermia didn't know what it was. But she didn't really know yet what anything was. The world was only forms, tastes, feelings and colours: a trillion pieces, still to be made into a coherent whole.

Potential.

EPILOGUE

They ate and drank. Gary joined them. Those working in the gardens gathered up their tools and returned to the warehouse.

The floodlights came on.

People, bare-armed and in t-shirts, walked along the paths, among the scents of stocks and nicotiana. The gardens filled. The play began. At the interval, the audience spilled out again onto the grass, onto the balconies.

Hermia fell asleep and Clem and Fay put things back in bags and baskets, hoisted Hermia onto Clem's shoulders and headed off to the house for a gossip and a nightcap.

Colin and Becs managed to persuade Henry, who did not like pubs, to come for a quick one down the Cock and Hen. Rick and Gary joined them. They tried to get David to go also, but he was in the mood to be alone for a while.

He sat on in that place by the Ebb, the food and bottles gone, the gleaming white cloth folded. The performance ended. For a while, people lingered in the gardens. Slowly, their numbers dwindled. Eventually, there was no one. The city fell silent also. A new moon came out, thin as a pencil-mark. The grass grew cold and damp. The cathedral clock struck midnight.

David stood, a bit stiffly, and started walking. He didn't know where he was going. He didn't want to go home quite yet.

This often happened when he thought about Merlyn.

David got clawed by a dangling frond of roses, felt, cool against his cheek, a cucumber; smelled the almost unbearable fragrance of the honeysuckle.

The Centre was silent. An ant-hill of sleeping individuals. In Weaver Street, all Henry Pearl's lights were out, and so were Rick's, but David and Clementine's sitting-room was still radiant. The women were still talking.

The High Street was very quiet, but not deserted. Hunched on a bench was the bunched shape of an alckie, his bottle carefully upright on the ground beside him. A stone-faced, slim-hipped young boy stood in a doorway chewing on his nails, sucking on a tightly-gripped fag. A police car crawled past. A young girl drooped over her crossed legs and her sleeping whippet by the glass frontage of Domicile Department Store, in the window of which was an enormous, rose-printed sofa, on it a Tudor sort of hat and a wooden musical instrument, shaped like half an onion. David heard a soft scrabbling coming from the back of Bigga-Burgers; where the dustbins were, presumably. It may have been cats or a fox, stray dogs or people.

The Cathedral Gate was closed. The Cathedral Inn was dark, except for some stingy light around Reception.

David turned to retrace his steps homeward, and realised that what he had thought was a rubbish bag, kicked along the pavement at chucking-out time, discarded outside Cagmag's, was, in fact, a person.

Beneath his eyes, the person took form. A woolly hat. Long legs. A hooked nose. A poet. A visionary. A bloody nuisance. Merlyn Orb. Merlyn Orb, come back. Not vanished without trace. Not disappeared without explanation.

The echo of David's footsteps slammed from wall to wall. Panting, he bent over the sleeping body. A pair of eyes opened. Wary. Threatened. Then, suddenly, unbothered, resigned to whatever might happen, good or evil, benign or violent. They closed again.

It was not Merlyn Orb.

And, suddenly, David knew that it was his destiny to do this forever: to check the faces of all he came across sprawled along benches, in doorways, on pavements, in gutters; just in case, just on the off-chance that one of them was Merlyn.

It was not Merlyn Orb.

But David got some money out anyway and placed it in the mittened palm, and closed the fist around it.

Because it was someone.